"Ireland itself becomes a character as Connolly adds description of the countryside and bits of history throughout the book . . . County Cork is surely a place you'd love to visit, and Sullivan's a great spot for a pint of Guinness and a bit of gossip." —*Kings River Life Magazine*

"[A] well-set and nicely paced cozy." —*Library Journal*

"Connolly has created some wonderful characters . . . You can tell the author loves her setting and has researched it thoroughly. Her love for the Irish countryside just glows throughout the story." —*Escape with Dollycas into a Good Book*

"Once you fall for Connolly's characters and the Irish beauty of the village of Leap, you might return for other reasons . . . Connolly's descriptions are enough to make anyone plan a trip to County Cork." —*Lesa's Book Critiques*

"The Irish countryside continues to enchant . . . Maura is a strong lead character, near perfect." —*MyShelf.com*

Buried in a Bog

"Connolly's latest is a captivating tale—sweet, nostalgic, and full of Irish charm, but also tightly plotted and full of twists, turns, and shocking reveals." —*The Maine Suspect*

continued . . .

"'Tis a grand thing . . . The prolific Sheila Connolly . . . pays tribute to her Irish heritage . . . Connolly invests this leisurely series opener with a wealth of Irish color and background."
—*Richmond Times-Dispatch*

"An exceptional read! Sheila Connolly has done it again with this outstanding book . . . A must read for those who have ever wanted to visit Ireland." —*Shelley's Book Case*

"Full of charm and mystery . . . The locals are warm and welcoming and the central hub of the village, Sullivan's Pub, is a slice of comfort. Throw in a dead body and a mugging in a nearby village and you have all the makings of a great whodunit." —*RT Book Reviews*

"Anyone with a trace of Irish in them, and all of us who wish we could claim an Irish connection, will welcome the first book in the County Cork series . . . And, with a country with Ireland's history, there's certain to be fascinating murders and mysteries to come." —*Lesa's Book Critiques*

PRAISE FOR THE *NEW YORK TIMES* BESTSELLING ORCHARD MYSTERIES

"Sheila Connolly's Orchard Mysteries are some of the most satisfying cozy mysteries I've read . . . Warm and entertaining from the first paragraph to the last." —*Lesa's Book Critiques*

"An enjoyable and well-written book with some excellent apple recipes at the end." —*Cozy Library*

"The mystery is intelligent and has an interesting twist . . . [A] fun, quick read with an enjoyable heroine."
—*The Mystery Reader* (four stars)

"The premise and plot are solid, and Meg seems a perfect fit for her role."
                                            —*Publishers Weekly*

"A fresh and appealing sleuth with a bushel full of entertaining problems. *One Bad Apple* is one crisp, delicious read."
    —Claudia Bishop, author of the Hemlock Falls Mysteries

"A delightful look at small-town New England, with an intriguing puzzle thrown in."
            —JoAnna Carl, author of the Chocoholic Mysteries

"A promising new mystery series. Thoroughly enjoyable."
        —Sammi Carter, author of the Candy Shop Mysteries

PRAISE FOR THE MUSEUM MYSTERIES

"Sheila Connolly's wonderful new series is a witty, engaging blend of history and mystery with a smart sleuth who already feels like a good friend."
            —Julie Hyzy, *New York Times* bestselling author of
                            the White House Chef Mysteries

"[The] archival milieu and the foibles of the characters are intriguing, and it's refreshing to encounter an FBI man who is human, competent, and essential to the plot."
                                            —*Publishers Weekly*

"She's smart, she's savvy, and she's sharp enough to spot what really goes on behind the scenes in museum politics. The practical and confident Nell Pratt is exactly the kind of sleuth you want in your corner when the going gets tough. Sheila Connolly serves up a snappy and sophisticated mystery."
                            —Mary Jane Maffini, author of
                            the Charlotte Adams Mysteries

An Early Wake

SHEILA CONNOLLY

BERKLEY PRIME CRIME, NEW YORK

THE BERKLEY PUBLISHING GROUP
Published by the Penguin Group
Penguin Group (USA) LLC
375 Hudson Street, New York, New York 10014

USA • Canada • UK • Ireland • Australia • New Zealand • India • South Africa • China

penguin.com

A Penguin Random House Company

AN EARLY WAKE

A Berkley Prime Crime Book / published by arrangement with the author

Berkley Prime Crime Books are published by The Berkley Publishing Group.
BERKLEY® PRIME CRIME and the PRIME CRIME logo are trademarks of
Penguin Group (USA) LLC.

For information, address: The Berkley Publishing Group,
a division of Penguin Group (USA) LLC,
375 Hudson Street, New York, New York 10014.

ISBN: 978-0-425-25253-6

PUBLISHING HISTORY
Berkley Prime Crime mass-market edition / February 2015

PRINTED IN THE UNITED STATES OF AMERICA

10 9 8 7 6 5 4 3 2 1

Cover illustration by Daniel Craig.
Cover art: *Celtic knots* © Shutterstock; *Vines* © Leone_V/Shutterstock.
Cover design by Judith Lagerman.
Interior text design by Laura K. Corless.

Acknowledgments

I first visited the pub Connolly's of Leap over fifteen years ago, when it was run by Paddy McNicholl and his wife Eileen Connolly. It was only the second pub I'd visited in Ireland, but it's been part of my life ever since, and it became the model for Sullivan's in this series. Back when I first visited, it was renowned for its music. Paddy was a musician, one of the founding members of a band called The Mighty Shamrocks, and he brought an extraordinary array of musicians to the place, where they played together in the narrow back room against the hillside. I was lucky enough to attend one of those events in that era. But when Paddy passed on a few years ago, the music stopped and the pub closed.

Two years ago I was talking to Sam McNicholl, the son of Paddy and Eileen, and a musician himself. He told me then that he wanted to bring back the music. He certainly had the energy and enthusiasm to do so. Last year I stopped in and found the pub newly polished without losing any of its character, and now Sam's only waiting on a few details (like licenses) for it to come back to life.

And that's where this story fell into my lap: this book is about bringing the music back. Memories are long in Ireland—and people remember the Connolly's that was. They'll come back.

ACKNOWLEDGMENTS

Like Sam said to me—and like Mick says to Maura in the book—it's magic. That's what I tried to capture here.

Some elements that I've included here serve as a reminder that Ireland is a part of the modern world. But when the music comes back to Sullivan's (or Connolly's), it's proof that the old ways survive as well.

Of course, there are others who have contributed along the way. Eileen Connolly McNicholl has been generous with stories of the pub back in the day, and some of her details have crept into this book and others. Skibbereen Garda Sergeant Tony McCarthy continues to provide helpful details about how the gardaí actually work in Ireland (and it's not quite like in the U.S.). As ever, if I've made procedural mistakes in this book, they are mine, not his.

Thanks as always to my amazing agent, Jessica Faust of BookEnds, and my tireless editor, Shannon Jamieson Vazquez; to the wonderful writers' community that provides so much support and encouragement, particularly Sisters in Crime and the Guppies; and to my blog sisters and brothers on Mystery Lovers' Kitchen and Killer Characters. And to my husband and daughter, who love West Cork almost as much as I do.

Is fada an bóthar nach mbíonn casadh ann.
It's a long road that has no turning.

—IRISH PROVERB

Chapter 1

Maura Donovan looked at the piles of paper spread out on her well-worn kitchen table and despaired. For six months now she'd been running Sullivan's, a small pub in a small town in County Cork, Ireland, and she had no idea if she'd made any money at all. She knew how to handle the day-to-day stuff like tending bar—she'd been doing that since she was legally old enough (and maybe a bit before), back in Boston where she'd grown up—but running a business was a different matter. At least it had been a good summer with nice weather, and the place had been well filled some nights. Not so well filled on others. She'd heard it was the poor economy everywhere that was keeping the tourists from other countries home watching their own pennies, but it was hard to get by with only the locals as customers. And even here in Leap there was plenty of competition, particularly from the inn across the street, plus the new bistro that just opened down the road—and even more competition in nearby Skibbereen, a thriving market town seven miles down the road and with ten times the population of Leap.

All of which was why Maura had been putting off doing the numbers for Sullivan's. She didn't have a computer or spreadsheets—just invoices and bank statements and lots of scraps of paper with scrawls that she couldn't even read. She had taken a couple of accounting classes back in Boston, but she'd never liked them and hadn't paid a lot of attention then. She'd paid the salaries of her employees—Mick, Jimmy, and Jimmy's daughter, Rose—but they were all part-time and worked erratic schedules, adjusting their hours from day to day or week to week. How her employees managed to live on what she paid them, she did not know, but closing down wasn't an option: she was pretty sure Mick could find himself another job, but she had her doubts about Jimmy. Jimmy was good at bantering with customers but when it came time to swap out the kegs of Guinness or wash up on a busy night, he always seemed to disappear. Then there was his daughter, Rose, who'd only recently turned seventeen, a sweet, bright girl who had little future in the small village but no plans to leave her father to fend for himself. Good for Jimmy, bad for Rose. Worse, there were hardly any young people Rose's age around: they'd all gone off looking for work in other places, not that Maura could blame them. The young men in particular seemed to have gone the farthest, not only to England or Spain but even to Australia.

Maura wanted the girl to have a life of her own, but she

couldn't offer much guidance, certainly not based on her own patchy history. Besides, she was still learning the ins and outs of Irish culture, and maybe she was reading the situation all wrong. But she was pretty sure there had to be something better for Rose than pulling pints part-time in a shabby small-town pub and going home to fix supper for dear old dad. Rose was quite a good cook, based on what she'd brought in to share now and then. Maybe she could find work in a restaurant locally. There was some money in the region, Maura knew—a conference center had opened over in Rosscarbery and a newer one in Glandore just up the harbor a bit. People were coming to the area, and they had to eat, didn't they? There were a few nice restaurants in Skibbereen. Rose should look to her future, rather than doing what Maura had done, which was drift along with no plan and no goals until her grandmother's death had blasted her out of her rut and somehow landed her in Ireland.

Well, now she was here, trying to scratch out a living, and responsible for employees. Maura herself took as little money out as she could, but even she had expenses, if only minimal ones.

Her house, for example, she'd inherited outright six months earlier, along with the pub from Old Mick Sullivan, but no matter how much she scrimped, she still had to pay for electricity, and gas for cooking and heating. She hadn't needed much heat yet, but that could change—she hadn't even been in the country through a winter yet. She'd been told that it never got really cold in this part of Ireland—something about the ocean currents. She'd even seen palm trees here and there, which always startled her. Still, these old stone and stucco cottages were hard to keep warm. Was she supposed to be laying in peat—or turf, as they called it here—or wood? She could just see herself in the middle of a damp winter, huddling over a small pile of smoky burning moss, trying to keep warm. *Not the life you imagined back in Boston, Maura.*

And then there was the car. She was driving an ancient Peugeot on an extended loan, somewhere short of a gift, from Bridget Nolan down the lane. But Maura couldn't expect Bridget to pay upkeep on the car that had belonged to her late husband, and she didn't like to take charity from anyone. She was happy to pay her own way and willing to work hard. But there was so much she didn't know.

Old Mick had kindly left her some money to tide her over when she took over the pub, but that wasn't going to last much longer. Which left the whole mess in her lap. For a moment Maura looked back on her days as a bar waitress with something like nostalgia: it sure was easier when all she'd had to do was show up and serve people, then collect a paycheck and some tips if she was lucky.

Of course, she *could* walk away from Sullivan's, if she couldn't make the numbers work. What would be the point of staying open just to lose money? The real estate market in Ireland was still down, but the pub license had to be worth something, didn't it? And it was hers to sell. She hadn't yet run through all the money Old Mick had left to her; she could take that and go . . . anywhere. Except she didn't know where to go. She didn't feel any strong need to go back to Boston— now that Gran was gone, there was nothing for her there. And she had Jimmy and Rose and Mick depending on her, and she didn't want to turn them out when there weren't enough jobs to go around. And maybe the new owners wouldn't be so kind to Old Billy Sheahan, a longtime friend of Old Mick's and a fixture in the well-worn armchair by the pub fireplace, or maybe they'd tear down the place altogether and put in a shiny modern place of some sort and change the town. Maura sighed. Not easy being an owner. Maybe it got better with practice.

She stretched, then checked her watch. Nearly ten a.m., and she should be opening the pub by ten thirty. *Too late to start anything now, eh, Maura?* she told herself. She stood up, pulled on a sweater hanging by the door, and went out the front door of her house.

She had no near neighbors. At one end of the lane, where it petered out, there was a house that hadn't been lived in for years, although the owners still kept sheep and cows on the pasture. The house on the other side of hers had been abandoned even longer, and she guessed it had been in ruins since before she was born. There were other, newer houses up the hill in front of her, and a few farther down the hill, not that she often saw the people who lived there. And then there was Bridget's cottage, on the lane that led from the top to the bottom of the hill. Maura decided to stop in and say good morning before she left for the village.

She picked her way along the muddy, unpaved lane toward Bridget's house, pulling her sweater close. It was September now, with the tourist season just ending. The days were getting shorter, and the wind sharper. She knocked on the front door of Bridget's cottage, which was smaller even than hers. She knew Mick, Bridget's grandson, made sure it was kept up and paid for his gran's phone so she could reach him in an emergency. Bridget was well into her eighties, but refused to consider moving in with Mick's sister a few towns over. This townland—called Knockskagh, or "hawthorn hill"—was her home, and she wouldn't be moved from it; she'd settled into the cottage when she married and had lived here all her adult life. Maura might have wondered if Bridget got lonely if she hadn't seen the steady trickle of friends and relatives who stopped by to make sure the old woman was all right and to swap gossip and news. It was nice, knowing that people were looking out for you. Her gran had done a lot of looking out for the struggling Irish immigrants who'd arrived in Boston.

"Ah! *Dia duit a Mhaire!*" Bridget opened the door with a broad smile.

"Dia's Muire duit, a Bride," Maura replied, with the little Irish she knew. Bridget had taught her a few phrases, like how to exchange a basic greeting.

"Come in, come in," Bridget said. "There's a bit of a chill in the air, isn't there?"

"Definitely. I can't stay long, but I was going crazy trying to sort out the finances for the pub and I thought some fresh air might help. Although I always like to see you."

"There's tea on the stove and fresh scones in the tin, if yer hungry."

"Thanks." Maura, long familiar with Bridget's kitchen by now, helped herself. "Can I pour you a cup?"

"That'd be grand, if it's no trouble."

"No problem." Maura filled two cups and carried them back to where Bridget now sat in front of a small fire. "Are you feeling the cold already?"

Bridget sighed. "Don't you be getting old, Maura—if it's not one thing, it's another. I can feel winter coming in my bones."

"Anything I can do?" Maura asked. She hated to think that

Bridget might be failing. Since she'd lost her grandmother—the only relative she'd ever known—less than a year before, somehow she'd come to count on Bridget to take Gran's place. It was because of Bridget that Maura had come to Leap in the first place, after she'd stumbled upon Bridget's long correspondence with her gran.

Bridget waved a dismissive hand at her. "Ah, don't be minding me. I'm just a fussy aul woman. And don't you be telling Mick that I'm complaining, either, or he'll be after me again to move in with my granddaughter over to Bandon. Which would not suit me at all, for she's got two loud children and little enough room as it is."

Maura knew Mick kept a close eye on his gran and would notice any decline in her condition on his own, so she wasn't about to go tattling to him. She took a sip of her tea—strong, as always. "I've been trying to figure out if Sullivan's is making any money. How did Old Mick manage?"

"He didn't ask for much. Many of his friends spent their time there of an evening. Not that they drank much. They could nurse a pint for hours, or so Mick used to say. They were there for the craic, not for the drink. God help the poor tourist who stuck his nose in while that crowd was in good form."

That wasn't hard for Maura to imagine, especially since she'd made few physical changes since she'd taken over in the spring, afraid to drive away what patrons she had. Besides, she'd never been big on prettying up a place. She tried to imagine track lighting and new curtains in the pub and had to swallow a laugh, though she had at least managed to introduce a few new paintings, which had brightened some of the darker corners. The paintings were the works of Gillian Callanan, an artist who lived over the hill in an old creamery by the lake, at least during the summer. Maura hadn't seen much of Gillian lately and wondered if she'd gone back to Dublin for the winter, as she had told Maura she usually did. Maura would miss her if she went, since Gillian was close to her own age and had quickly become a friend—one of the few Maura had made since she'd arrived—but she knew that Gillian couldn't make a living selling her paintings during the winter around here. Besides, the creamery building wasn't heated, certainly not well enough to withstand the wind rushing across Ballinlough. Maura could tell already that this could be a lonely place in winter.

She stood up. "I should probably be going. Can I pick up anything for you?"

"No, love, I'm grand. Mick came by yesterday. And don't worry yerself about the numbers—I'm sure things will come right."

"I hope so, Bridget. See you later."

She shut the door on her way out, then trudged back to her place. She wasn't sure why she'd asked Bridget if she needed anything, when Maura was the one with a bare pantry. There never seemed to be any time to shop, much less prepare meals, and she spent most of her waking hours at the pub. It was easier to walk down to the Costcutter at the gas station and pick up something quick.

She drove into the village, glad in a way that the few clueless tourists who had ventured along the lanes had gone home now. To be fair, she'd been in the same boat herself not that long ago. It was hard for some people to accept that there were no road signs, except on the biggest of the main roads, and that most people gave driving instructions along the lines of "Turn left at the abandoned church and go up the hill until you see the field with the bull, then turn right at the fallen tree." It took a bit of getting used to, and by the time most people did, it was time for them to leave. Luckily most of the time there were no cars on the lanes, which were pretty much one lane wide anyway.

Maura parked her car well away from Sullivan's—parking was at a premium along the main road and she didn't want to discourage any potential customers—and went toward the front door of the pub, keys in hand. She was surprised to find the door already unlocked and Rose behind the bar. She stepped into the dark interior and took quick stock of the scene: no customers except for a casually dressed young man seated on a stool at the bar and talking to Rose with great animation.

Rose looked up and saw her, then beckoned her over eagerly. "Maura, this is Timothy Reilly. He's a student from Trinity up in Dublin and he's here to work on a project, he says. Tim, this is Maura Donovan—she's the owner here, since March. Mebbe you'd best explain what it is yer after." Rose was as animated as Maura had seen her in a while, but then, Tim was a fairly attractive young man. He looked to be around twenty, putting him about five years younger than Maura, and he had an open, eager face.

"Nice to meet you, Tim," Maura said. "What brings you to the Wild West of Cork?"

"It's a pleasure, Maura. It's the music that brings me— the music here at Sullivan's."

Chapter 2

For a moment Maura stared blankly at Tim: this was the first she'd heard anything about music at Sullivan's. She glanced at Rose, who shrugged, apparently as ignorant as Maura. She pulled out a stool and sat down next to the young man.

"Can I get you anything, Maura?" Rose asked.

"A coffee, please. Tim, are you set?" He had an empty cup in front of him, so he must have been here for a while, even though the pub wasn't officially open yet.

"Another coffee would be grand, if you don't mind, Rose." He smiled at her.

Rose blushed. "Right away."

Maura turned to face Tim. "So, what's this about music?"

He cocked his head at her. "American, are you? How do you come to own this place?"

Maura noticed he hadn't exactly answered her question, but by now she was used to the roundabout path most conversations here took. "I grew up in Boston, but my grandmother was the niece of the late owner, Michael Sullivan—that'd be Old Mick. I took over about six months ago."

Tim looked disappointed. "So you'd know little about the history of the place? Did you know this Old Mick?"

Maura shook her head. "I never met the man, I'm afraid. And I kind of hit the ground running here, so there hasn't been a lot of time to ask about what happened before I showed up. What are you looking for?"

Rose set two mugs of coffee on the bar in front of them. Tim smiled his thanks, and Rose's blush returned. "As Rose here said, I'm a student at Trinity in Dublin—do you know it?"

"I haven't seen Dublin yet, only this part of the country." To be fair, Maura *had* seen the airport and the bus station, but she didn't really think those counted. After arriving on a red-eye flight, she hadn't noticed much about the scenery she'd passed on her way to Cork.

Tim filed that fact away. "I'm doing an arts degree in musicology." When Maura stared blankly at his description, he explained, "It's the history of music, and to finish I have to write a dissertation—that's a long paper—so I'm here fer the research. The department requires we know a bit about playing music, and I'm not a bad aul player m'self, but what I'm looking to do is teach music history and theory. Do you know anything about Irish bands?" He looked hopefully at Maura.

She hated to disappoint him again, but she'd never been particularly interested in music. "You mean all that tin whistle and fiddle stuff?"

Tim smiled. "That's the traditional side of things. Which is all good and well—and some of the tunes go back for centuries, so it's interesting to see them surviving today and still being played. But what interests me now is more the contemporary scene, and how modern musicians have borrowed elements of the old forms and made them into something new."

Maura glanced quickly at Rose, who had to know more than she did. "Like the Saw Doctors and the Cranberries," Rose volunteered. "Is that what you mean, Tim?"

The names meant nothing to Maura. Were those current bands? Or ancient history?

He nodded vigorously. "Yes, but they're not the only ones. Where do you come from, Maura? Did you mention Boston?"

"Yeah, I grew up in South Boston."

"Grand—then surely you know of the Dropkick Murphys?"

Maura smiled. It was impossible to grow up in Southie and not know the Dropkick Murphys; impossible to work in any local bar and not hear their songs in the background, over and over. "Them I know."

Tim beamed. "Well, there you go. They're American, of course, but there's still that element of the traditional in what they write, what they perform, even today. Maybe it's in the genes, but that's a study for a different department, for sure. What I'm looking at is the evolution of recent Irish music over the past couple of decades and its debt to the traditional."

"That sounds interesting," Maura said politely. "But where does Sullivan's fit?"

Tim looked incredulous. "Do you not know? Sullivan's was the heart of the music scene for this end of the country, back for a decade or more in the nineties."

Back in the nineties, Tim would have been in diapers. Why would he be interested in the music? But then, Maura didn't claim to understand how colleges worked. She had a vague idea that when you wrote a paper you had to do something that hadn't been done before. In that case, writing about the history of Sullivan's definitely qualified. Maura searched her memory and couldn't recall anyone mentioning music and Sullivan's in the same breath, although now that she thought of it, there were some posters of bands tacked up in the little-used back room . . . "Here? But this is the middle of nowhere!"

Tim nodded. "It is that, but who's to question how these things come about? In its day, Sullivan's drew players from all over. It was Mick Sullivan brought them together, and he sat in often enough. Or so I'm told."

Old Mick had been a musician? One more thing Maura hadn't known about him. He must have had a wealth of stories to tell. And Tim here had missed him by only six months. Too bad. "It's a shame you can't talk to him," Maura said.

"It is," he agreed. "I should have sorted things out sooner, but I've only just scratched the surface. But surely there are others around here who remember? Who knew the place back then?"

Maura and Rose exchanged looks. "Before I was born," Rose said. "Me da might know."

"Or Mick—young Mick, that is," Maura explained to Tim.

"No relation to Old Mick. But young Mick's old enough to remember—he had to have been a teenager then, right, Rose?" Rose nodded.

"And where might I find these fellas?" Tim asked.

"Here," Maura said promptly. "They'll both be in sometime today—they work here. And they worked for Old Mick, before. I'm sure they'll be happy to help. And, of course, there's Billy Sheahan."

"Who's he?" Tim asked.

"An old friend of Old Mick's—and I mean 'old' in both senses." Maura smiled. "He's in his eighties, and he and Old Mick were friends for decades. He usually comes in about now, and he's here for most of the day." Billy hadn't yet arrived, but it was early yet. Maura wasn't worried, since he lived on the ground floor at the other end of the building and could make his way to the pub blindfolded; once he arrived he'd stay most of the day, spinning tales for any tourists who wandered in and swapping stories with his local friends. Maura happened to know that most of Billy's stories were true, although he wasn't beyond throwing in a bit of creative detail, depending on his audience. She had come to realize that often in Ireland the telling of the story was more important than the truth of it. She had no idea what tourists made of him, but she was pretty sure they went away believing they'd had a taste of Auld Ireland.

"Brilliant! That's exactly what I was hoping for—an oral history of the way things were. I'd planned to poke around for a few days anyway."

"Do you have a place to stay?" Maura asked. So far her impression was that most people from outside County Cork assumed there were plenty of bed-and-breakfasts and hotels to be had, but the reality was a bit different: the Leap Inn, locally more often called Sheahan's, across the street catered to fishermen and had only a handful of rooms; the hotel in Skibbereen was kind of upscale for a student; and the conference centers that were popping up here and there were probably far beyond his means.

"I thought I'd look for a hostel or the like," he said. "Do you know of one?"

"I hear there's one in Skibbereen, if you don't mind dormitory style," Rose volunteered.

"That'd be grand. By the way, what music do you listen to here now? I don't see any jukebox in the place."

"Nothing," Maura admitted. "I don't have time. There's the television for the customers, for sports. When the place is busy, it's too loud to hear anyway." She spotted a couple of men coming in the door and excused herself to go over to greet them and take their orders as they settled themselves at a table. When she looked back, Rose and Tim were deep in conversation, no doubt comparing bands, local or other. For a moment Maura felt old, even though she was probably only a few years older than Tim. But, she told herself, she'd had much more life experience than a sheltered college student like Tim could have had. It was small comfort.

There were a half dozen people in the place by the time Old Billy Sheahan made his slow way into the pub, headed for his accustomed chair like a stately tugboat.

"Good morning to you, Maura, or, no, I should say, good afternoon," Billy greeted her. "As the cold sets in, I move a bit slower."

"That's what Bridget said too. What can I get you?"

"A pint, if you will."

"Coming up." She went over to the bar and went behind it to start pulling Billy's pint.

Rose turned to her and said tentatively, "Maura, would you mind if Tim and I went out for a bit of lunch? It's quiet here."

"Sure, go ahead. I think I can handle it." She smiled to indicate her sarcasm. And she wanted some time to talk to Billy alone about this whole music thing, of which she knew absolutely nothing. She had trouble picturing any friend of Billy's as a music guru, although Old Mick and Billy would have been in their late sixties back then. Now that she thought about it, she could name a lot of performers who were still going strong in their sixties and even seventies, touring and everything. Like the Rolling Stones. Maybe she'd been too quick to judge.

Rose and Tim went out the door, and Maura topped off Billy's pint and took it over to him. She checked to make sure everyone else was well supplied with drink, then sat down next to Billy.

"Who's that young man who left with our Rose?" he asked. "Not from around here, is he?"

"No, he's a student, from Dublin, he says. His name's Tim Reilly. He said he wants to find out about the music scene here in Sullivan's in the nineties. It's the first I've heard about it."

Billy's eyes lit up. "I hadn't thought of that in years! This used to be quite the place to play."

"So he was right about that?" Maura asked.

"Oh, yes, musicians would come from all over. Not for

concerts, as such, but to—what should I call it? Jam?—with each other. Like a *seisiún* is for the traditional kind of music."

"What they were playing wasn't traditional?"

"No, these were players of popular stuff. Not always the lead singer of this band or the other, but a lot of the sidemen. Word would go out—don't ask me how, it was before all this electronic nonsense—and the players would come together here of an evening, late, and settle in the back room and go on half the night. And people would come to hear them. I don't know how they'd find out it was happenin', but they'd start appearing early in the evening, and they'd stay 'til the end. Packed, the place was."

"Was Old Mick a musician?"

"He'd been known to pick up a fiddle now and then, but mostly he kept the drinks flowing."

"How'd they get around the regulations about closing times, if they stuck around all night? Even I know you can't keep serving 'til dawn." Maura knew there was some give-and-take, depending on the attitude of the gardaí, the local police, but she didn't think the rules could be stretched that far.

"You'll have heard the term 'lock-in'?"

"Yes, but I'm not sure how it works."

"If you want to keep yer pub open after legal closing time, you ask that yer patrons pay for their drinks beforehand, and then after closing time you lock yer doors and it becomes a private party, with no money changing hands."

"Ah." Maura could see a lot of room for interpretation of the law there, but it made a kind of sense. "What about you, Billy? Did you join in?"

He grinned. "You've never heard me sing, have you?

Like a gate that needs greasin'. No, I'd keep an eye on the front of the house while Mick covered the back. Grand times they were."

"That kid who was talking with Rose—he says he's a student at Trinity, studying how popular music changed in Ireland in the nineties—not the old stuff. He seems to think Sullivan's was like the center of the music universe, at least around here. Would you be willing to talk to him? I can't tell him anything, and Rose is too young to have known about it then, but I'm sure you could fill his ear for quite a while. Do you mind if I turn him over to you?"

"I'm happy to go on about those days. And if he's to be around fer a few days, then he and Rose can spend some time together as well."

Maura was struck once again with how perceptive Billy was. He might look like a doddering old man, but he was shrewd enough to recognize that Rose was enjoying Tim's company. "You playing matchmaker now, Billy? I don't know how long Tim will be around, but he was asking about a place to stay."

"Assuming he needs to get back to Dublin for the start of Michaelmas term, that's not 'til late in the month. So he's got a bit of time free."

Michaelmas? Another label that meant nothing to Maura. In any case, Tim would have a week or two to find out whatever he needed for his paper or whatever. "When he comes back, I'll tell him to talk to you."

"My pleasure. You might tell him to talk to Mick as well."

"You don't mean Old Mick, do you?" Maura teased.

"Sure and he's dead, isn't he? No, Mick Nolan. He was

still at school when all the bands were playing here, but he hung around as much as Mick would let him."

"Huh," Maura replied. She'd never seen Mick show the slightest interest in music, but then, he was certainly close-mouthed about his own life. Maybe he had hidden depths. Or maybe she should talk to him first, before siccing Tim on him.

Chapter 3

By the time Rose and Tim returned an hour later, business had picked up a bit—now there were six men and a lone woman in Sullivan's, each looking for a quick pint or a cup of coffee before taking off to do errands. Or filling their time, if they had no jobs to go to. About normal, but any one customer made a noticeable impact on the day's intake. Rose took a quick glance around then hurried to the bar. "Sorry I've been so long, but we lost sight of the time."

"That's on me," Tim said quickly. "It helps me to talk through what I need to know, and what questions I want to ask, so I was trying them out on Rose first."

"It's okay, Rose. Relax," Maura said, nodding in Billy's direction. "By the way, Tim, I talked to Billy over there, and he said he'd be glad to fill you in on what used to go on here."

Rose beamed. "Oh, that's brilliant! Tim here was telling me about all the bands back then and all the people who played in 'em. Seems hard to believe, doesn't it? This place filled with people and music?"

Sad but true, Maura thought. "Was it the times that changed, or did Old Mick just let it go downhill? He was getting old."

"I couldn't say," Rose said. "Old Mick never mentioned the past, at least not to me, but I didn't know him long. You can try asking young Mick, though."

"Has he ever talked about music with you? I mean, not just music here, but anywhere else?"

Rose considered the question. "Not that I remember. He's not one for those little music players, like so many of the lads."

Mick was hardly a lad, Maura thought, since he was probably ten years older than she was. But MP3 players or mobile phones that played music were nearly universal these days. Not that she'd ever had the money for either one. Shoot, that reminded her of another expense to consider: her pay-as-you-go phone was almost out of minutes. Now she'd have to figure out what she wanted in a phone—and what she could afford. She didn't have many people to call, but it was good to have a phone just in case.

Her mind was drifting, so she straightened her shoulders and told Rose, "Will you take over the bar for now? I'd like to hear what Billy has to say too, I guess. Tim, you come with me and we'll talk to Billy together. The price for his talk is usually a pint."

"You said his name was Sheahan? Is he related to the people who run the hotel across the road? The sign there's kind of hard to miss."

"He is, but don't ask me exactly how. I keep finding that everyone around here is related somehow, even to me. They can't always explain *how* we're related, though, so they just call us cousins," Maura said. "Anyway, come on over and let me introduce you to Billy." She led the way to the corner next to the fireplace where Billy held court. Billy looked up, delighted at the idea of a new audience.

"Billy, this is Timothy Reilly from Dublin," Maura said. "He wants to talk about the music at Sullivan's, back in the early nineties."

"*Fáilte romhat, mo bhuachaill,*" Billy said, laying it on thick.

"*Go raibh maith agat, a dhuine uasail,*" Tim replied promptly.

Billy smiled broadly. "Ah, the schools are doing a sound job of keeping the language alive these days! So, Timothy Reilly. Where are yer people from?"

"Me ma was from Clonakilty, sir, but she left there early for Dublin."

"And now yer doin' a degree at Trinity. In music?"

"I am, sir. I'm interested in the persistence of musical traditions as they've been carried over into contemporary forms. I've been told that Sullivan's here was a sort of nexus."

Billy looked blank at the unfamiliar word, but Tim was quick to realize it. "Sorry, kind of a crossroads, where the old and the new came together. I've heard that a lot of sidemen from some of the big-name groups made it a point to drop in here just to play with whoever was handy. And whoever wandered into the pub was the happy beneficiary."

"Yer not far wrong, my boy. Let me tell you . . ." And Billy was off. Maura sat back and contented herself with listening, while keeping an eye on Rose behind the bar, but there were few new customers in the midafternoon. Tim, on the other hand, pulled out a small notebook and was trying to keep up with scribbled notes, stopping Billy every now and then to clarify a point or check the spelling of a name. He seemed to grow more excited the longer Billy talked, almost bouncing in his chair. After an hour or so Billy cleared his throat and, with a pointed glance toward the bar, said, "All this talkin' is dry work. I wouldn't say no to a pint."

Tim looked startled, until he figured out what Billy meant. "Oh, right, of course. I'll be just a minute."

When he had walked away, Maura leaned in toward Billy. "You don't mind, do you? He seems very eager."

"Saints, no! It's a rare treat to talk about those days, those people. There are few who know about it anymore; fewer still who ask."

"This is the first I've heard of it," Maura said. "Was it really a big thing?" She wasn't even sure what a "big thing" would mean around here. "Old Mick had regular music events here? Not just a guy with a fiddle and someone with a drum or that bagpipe thing?"

Billy nodded. "That's the traditional style, and it's an uilleann pipe, not a bagpipe. Mick pulled in a few of those, now and then. The tourists like it. But that wasn't where his heart lay. He brought the new music in—the bands on the way up or the ones on the way down, and anywhere in between." Billy cocked his head at her. "Yer not one for the music, are you, now?" When Maura shook her head, he went on, "How do I say it best? There are the stars—the bands that play in the big stadiums in the big cities—and no doubt you've heard of those. Then there are the others who play with them now and then, when the schedules fit. They aren't always part of the band, see, but they're on tap fer when they're needed, and you might never hear their names. And those are the ones, who aren't working steady, who come together at places like these to keep their hand in, and to swap gossip."

"Okay, I can understand that. But what was special about Sullivan's? Was it the only game around?"

"It was Mick made it into something more, you see. He knew music and he knew people, and he knew how to put them together. So the fellas that showed up here of an evening were fair talents on their own, and the word got 'round. They came from all over, and they knew Mick would give them a hot meal, as much as they could drink, and a bed for the night—or the floor if all the beds were filled. All they had to do was play, and play they did. The lads would have played anyways, but when they were into it, it was something special, and the audience knew it."

"How did people find out they were playing here? I mean, this was before the Internet or even cell phones. Or didn't it matter? I mean, were they just playing for themselves, or did they need an audience?" Maura asked.

"The people came. I couldn't tell you how they heard, back then, but they found their way here."

"How long did all this last?"

Billy contemplated the flaking plaster of the ceiling for a moment. "A decade, maybe? Times changed, and so did the music. After a while the players stopped coming around so often, and I guess Mick got tired." Billy paused as Tim reappeared. "Ah, Timothy, there you are—I'd started to wonder if you were brewin' the stuff yerself. Or was it that yer brewin' something with that lovely young girl over there?"

Maura watched with amusement as Tim blushed.

Tim set the brimming pint down where Billy could reach it and turned to Maura. "Hey, it sounds like you've got loads of great stories, and there are probably other people around here that I should be talking with. I don't suppose Mick Sullivan kept any written records, did he?"

Maura suppressed a rude snort. She herself now had the sum and total of Mick's documents, which consisted of a single battered file folder holding a list of his suppliers and a few other pieces of paper. All other details—about ownership of the place, taxes paid, and the like—were in his lawyer's hands, along with his will. Or rather, *her* lawyer—solicitor?—now. "Sorry, Tim," Maura said, "but Mick ran the place to suit himself and no one else. I don't think he was thinking about preserving the history of the place."

"That's all right—an oral history will do just as well." Tim stood up and faced Billy again. "Thank you, Mr. Sheahan. May I spend some more time with you tomorrow?"

"Mr. Sheahan was me da—I'm Billy to one and all, save that the boys call me Old Billy when they think I can't hear them. But I can't say they're lyin', for I know I'm old. I'd be happy to ramble on tomorrow. Stop by 'round lunchtime, will you?"

"I'll do that, thank you."

Maura looked over at the bar to see Rose getting ready to go home and fix her father's supper. Still no sign of Jimmy, but she saw Mick through the window, heading her way. "Tim, why don't you catch Rose on her way out, and she can give you directions to that hostel she mentioned earlier? We'll see you tomorrow."

"I'll be here. Thanks, Maura." He ducked his head and hurried over to the bar, where Rose gave him a huge smile, which in turn brought on another vivid blush from Tim. Rose slipped on a sweater, and he held the door for her, then followed her out. Mick slid in as they left, giving Tim a speculative look as they crossed paths.

"Evenin', Maura. What's his story?" Mick nodded in the direction of Tim and Rose, who were now standing on the sidewalk outside the pub. Rose was gesturing broadly toward the west and Skibbereen. But before Maura could explain, a group of customers came in, and she and Mick got caught up in serving them.

"I'll fill you in later," she said, as she busied herself pulling pints.

Chapter 4

Their steadiest crowd at Sullivan's was made up of men who stopped by nearly every day on the way home. Whether they had jobs, Maura didn't know for sure, nor did she feel she could ask; she'd make conversation with them, but never about anything serious, and only if they seemed to want to talk. But they all seemed to know one another. They'd drift in and settle in for a pint or two, in no hurry to go home to their dinner. Or maybe there was no one waiting for them, and Sullivan's was as close as they came to a home. As long as they bought their pints, Maura wouldn't complain, and it wasn't as though other people were clamoring for their seats. On average each man stayed a bit over an hour, then drifted out the way he'd come, with a raised hand or a tipped cap as he went out the door.

When they'd gotten everyone served, Mick found time to ask, "Right, so—who was that boy in here earlier?"

"The one Rose was talking to? What, are you looking out for Rose now?" Maura swallowed the rest of what she wanted to say, which was that someone had to: Rose had no mother to look after her, and her father, Jimmy, was all but useless. "I worry about Rose," she said.

"You've said that before. She's got a good head on her shoulders, Maura. Let her work things out for herself. You've got enough on yer plate with this place without worrying needlessly about things that don't require yer assistance."

"I know, but there's not much of a future for her in this place."

"Maybe some Prince Charming will walk in and sweep her away," Mick said, unruffled. "Which brings me back to my original question. Who was the fella I saw her leaving with? We don't get many around here who are both young and unfamiliar. Tourist?"

"Not exactly." Maura filled Mick in on Tim's musical quest. "Since I didn't know squat about that, I handed him over to Billy, who was happy to explain. Or start to, at least. It sounds like Billy has plenty of information. What about you? Do you know about what went on here?"

Mick stared over Maura's head, lost in thought. "Right, you wouldn't know," he said, almost to himself.

Maura turned to face him. "Well, of course I wouldn't! I've barely been here six months. Tim's asking about twenty years ago. So unless U2 played here or something, I doubt I'd have heard about it."

Mick smiled. "No one quite so grand. But not so far from it as you might think, looking at the place."

"So fill me in. I hate looking stupid."

Mick didn't answer directly. "You've seen the back room?"

Maura nodded. "I've looked at it, and I shut the door as fast as I could. It's a mess, and I haven't had time to worry about it. Why?"

"That's where the music was. Did you not notice the equipment?"

"Not really. If the stuff crammed in the corners there is music equipment, it looks pretty ancient."

"Maybe, but back then it was top of the line, especially for a small place."

"So how many people does this 'small' back room hold?"

Mick's mouth twitched. "There's some legal piece of paper somewhere that says this place can accommodate up to two hundred people—that's back and front combined. I'd say we often had closer to three hundred, at least a time or two."

"And the building didn't fall down?" Maura was having trouble wrapping her head around the idea of crowds in the hundreds in Sullivan's. She'd never seen more than fifty people in the pub at one time; she couldn't begin to imagine it holding three hundred.

"In case you haven't noticed, the back wall is built against the stone of the hill, so it can't go anywhere. The building's well over two hundred years old, and solid—have you not seen how thick the walls are? We did have to reinforce the balcony, though."

Maura interrupted him. "Whoa, wait—there's a balcony in there?"

"It runs around the room, upstairs. It's not so big, maybe one and a half meters deep. But then, the stage is no more than four and a half meters square. Cozy, you might say."

So about five feet deep. Maura worked it out in her head. "There's a second bar back there, right?"

"There is," Mick told her. "Not as big as the one out here, maybe three meters across."

Maura was still trying to sort out how much she didn't know about her own building. Balcony? Stage? She really needed to take a better look at that back room. "When did all this happen?"

Mick leaned back against the bar and checked the room: nobody appeared to need a drink topped off. "The nineties? I was still in school, but I hung out here whenever I could. I did odd jobs for Old Mick, and he let me sneak in to see the bands."

Maura studied Mick's face in surprise: she'd never seen him this enthusiastic about anything before, and it made him look somehow younger, his eyes bright with memories. "Did Old Mick play?" she asked.

"That he didn't, or not seriously. Not like the ones who came from all over. Call him an entrepreneur, an impresario. Or maybe a wizard. He called them here, though I never knew how. The musicians just appeared, and then the people followed. And it was grand."

"Why'd it stop?" Maura asked, although she thought she could guess. Old Mick had been well past eighty when he died, and wasn't live music a young man's game?

Mick shrugged. "Hard to say. Old Mick got tired, and the music world moved on. I'm not sure he ever came to terms with some of the changes in the music. Are you much for the music yerself?"

That matched what Billy had told her. Maura shook her

head. "Not really. I mean, I worked in a few bars in Southie, or around Boston, mostly the ones with a lot of Irish guys in 'em. Give them a few pints and they'd start singing the old songs. Seemed like everybody knew the words to them. Sometimes they'd get stirred up and there'd be a fight or two. Other times they got kind of sad and quiet. Either way, they bought a lot of pints."

"I could name names for you, for the bands, but you wouldn't know them. So you've never been to a live concert, then?"

"No," Maura said curtly, feeling defensive. Popular music had never really appealed to her, and while it had always been on in the background in the bars where she worked, she'd never paid much attention and always had trouble identifying any particular group. Half the time the music was drowned out by the noise in any of those pubs, especially on weekends. And none of the places had been the kind to bring in live bands. "Not interested." A lame excuse, but at least partially true.

Mick looked at her with something suspiciously like pity. "We Irish love our music. There's hardly a man or woman 'round here who doesn't play some instrument, or is willing to pick one up if a *seisiún* starts up. And if they've no instrument, they'll sing. We all share the words and the tunes. Some go back centuries, even. You've probably heard yer fair share of them even in America—many of the folk singers back in the sixties picked them up again."

Maura held up a hand. "Okay, you can stop now. I get it. There's a lot of Irish music history, and some part of it took place right here in Sullivan's, right?"

"Right. This Tim will be getting a true oral history from Billy there." Mick nodded toward the old man, dozing in his corner.

"Yeah, they both seemed pretty happy earlier." Maura wondered if there were any other surprises about the pub she now owned. "You aren't going to tell me that Michael Collins spent his time off here, are you?"

Mick smiled. "Yer all but an idiot when it comes to Irish music, but at least you know that the founder of the modern Irish state was from a Cork family not far from here. No, he did his drinkin' at the Eldon Hotel in Skib. And Clonakilty, of course, although that's not to say he didn't stop in here for the odd pint—this place has been around for a long time." He turned away to take the orders of a pair of men who had just come in.

Maura wondered for a moment whether she should tell Mick about her concerns about the cash flow at Sullivan's. After all, he'd worked here a lot longer than she had. She knew exactly what she was paying him, and he hadn't asked for anything more. But then, she had no idea what his expenses were. In fact, she realized that she knew next to nothing about Mick's life outside the pub—not only did she have no idea where he lived, she didn't even know if he lived with anyone else—family, friend, or partner. He'd never mentioned a wife or girlfriend and didn't seem to answer to anybody else. How had he managed to remain single so long? What did he do in the time he wasn't at Sullivan's, other than visit Bridget? Where would he go if she shut down the place? When he'd learned that Old Mick had left the pub to Maura, he hadn't quit (which she was afraid he would), but neither had he offered to buy her out. Assuming he could've afforded to.

Rose's dad, Jimmy, had been more difficult about her inheritance, but Maura was pretty sure he couldn't pay for a share of the place even if he'd wanted to. But Jimmy was the type of guy who would probably land on his feet no matter what, even if he never did more than scrape by. Besides, it was Rose who Maura worried about. Mick and Jimmy were grown men and would just have to deal with whatever came along.

Business picked up gradually through the evening. Billy garnered his share of attention: he looked almost like royalty, enthroned in his well-worn chair by the fire, spinning tales to all who would listen, tourist and friend alike. His glass was seldom empty. Jimmy came in a bit after six, presumably well fed by Rose, and set about clearing used glasses and wiping down empty tables with good cheer.

Maura greeted at least half the people who came in by name, which was a huge improvement over the past couple of months. On the other hand, did it matter if she charmed whoever walked in the door? She was still trying to figure out what her role at Sullivan's was: she wanted to make it clear that she was the owner, not a barmaid, but she admitted to herself that she still had to make an effort to welcome people and schmooze them while they waited for their pints to settle. One thing she'd learned since she'd been in Ireland, however, was that a pub owner, especially a woman, was expected to chat with customers, create a relationship with them, so they'd come back regularly for a pint and some craic. That was the way the business worked, but it was hard for her. A lot of that came from how she'd grown up, with her father dead and a mother who'd run off, God knew where, when Maura was a baby. Plus she'd lived in a rough neighborhood where it didn't pay to reveal too much of yourself, in case it made you look weak and vulnerable. Back when she'd been waitressing or tending bar, she'd always tried to be as bland as possible. She knew she could have made bigger tips if she'd been friendlier or flashed more skin, but she'd never been comfortable doing that. She'd accepted the price of smaller tips in exchange for clinging to some of her dignity.

But now she was the owner, the "face" of Sullivan's, and the rules had changed. Could she change along with them? Did she want to?

Jimmy deposited a double handful of empty pint glasses on the bar in front of her. "Penny?"

Maura looked blankly at him for a moment. "What? Oh, for my thoughts, you mean."

"I do, that," he replied. "Yer looking pretty somber for such a fine evening. Troubles?"

"No, everything's fine. I was just thinking."

He accepted her explanation without comment. "What's this I hear about a college boy nosing around, talking about the music?"

Had Rose mentioned Tim to him over supper? "That's about it. He's at Trinity in Dublin, and he's doing some kind of research on Sullivan's back when it was the music capital of West Cork, or something like that. He talked with Billy for a while, and he'll be back tomorrow. Do you remember those days?"

Jimmy leaned against the front of the bar. "Some. I was working in town back then, before I started here, and newly married, so I didn't have much time of my own. But there was always talk of who might be showin' up at Sullivan's of a weekend."

"Sounds like there was a lot going on back then. Mick says they packed this place, front and back. Must have been like sardines." And no doubt a fire hazard and hot and damp, and Maura didn't even want to think about the state of the bathrooms during such an event. Maybe the guys just went out the back door and did what they had to do, although maybe they might not be let back in. All in all, hard to imagine. "Table in the corner is looking for drinks, Jimmy."

"I'll see to it," he said and went over to greet the customers there.

Maura was left with her own thoughts again, once everyone was supplied with pints. She couldn't imagine this place as the hub of anything, but it seemed to have been true once. The space in the back looked unlikely, what little she'd seen of it, but it had worked once. Could it happen again? Even she was aware that the music world had changed a lot in the past twenty years. Everything was electronic now, and people could carry or access their entire music library on a tiny device or through their cell phone. She'd heard that the old bands who still toured often priced their tickets beyond the reach of everyday fans, at least back in the States. She had no idea where to find small start-up bands in Boston; where could she look in Ireland? And where on earth would a small place like this, far from any major city, fit in the music world now?

But. The real question, now taking shape for Maura, was: could Sullivan's make money, if she could bring the music back?

She knew up front that she couldn't do it herself. She'd need help, since she knew next to nothing about current music, at least beyond the big names. She wasn't sure if whatever pub license she had would cover live performances. She'd have to check legal capacity. She'd have to see what advertising would cost and if it even reached the right people.

But could it work? It was something to think about, but she had to shelve it then as another group of men came in. Mick left around ten, and Maura and Jimmy closed up the place after eleven, as the last patrons scattered into the night. "You go on home, Jimmy," Maura said. She wasn't just being generous: she wanted a little time alone in the place.

Jimmy grabbed his jacket and left quickly, with a "ta" on his way out the door. Maura finished rinsing glasses and cleaning the tables, then swept the floor. Then she looked at the long room, parallel to the road. The walls were dark, as was the battered, mismatched furniture. Of course, when the place was full, none of that showed. She wandered toward the back room and paused in the doorway, listening. For what? The ghosts of long-gone musicians? In the murky light from the weak lightbulbs, the empty room looked sad and shabby. Again she tried to imagine it packed wall to wall with bodies, moving to whatever beat the band generated. It wasn't easy. The rock face at the rear was cold, and she'd been told that when it rained it got pretty damp back here. To be honest, the place just didn't look all that impressive. So what had drawn so many musicians to it? Maybe the acoustics were spectacular. "Hello?" she said tentatively, feeling foolish. Her voice echoed hardly at all. With a sigh she turned off the lights, locked up, and walked out to where she'd parked her car.

Chapter 5

The papers she'd left scattered on her table on Thursday didn't look any more appealing to Maura the next morning, and she had no new insights to add. If she was lucky, the pub was breaking even, with maybe a bit left over. But the slow season was looming, and there wasn't much to be done about that. Unless . . .

Maura knew a little bit about the traditional side of Irish music, as she'd told Billy. With Boston's Irish population, it was hard to avoid. She didn't particularly like it; she'd always found it kind of sloppy sentimental or sad. Lots of dying and mourning—or being betrayed by a fair maiden. Not really her thing. Nor were the endless celebrations of battles bravely fought and almost always lost. Had the Irish ever won a battle?

Once she was dressed, she stuck her nose out the front

door and found the temperature cool but not unpleasantly so. She pulled on a sweater and stepped out. Walking to the end of the lane, she saw Mick's car parked in front of Bridget's house and didn't want to intrude, so she turned around and walked toward the other end, where the lane petered out in a farmyard with the abandoned house and a barn that housed mostly hay. She listened to the birds in the hedgerow on the other side: they were still busy. The cattle in the field off to her right looked up with mild curiosity and, when she didn't offer them any food or entertainment, went back to cropping the still-green grass. As a born-and-bred city girl, Maura was still surprised by how loud a group of cows tearing and chomping could be. There were maybe fifteen cows in the field, and she idly wondered how many cows it took to make a herd. Was this enough? They were black and white, a pretty contrast to the mostly green landscape, but Maura had no idea what breed they were.

Someday, Maura thought, she should introduce herself to her other neighbors, beyond Bridget and these cows. There *were* other people living nearby who occupied nice houses that had been built when the Celtic Tiger was briefly thriving, although uphill the new houses alternated with older houses, now abandoned. Some of those looked to be in decent shape, like hers, while others had been left to fall to pieces, like the one directly next door. *Why is nobody living on this farm?* Maura had trouble imagining people just walking away from a perfectly good house in the country, although she knew that even in cities like Boston it happened quite a bit. But those places were usually owned by absentee landlords, who refused either to pay taxes and manage them or to give them up to the city (which probably didn't have the money to do anything with them anyway). She sighed. Maybe she should ask Bridget for the history of the hill.

Maura figured she might as well head for the pub, and when she pulled up in front of Sullivan's, Tim Reilly was already there, leaning against the wall next to the door, hands stuffed in his pockets. He straightened up when he saw her. "I didn't know what time you opened," he called out when she opened the car door.

"It kind of changes day to day," Maura said. "Technically it's ten thirty, but we don't always follow that if there are no customers. Usually we're open before twelve, at least, during the week."

"I can go away and come back later, if I'm in the way," he volunteered.

"You don't have to do that—I'm happy to have company. I can offer you coffee, but nothing to eat," she reminded him.

"You don't do food here?" Tim asked.

"Not at the moment. The former owner didn't, and I haven't changed much since I took over. There's a kitchen behind the bar, but I hear from other people who are doing it that it's a real pain to meet all the European Union regulations these days, so I haven't done anything about it." Maura got the door unlocked and pushed it open. "Come on in."

Tim followed her into the empty pub. "Thank you. When will Billy be in?"

"Whenever he decides to come in. He lives at the other end of the building, so he doesn't have far to come. But he knows that you'll be waiting for him, so I'm sure he'll be here soon." Plus Maura suspected Billy knew Tim would be good for at least another pint or two. Did Tim have the cash to keep Billy—or anyone else he might interview—supplied with Guinness?

"I like yer paintings," Tim said, pointing to the large ones that flanked the fireplace.

Maura went around turning on lights, and then she figured she might as well start the fire, take the edge off the room after a cool night. "They're done by a local artist who lives nearby. You might see her in here if you're around for a bit longer."

While Maura stacked turf in the fireplace, Tim wandered around the room, peering at the photos and flyers and even a few posters tacked or stapled or taped to the walls—growing more and more excited as he went. "Do you know what you have here?"

"You mean, all that stuff? Not a clue."

"This is amazing! It's like a history of music for the last few decades, all jumbled up with tourist shots and sporting events and who knows what. You mind if I take some photos?" He reached out a reverent hand to touch one of the posters, as if to make sure it was real.

"Knock yourself out. Maybe when you're done, you can tell me who some of those people are—the ones on the posters, I mean. Do you have a schedule for this project of yours?"

Tim sat on a bar stool and continued to look around, his mobile in his hand. "Did you say something about coffee? As for the schedule, this is kind of an exploratory trip, you know? I mean, I didn't know what I'd find here, if anything at all. All I had to go on were some comments from people, and I've seen a couple of references to this place here—Sullivan's—in the newspaper archives. I kept finding not big articles or profiles, but more like a mention here or there in a music mag that folded ten years ago, that kind of thing. The name Sullivan's popped up often enough that I got curious, and I thought I'd come see for myself. Now, even though me ma was raised near here, I'd never been to Cork, and I couldn't figure how this out-of-the-way spot could pull in big names, since it looked kind of an unlikely spot for a music mecca, doesn't it? Sorry—I don't mean to offend you."

"I know it's a dump, but apparently that's the way some of my customers like it," Maura said as she set a cup of coffee in front of him. "I've been taking it slow, because I'm afraid if I change anything I'll drive away what few I have, and I need every one of them."

"You haven't been here long?" Tim asked.

"I told you, barely six months, which is why I don't know anything about what you're looking for. I haven't even looked hard at that back room, because we've never had a big enough crowd to need it."

"It must've been grand back in the day," Tim said dreamily, looking past her without seeing.

"Why are you so interested?" Maura asked, making herself a cup of coffee as well. "You said your mother came from Clonakilty? That's not far."

"Yeah, but once she got to Dublin she never looked back. She's got no family left there."

"Was Sullivan's unusual, or were there places like this all over Ireland? That brought in musicians, I mean—I know there are plenty of places to drink and talk."

"Ah, that's the real question, Maura. And that's what I want to understand. You have to remember how far back our traditions in music go, along with our poetry. We were often a people who were afraid to commit words to paper, even if we could write, so we committed the words to memory instead, and we passed them on. We're a nation of poets, or bards, if you will, and that may be why the old forms have persisted, even in modern rock music. You must have heard enough of it to know that."

"Okay, I get that, Tim, but you didn't really answer the question: what made *this* place special?"

"To be honest with you, I don't know. That's why I'm here. That's why I want to talk to the people who were part of it, because maybe they can explain how it all happened. Or maybe we'll never know. But it did happen."

"I'm sorry I can't help you more."

"Ah, don't worry yerself—there'll be plenty who were around back then. Billy's a grand man fer the stories." He turned eagerly as Rose came in. Maura noted that Rose was wearing a sweater that she'd never seen before—for Tim?

"Good morning, Tim," Rose said brightly. "Did you find the hostel all right?"

"I did, and they fixed me up for a bed," he said.

Something in his tone made Rose look more sharply at him. "Is it not to yer liking, then?"

He shrugged. "I'm in a room with three Norwegian guys who seem to have visited every pub in Skibbereen yesterday. Even asleep they were loud."

"I'm sorry if I steered you wrong. Maura, do you know anyplace else Tim might find a space?"

"The hostel's all right," Tim hurried to assure her—Maura assumed because he didn't have the money for anything better. Even if he hadn't been a complete stranger, she couldn't exactly offer to let him stay with her, since she hadn't done a thing with the tiny second bedroom upstairs—the sprung bed in there looked older than either of them—and she only had Old Mick's battered easy chairs downstairs, not even a sofa.

"Maybe Mrs. Keohane could take him in," Rose said to Maura eagerly. "Will it be fer long, Tim?"

The Keohanes' place was a good suggestion, Maura thought. Ellen Keohane, who lived across the road, let a couple of rooms, although it wasn't exactly a B&B. Maura had stayed there when she'd first arrived in Leap.

"Through the weekend, at least," Tim said. "Depends who I can find to talk to. But don't put yourselves out for me."

"Won't hurt to go over and see if the Keohanes have space for you," Maura said. "Do you have your stuff with you?"

"I do. I was afraid to leave it lyin' about in that room, and there isn't much anyways."

There wasn't a customer in sight, although it was still early. Tim kept bouncing from foot to foot, uncertain about what to do, where to go. Maura decided for him. "All right, let's go talk to Ellen Keohane now and get one thing done. Rose, can you cover?"

Rose looked at Tim but said, "Right so, Maura. I'll be here."

"Tim, let's go." Maura resisted the urge to take him by the hand and lead him across the street. Not that it was necessary: she could see only one car on the road, a half mile away. The traffic wouldn't pick up for another half hour at least, when people started in on their lunch errands.

"Where is it we're going?" Tim asked.

Maura pointed across the road. "The Keohanes live down below, on the harbor—you can't really see the house from here. They're nice people. Oh, they do have kids, if that's a problem."

"Not at all."

They turned down the driveway that descended toward the Keohane house. At the front door Maura rapped, and a harried Ellen opened it. "And a good morning to you, Maura. How are yeh? Sorry I haven't stopped by, but the wee ones keep me busy."

"I'm great, Ellen. Look, I have a favor to ask. This is Tim Reilly." Maura nudged him forward. "He's a student from Dublin and he's here for a few days. I wondered if you had a room free for him? If it's no trouble."

Ellen smiled warmly at him. "Ah, sure, not a problem. We don't get much in the way of visitors once the summer's over, and truth be told, I don't go looking for them, what with the children and all keeping me busy. But yer welcome to stay, Tim. Will you be here long?"

"Thank you, Mrs. Keohane," Tim said politely. "Only a few days, I think. I'm doing research for university, and I'm not sure how much I'll find. But this would be great, right across from the pub."

"Then we're fixed. Maura, I've got a women's club meeting at the church, while the babes are in school. Tim, you can stop by later and I'll give you the tour of the place and a key, if that suits?"

"That's great, thank you."

"Thanks, Ellen," Maura added. "Stop by the pub if you can—I've put in a new coffee machine."

"Grand! See yeh."

Ellen shut the door with a smile, and Maura turned to Tim. "There, that's one thing taken care of. Let's go back and see if Billy has arrived."

Chapter 6

Billy was settled in his usual spot by the time Maura and Tim returned, and Tim made a bee-line for the fireplace corner. Billy welcomed him. "Ah, the very lad! I've been thinking back to the days yer asking about, and I have a lot to tell yeh. But my throat's a bit dry, so it is." He looked expectantly at Tim, although with a twinkle in his eye—Maura knew Billy was never offended if someone ignored his broad hints.

This time around Tim knew what Billy meant. "Oh, right. Be right back." Tim went over to the bar, where Rose greeted him as though he had just returned from the war front, even though he'd been gone all of fifteen minutes. Tim relaxed against the bar while Rose started a pint and waited for it to settle.

Maura pulled up a chair next to Billy's. "You aren't just yanking his chain, are you?" she asked in a low voice.

Billy regarded her, not in the least insulted. "I might give the tourists a bit of fancy talk, but I've more than enough real history to make the lad happy. It's been a while, but I'm glad to revisit the memories."

"You'd known Mick a long time, hadn't you?" Maura asked softly.

"Only all me life."

Tim returned quickly, carrying the brimming pint with care. "There you go, sir."

"So yer back to 'sir,' are you? It's Billy to my friends, and I'd be proud to count you among them."

"Thank you . . . Billy. Do you mind if I take notes again about what you tell me? Or even record it? I'd hate to miss something important."

"Whichever yeh choose is fine by me. I won't say that there was anything so important as all that went on here, but we saw many well-known faces now and again. There was this one time . . ." And Billy launched yet another story, with Tim scribbling fast in his pocket-size notebook. Maura would have loved to stay to listen, but it was nearly noon, and the pub was beginning to fill with people stopping by on their way to or from somewhere.

Back at the bar, Rose said, "So he tells me he'll be stayin' at the Keohanes' place, then?"

"Yeah. Tim seems like a nice guy," Maura said, looking at Rose out of the corner of her eye. "But he won't be sticking around, you know."

"Ah, Maura, that sounds like something me mother

would say, God rest her soul," Rose answered, and a brief shadow passed over her face. "I'm not an eejit, but there's few enough young fellas in here to talk to. Can't I enjoy the company for a while?"

"Sure you can."

"It's kind of you to worry, though. You worry a lot, don't you?"

"Do I?" Maura asked. She did, of course, but she tried not to share her worries much. Was she that obvious?

"You do. You get this kind of frown, like yer thinkin' hard. Is there anything wrong?"

"No more than usual, Rose," Maura said. "Mostly about how to bring in enough customers to pay the bills."

"It's as busy as I've ever seen the place, this time of year," Rose said, "not that I've been here long, but me da has and he says the same."

"I'm sure that the people around here have been curious about me, the new American who kind of dropped out of the sky and ended up here. But will they keep coming, now that they've met me?"

"Sure and they will. Yer right that they were curious, but I'd say they liked what they saw. And there are those that are happy that you haven't tried to change things, or not too fast."

"If it ain't broke, don't fix it." Well, that didn't strictly apply, since Old Mick had let the place decline slowly over years, as far as Maura could tell, and there had been a number of things that needed fixing sooner rather than later. But she didn't see the point of changing things until she had a better idea of what was working and what wasn't.

The door swung open, and a guy came in, someone

Maura didn't recognize. Tall, thin, midfifties, his dark hair long and laced with gray. He was dressed in jeans that looked honestly (not fashionably) faded by time and wear, an equally faded shirt, and an old leather jacket over it. He paused in the doorway and looked around the room with a half smile on his face. Then he walked over to the bar.

"What can I get you?" Maura asked.

"I'm lookin' for Billy Sheahan." His accent was Irish, but not local, Maura decided. In her six months in Ireland she'd learned to distinguish among a few of the regional accents, and his was neither town nor farm in Cork. Dublin, maybe?

She nodded toward Billy and Tim, next to the fireplace. "Over there."

"Ta," he said and strode across the room on long legs.

Billy tore his attention away from Tim to look at the stranger. His eyes lit up. "Well, and if it isn't Niall Cronin! What brings you to this far corner of the west?"

"I heard there was someone askin' about the auld days, when me and the fellas used to play here. I thought I'd stop by and see what was what."

"This here's the young man himself"—Billy nodded toward Tim, who jumped to his feet—"Timothy Reilly. Tim, my boy, this is—"

Tim spoke in reverent tones before Billy could finish. "Niall Cronin!" He stuck out his hand. "I've been listening to yer albums half my life. This is fantastic! Can I talk to you? Do you have the time? Not like an interview, exactly, but—"

"Slow down, Tim," Niall said. "I'm not going anywhere right now, and I'd be happy to talk. But it's been a long drive today from Dublin and I'm parched."

This time Tim was even quicker on the uptake. "Can I get you a pint?" he asked. "Billy, you need another one yet?"

"Nah, I'm fine fer now. You go on, then, take care of Niall."

Tim all but bounded over to the bar. "I need a pint," he told Maura.

"So we heard," she replied as Rose set about pulling a pint. Maura leaned forward on the bar. "So who is that guy who has you so excited?"

"You don't know Niall Cronin? He was the lead singer and bass player for the Weeping Chestnuts."

"The what?" Maura couldn't dredge up any memory of a band with a name involving chestnuts, but apparently a lot of Irish bands had never made it across the Atlantic.

Tim's eyes widened. "You really haven't heard of them? They were absolutely pivotal in the early nineties—pushed the Irish music scene in a whole new direction. I mean, this man is legend, like rock royalty around here. And he's willing to talk to me!"

"That's great, Tim. You're off to a good start. You know, he asked for Billy when he came in. I wonder how he heard that someone was interested."

"I don't know and I don't care, so long as he's here now," Tim said happily. "Is his pint ready?"

"That it is," Rose said and slid it across the bar.

When Tim turned to deliver the precious pint, trying hard not to spill it, Maura turned to Rose. "Have you ever heard of this Niall guy?" she whispered.

Rose shrugged. "He looks older than me da," she whispered back.

A few more people came in, and there was no more time to talk. But every time Maura looked over at the three men

50

in the corner, they were deep in conversation. Or at least the two older ones were, while Tim looked like he wanted nothing more than to sit at their feet in worship while writing madly in his notebook, which wouldn't last the day based on how quickly he was turning the pages. Again Maura wondered how it happened that Niall, whom Tim had called rock royalty, had appeared at this particular moment, asking for Billy. As far as she knew, Billy didn't even have a phone, let alone a computer or Internet access to put the word out.

The three men spent the afternoon in the corner, ignoring the startled looks from those few customers who wandered in and recognized the star. Tim ran out for sandwiches and chips early in the afternoon, but he resumed his former position in record time. A few more pints were ordered and delivered. Rose went home at five, pouting a bit because Tim had paid her no attention at all during the entire afternoon. Mick came in shortly after Rose left, and Maura enjoyed witnessing his double take when he scanned the room and then fixed his gaze on the trio.

He came quickly around the bar. "Do you know who that is?" he said in a low voice.

"Only because Tim told me. You're impressed?"

"I am that! What in the name of all that's holy is Niall Cronin doing here?"

"He came in around noon looking for Billy."

"What for?" Mick asked.

"How would I know? They've been talking all this time, and I think Tim there is in hog heaven."

Mick looked briefly bewildered by her metaphor but then went on, "Would he mind if I went over and introduced myself?"

"You're asking my permission? Go for it."

Mick tucked in his shirt and strode over to where the men were sitting. Maura couldn't hear their conversation, but watching the pantomime was entertaining in itself. Billy was in his element, presiding over the gathering. Niall sat beside him, relaxed and expansive. Tim had claimed a low chair a bit farther from the pair and looked annoyed at Mick's intrusion. Mick—normally reserved— was as effusive as Maura had ever seen him and seemed a bit awed at the company in which he found himself. After a minute or two, Mick pulled up a chair and joined the group. Maura might have resented him leaving her alone with all the pub duties, but she was having too much fun observing the impression Niall had on the customers—a couple of whom showed the same reaction as Mick.

The door swung open to reveal another stranger, who hesitated as he scanned the room. His face lit up when he spotted Niall. He approached tentatively, but when Niall looked up, he stood and greeted the newcomer warmly. The crowd had thinned enough that Maura could hear their conversation now.

"I wasn't sure you'd come," Niall said. "I would've given you a lift."

The man waved a dismissive hand. "No worries. I took the bus—had some business to take care of. But I brought me fiddle." He held up the fiddle case as evidence.

"Good man," Niall said. "These two here are Tim Reilly, who's asking about the likes of us for some research he's doing, and Billy Sheahan, who started things rollin'. And I don't recall this other lad," he added, looking at Mick.

"Mick Nolan." Mick introduced himself.

"Pleasure," the new arrival said. "What's a man got to do to get a pint around here?"

Maura had been watching them and decided it was time to introduce herself. She came out from behind the bar and walked over to their table. "You ask me—I'm the owner, Maura Donovan." Maura held out her hand.

The man took it and shook. "It's a pleasure, Maura Donovan. Do I take it Old Mick has gone to meet his maker?"

Maura nodded. "Six months back. He left the place to me. A pint?"

"That would be brilliant. Oh, where are me manners? I'm Aidan Crowley. Niall and me, we started out together and played here a few times. But we haven't seen much of each other for . . . how long is it now, Niall?"

"Donkey's years," Niall said. "Sit down with us, will you, Aidan? We're telling Tim here stories of the old days."

Maura glanced at Tim, who looked somehow less excited than he had only minutes before. Maybe he didn't want to share Niall's attention. Or maybe this Aidan guy didn't measure up to Niall's standard. But he seemed to be a friend of Niall's—and he wanted a drink. Maura filled a pint and brought it over, though the men all but ignored her, lost once again in sharing reminiscences.

It was close to six when the group broke up. Mick stood up first and shook hands with Niall and nodded at Aidan. Niall said something to Tim, who looked like he'd been struck by lightning, and then the two left together, trailed by Aidan. Billy stayed where he was, looking as pleased with himself as a contented tabby cat.

When Mick returned to the bar, Maura asked wryly, "Did you have fun?"

"Sorry, I know I left you holding the bag. But how often do I get the chance . . . That was brilliant!"

"Are the guys all off to find dinner?"

"They are."

"Is Aidan someone I should recognize?"

"He was never as big as Niall, but Niall's always been generous to his friends, and they go way back."

"That's nice. Did they pay for their drinks?"

"I told them they were on the house," Mick said. "I'll cover it."

"I'll split it with you," Maura said, deciding quickly. "It might be good publicity for us, if word gets out." It added up to nearly a dozen pints between them all, and Maura hoped it would be worth it.

Mick guessed where her thoughts were going. "Don't worry, they'll be back. And I think they'll bring some others along. Maura, I think we have something to talk about here."

Maura smiled. "And I think I might know what it is. Later, then, after the rush." Which, if word got out that Niall Cronin was in town, might actually exist for once.

Mick smiled back. "Count on it."

Chapter 7

Her prediction, or her hope, was right: even for a Friday evening it was respectably busy, and it was close to eleven when the last patron headed out the door into the night. Jimmy hadn't come in until after six, but Maura let him off the hook for final cleanup, because she wanted time to talk with Mick.

When the chores were done, Mick poured himself a pint of Guinness. "Will you join me in a drink?" he asked Maura.

"Sure, but I'll have a coffee. I've got to drive home, and I can't risk losing my edge when I'm driving the lanes after dark. I think my car is wider than they are."

She made herself a cup and leaned on the bar. "So, you going to fill me in on what you guys talked about?"

"Young Tim seems to have set off something with his questions."

"That's what I thought, but I don't begin to understand what or how. Let's start with how this Niall person in Dublin knew that Billy Sheahan in Leap was interested in talking to him at this particular point in time."

Mick smiled into his glass. "It was always like that."

Maura felt like stamping her foot in frustration. "Mick, that doesn't explain anything. If you wish for it, it will happen? Some kind of psychic network? I'm not buying that. Someone sends out a call and the troops gather? It's not like Billy signed on to his Facebook page and told all his followers, so how does this work?"

He looked at her then. "Maura, why do you have to know? What's it matter? Twenty years ago Sullivan's drew people in from all corners of the country, but nobody could say how. You'll jump down my throat, I have no doubt, but I'd say there *is* something magic about it all." Seeing the expression on Maura's face, Mick hurried to add, "Leavin' out the pesky details, it's probably something like Billy spoke to someone yesterday, and that person told someone else, who knew someone, and eventually it made it to Niall, who after all was somewhere in the country, rather than on tour in Thailand. Ireland is a small island, you know."

"Yeah, but then what? Niall immediately dropped everything to drive here and see Billy? Why?" Maura said dubiously.

"For the music, of course. It was always about the music."

"Will there be more people just showing up tomorrow?"

"Count on it—if Niall's here, and his old friend Aidan, there'll be more."

Maura wasn't sure what she thought about that. "Great. Like I said, send out an order to the universe, and your wish will be delivered the next day. Why didn't I think of that?"

"It could do. You should be happy—tomorrow night we'll be filled here. I'm guessing Tim will be a happy man by the end of the day." Mick took a sip of his pint. "Was there something more yeh wanted to talk about?"

"Yes, but I'm still thinking it through. I've been going through the numbers—you know, money in, money out— for this place, and it's not pretty. We're getting by, but there's nothing left for improvements or upgrades or changes. Or raises." Not that anybody had asked for one, Maura admitted to herself. "But after hearing today about how Sullivan's used to be *the* place for live music from current bands, not just in this neighborhood but in the whole county, I'm wondering if maybe we can bring the music back if enough people remember. Does that make sense?"

"Possibly," Mick said thoughtfully.

From the tone of his response Maura couldn't tell what Mick was really thinking. "Thing is, I don't know squat about the music scene around here—I don't know performers, let alone what the competition is like, or what Sullivan's could offer that they don't. I mean, don't we need a hook or something?"

"A gimmick to draw them in? I see." Mick thought for a few moments, in no hurry to answer. "There's the places that do traditional *seisiúns*, and not just for tourists. There are plenty of players who enjoy getting together when they have the time. The groups aren't fixed—whoever shows up with an instrument can join in. And there's some clubs in

Skib, but from what I've heard, they go more for quantity than quality of music, if you know what I mean."

"Loud?"

"Bang on. The kids like 'em, but you could paint this old place pink and add neon all 'round and you still wouldn't bring that lot in here."

Maura had to grin at the image of Sullivan's tarted up with neon. "Ick. Like dressing up a pig, eh?"

Mick smiled. "You could say that. What made this place special was that for a lot of the players who came here, this was just a back room to hang out in with the boys—and the occasional girl—and maybe play some tunes if the spirit moved them. They weren't performances for an audience, like, although sometimes it was hard to tell the difference. You never knew who might show up, but they all played together and the music was brilliant. There were even some recordings made, although I've no idea where those might have gotten to. If they survived at all."

Maura digested what he had said. "Did the performers get paid?" she asked bluntly.

"They'd have been insulted if yeh offered them money. They played for the love of it."

And maybe the free drinks? No, that was cynical: Maura figured she should at least try to believe that the music had been more important. "So the bar stayed open? There was some income from selling drinks?"

"Of course. What is it yer gettin' at, Maura?"

"Mick, here's the thing: we need to bring more people in if Sullivan's is going to survive. If we had a rep in the past for good music, do you think we can do it again?"

"With you knowin' nothin' about the music?"

"*You* do. Don't you?"

"Are you askin' me for my help in this?"

Much as Maura hated giving up any part of her control over the pub, this was something she couldn't do by herself. "Yes, I am."

Mick almost smiled. "Indeed. And what is it yer expecting me to do?"

"I don't know. Make that magic happen. Bring back the bands, and hope that the people will follow. And then they'll buy drinks. And talk up the whole thing and bring in more people."

"And then that'll fix all yer problems, eh?"

"Don't laugh at me, Mick. It's a start. Otherwise Sullivan's may just die a slow death. Is that what you want?"

Mick gave her a searching look. "You want to keep this place going."

Maura thought long before replying. "I guess I do. I may not have been here for long, but I can see how people feel about this place and why they kept coming even while it went downhill. Part of that was out of loyalty to Old Mick, and obviously I'm not him. But he left the place to me, and I don't want to see it go down without a fight." It was the first time she'd put it into words, and as Maura said it, she realized she meant it.

Mick slouched against the bar, looking vaguely interested. "Fair enough. So what's yer plan?"

"I don't have one. That's the problem. But if Niall Cronin is as important as you say he is, and *he* came, then maybe we've got an opportunity here. Maybe we could ask him to do a benefit concert or whatever you want to call it for Old Mick, and that could kick things off. Could that work?"

"Maybe." Mick fell silent, thinking. Finally he said, "Let me suggest this: see what tomorrow brings."

For some reason, that annoyed Maura. Wasn't he taking this seriously? "You're throwing stupid sayings at me?"

"Not at all. I'm saying, give it a day. If what I think may happen does happen, and Niall and Aidan were just the first wave, then we'll have a better handle on things by tomorrow night. Or maybe Sunday morning. If nothing's changed, you can think again, and you've lost nothing but a day."

Maura considered. Mick *had* listened to what she'd suggested, and he hadn't rejected it entirely. If he was right, tomorrow might be a very interesting day. If he was wrong and nothing happened, no loss, as he pointed out. Besides, it was late, it had been a long day, and there was nothing more to be done at the moment. "All right. We'll wait and see what happens tomorrow."

Mick drained his glass, then rinsed it and set it to dry. "Right. That's me off fer the night, then. I'll be in tomorrow afternoon, although if they're spillin' out the door by midday, give me a ring."

"Just in case something magical happens?" Maura said with a smile.

"Just so. Good night."

Chapter 8

It rained during the night, and on Saturday morning when Maura opened her front door a sliver, she could see that the lane was muddy. Not exactly what she wanted to wade through to visit Bridget, but she wanted the older woman's opinion about the ideas that were bouncing around in her head. On the other hand, a woman of Bridget's age probably wouldn't have spent much time listening to music in a pub. Had women gone to pubs at all a half century ago, when Bridget was young? Practically speaking, there would have been kids at home and chores to be done in the evenings, from which the men were often exempt, given that they'd spent their days outside dealing with cattle or sheep or crops, or some combination of the three. It must have been a hard life; the idea of trying to feed everyone by cooking over an open fire, not to mention just fitting mom, dad, and a bunch of children (maybe even an in-law) into a typical two-bedroom home with no plumbing, was daunting. Maura still had trouble wrapping her head around how people had done it. She lived pretty high on the hog by those old standards: she lived alone in her four-room house and didn't have to worry about an outhouse. Now, of course—or at least until a few years ago—rich Dubliners or people from England or even Germany had been snapping up cottages like hers and calling them quaint and charming (after they'd added plumbing and electricity). What a strange turn of events!

Despite the mud, Maura squared her shoulders, grabbed her sweater, and marched down the lane toward Bridget's house. No sign of Mick's car this morning, so she was free to get Bridget's opinion of her plans.

She rapped on the front door, which faced the rising sun. Bridget opened it after a half minute and smiled up at her. "*Fáilte romhat*, my dear. I wondered if you'd be stoppin' by this morning."

"Good morning, Bridget. I thought I'd let you and Mick have some time together yesterday. Have you talked to him since?"

"About what yer plannin' for the pub? No, he hasn't said anything."

Maura laughed. "Hang on—if he didn't tell you, how did you hear about what I was thinking about? Mick and I didn't really talk about anything until after closing last night."

"From Billy Sheahan, of course."

Maura cocked her head at Bridget. "How so? That doesn't make sense. I know Billy doesn't travel around, especially at night. Does he have a phone I don't know about?"

"No phone—he says he can't abide those tinny little voices squeaking in his ear. But Billy has friends, and his friends have friends, and the word gets around. Would you care for tea?"

"Yes, thank you, I would like tea. And more of an explanation." Maura walked into Bridget's spotless home and closed the door behind her.

"It's made already. Help yerself and then sit with me."

Maura followed instructions, after making sure Bridget was also well supplied with tea. "All right, tell me: how do you know about my plans?"

"Maggie Sweeney, who lives down the hill—she told me that her brother stopped by Sullivan's yesterday. He lives over to Union Hall but he stops by regular, and he recognized Niall Cronin."

Unlike me, the clueless American. Well, at least it wasn't voodoo that got the word out locally. "Have I met Maggie? Or her brother?"

"You might have seen him at the pub, but he's a bit shy so he might not have talked to you. He's a fine man, though," Bridget said.

"I'm sure he is," Maura said impatiently. "So he came in for a pint and recognized Niall, and he told his sister? Did he talk to Billy?"

"He didn't have to. He remembers back in the day when Niall and the lads would stop by of an evening and play the night away. Is that not what you'd be thinkin' of, dear? Goin' back to the way it was?"

"Sort of. What do you think? If we started offering music again, would someone like Maggie's brother come? Would his friends?"

"Now and then, I'd guess. If you don't make a big thing of it."

"What on earth does that mean?"

"No big push to get the word out. Just let it happen, the way it used to."

Bridget's advice ran counter to anything Maura had heard about modern promotion: ads in print publications, radio spots—where was the nearest radio station? Cork?— invitations to everyone via some mailing list she didn't even have, not to mention "social media" like Facebook and Twitter, about which she knew little and cared less. Oddly, Bridget's suggestion not to promote at all would make things a lot easier, if she decided to go ahead with this thing. All Maura had to do was gather the musicians at Sullivan's—although how she was supposed to make that happen mystified her—and the rest would apparently follow. Her only job would be to serve drinks and make nice. Could it be that simple? She shook her head, smiling.

"You don't think it will happen, do you, now?" Bridget asked softly.

Maura sipped her tea, stalling. "Bridget, I don't know what I think. It seems crazy, but I was there when Niall Cronin walked in. I've never heard of him, but I could see how excited Mick was to see him there, and Tim Reilly looked ready to explode. If there were enough people who felt like that, it could work, I guess."

"And who would this Tim Reilly be?" Bridget asked.

"Oh, right. It seems like a whole lot has happened in the last day. Tim is a student at Trinity, and he's looking into the music from the time when Sullivan's was big. That's why he was so excited to see Niall—it was like one of his heroes just walked in the door. Me, I had no idea who he was."

"Have you no liking for the music?" Bridget asked.

"Everyone keeps asking me that. I guess I never realized that it was odd, but no, I've never been musical. We all had to play an instrument at school, but the music teacher figured pretty fast that I wasn't cut out for it." And then funding for the school district's enrichment programs had been eliminated anyway, and the music program went away along with the teacher. "And I was never into buying CDs or downloading stuff. Seemed like a waste of money to me. I mean, songs are popular for a short time, and then everybody goes on to something else."

"You wouldn't say that about Irish music. There's a long history to it, even for the young ones playin' now."

"So people keep telling me," Maura replied, draining her mug. "Well, Mick said we didn't have to decide anything until we see what happens today. Which may be nothing at all out of the ordinary."

Bridget smiled. "Wait and see."

"You sound like Mick. Or maybe he sounds like you. Want me to wash your cup?"

"I'd be glad of a top-up instead, if you don't mind."

"No problem," Maura said. She refilled the cup, added sugar and milk, and set it next to Bridget. "I guess I'd better get down to the village and prepare for . . . whatever happens. I'm sure Mick will fill you in later."

"He will that. *Slán go fóill*, my dear."

The sun had climbed over the hill to the east by the time Maura went back to her own cottage, then set off for

Leap. This whole thing seemed absurd: some kid showed up from Dublin and suddenly she was talking about reviving a long-standing musical tradition she hadn't even known about two days earlier? Maura Donovan, with the tin ear? It was a joke . . . wasn't it?

When she walked into Sullivan's after parking her car, Rose was already there, polishing the top of the bar with unprecedented energy. Tim and Mick were moving chairs and tables around and didn't even notice Maura's entrance.

"Uh, hello?" she called out as the men disappeared into the back room. "Anyone want to tell me what's going on?"

"Good morning, Maura," Rose said cheerfully. "Isn't it grand?"

"Isn't what grand?" Maura demanded.

"The old place is comin' alive, isn't it? There'll be music here tonight."

"How do you know? When I left last night, Mick and I had kicked around a few ideas, but that was as far as we got."

"That'd be my doing." Maura turned to see Niall Cronin slouching in the doorway. "I might've rung a coupla fellas last night."

"What's a 'couple'?" Maura asked.

"Enough. I told your guys here I'd stop by and see to the equipment. What you've got looks old but sound. What can you tell me about it?"

Maura looked blankly at him for a moment, trying to remember if she could even identify some of the items in the back room. "Uh, nothing? I didn't even know there *was* equipment. Apparently there's a lot I still don't know about Sullivan's. For example, nobody mentioned the music."

"Then you're in for a treat. Ah, here's Billy."

Maura spied Billy Sheahan making his slow way toward the door. She couldn't recall ever seeing him at the pub this early—it wasn't even opening time. "Good morning, Billy," she called out when he came into earshot. "Is this more of your doing?" She gestured around the room; she could hear ominous thuds and clanks from the back room, where Tim and Mick were most likely moving large, mysterious objects around.

"I might have made a small suggestion or two. Ah, Niall, it's grand to see you here again."

"Yeah, I'd almost forgotten what morning looks like. Look, I've been in touch with some of the lads, and things are looking good. Thanks for the heads-up."

"Can I get you something, Billy?" Maura asked as he settled himself in his usual chair.

"It's a bit early for the black stuff, even for me. Can you manage a cup of tea?"

"Of course. Mr. Cronin?"

Niall clutched his heart theatrically. "Oh, darlin', you cut me to the quick! Am I that old? It's Niall to pretty ladies like you. Tea would be grand."

"I'll do it," Rose volunteered, clearly starstruck.

Maura leaned closer to Rose. "When's your father coming in?"

"He'll be around directly, he said," she answered, her eyes on the metal pot she was filling with boiling water.

"How long have yeh been doin' this?" Niall asked Maura, waving a hand at the bar.

"Tending bar or running Sullivan's? I've worked in bars maybe eight years, starting before I wasn't exactly legal. I inherited Sullivan's from Old Mick about six months ago. Why?"

"I knew Old Mick, years ago. He was a force unto himself. Kind of magnetic. He drew people in to this place, against the odds."

"What happened? Why do you think it stopped?"

"Time passed. We all grew older. Makin' music isn't easy, and most of us ended up with families and responsibilities, so we couldn't go roaming about the countryside playing gigs here and there. Life moved on."

"You married?" Maura asked.

Niall gave a short laugh. "You interested?"

"Not right now, but I could add you to the list if you want," she said, surprising herself. Well, he was an attractive man. Maura found herself wondering what he was like when performing onstage.

"Wait much longer and I won't be worth much," Niall shot back, but at least he was smiling.

"Hey, we could use a hand over here!" Mick called out from the back as Rose poured a mug of tea for Niall and handed it to him, then filled another one for Billy.

"Shall we?" Niall said with exaggerated gallantry, letting Maura go before him.

"As long as you'll tell me what I'm looking at and promise it won't all blow up when you plug it in." Maura led the way into the back room. She was surprised by how much larger it looked now that a lot of the junk had been cleared away. (She had no idea where it had gone. Would she ever see it again? Did she care?) Things were moving fast. Mick and Tim had pulled out the old music equipment—Maura could do no more than lump all the pieces together under the heading "amplifiers"—and assembled it in the middle of the floor. Niall went over and ran his hands over the biggest piece with something like affection.

"I haven't seen one of these beauties for a long time. Does she still work?"

"One way to find out," Mick said and began hunting for an outlet. There weren't many in the room. "We may have to beef up the power supply a bit."

"Can you do that?" Maura asked skeptically.

"Short term, sure. In the long run we might need to do a bit of wiring. Although the equipment has changed some. We'll see."

"Uh, Mick, is there a fire department in Leap?" Maura asked, stymied by the electronic side of things. She looked around the room. She'd spent so little time in it, she had no idea what was really in here. Was there even any heat? No fireplace, though if the space was packed full with moving bodies, a fire might've been a hazard, and all those bodies probably provided plenty of heat. Maura shook her head, still having trouble believing this empty room could ever be "full" or "packed." She'd never seen more than two people in it before now. But best to keep the possibility of a crowd in mind, she supposed. Were there any access doors? There appeared to be one on the side, past the small wooden stage. Although maybe "stage" was an exaggeration: it was a roughly square wooden platform that rose no more than a foot from the floor. One more door opened out the back, up at the balcony level. The bar Maura remembered ran along the width of the room opposite the stage—and it was filthy. How long since anyone had used it? There were glasses lined up, but they'd all need washing. No liquor on the shelves, though, and probably no kegs for the taps.

"Mick? Can we serve from here? Or does it all have to come from the front? And what about supplies?" she asked.

"I've already laid in two more kegs—they'll be here this afternoon," he replied absently, studying a cluster of electric cords in his hand. Niall went over to help sort out which was which.

"Should I ask Rose to wash the glassware?"

"Good idea."

"I'll help," Tim volunteered, which surprised Maura: he'd been gaping at Niall like a lovesick puppy since the man had walked in. Rose should be flattered, if she knew.

Maura felt like a third wheel, so she left Niall and Mick to their electrical issues and went back to the front of the house. She stopped first at the bar. "Rose, can you figure out what needs cleaning up in the back? And make sure we've got enough glasses out for . . . whatever. Tim said he'd help you, if you need to carry stuff."

"Right away."

When Rose disappeared to the back, Maura went over to talk with Billy, who was happily settled with a thick mug of dark tea. She dropped into a chair beside him and checked her watch: still an hour from opening. What had she just gotten into?

"Yer lookin' a bit unsettled, Maura," Billy observed.

"I am. Suddenly there are all these people setting up for something I don't even understand. Even you—I'm not sure I've seen you before opening time more than a few times since I took over here. I feel like I walked into a different universe. I have no idea what's going on right now and even less of a clue what's going to happen later today. That is, if something *is* going to happen." She cocked her eyebrow at Billy.

He smiled benignly at her. "Sure and it is. We've set the bird to flight and the ball to rolling and the clock to ticking. It'll be a day like no other since yer arrival."

Maura shook her head, more from confusion than because she disagreed. "I don't understand the 'what,' and I definitely don't understand the 'how.' You really think people are going to just show up?"

"That they will, when they hear that the music's back at Sullivan's. It'll be grand, you'll see."

There was a tentative rapping at the door, and through the glass Maura recognized Aidan from the day before outside. She figured Niall must have asked him to come help out, so she went over to open the door. By daylight he looked a bit frayed around the edges. "You're Aidan, right? Come on in. If you're looking for Niall, he's in the back. Can I get you some tea or coffee?"

"You'd be the American, Maura, right? Tea would be grand, ta. Hey, Billy!" Aidan nodded toward Billy, who raised a hand in salute. He followed Maura to the bar, clutching a battered fiddle case.

"Are you from around here, Aidan?" Maura asked as she prepared his tea.

"I live up to Cork these days." He didn't explain. Aidan was clearly not the chatty type. Maura hadn't visited Cork city, an hour away—with the exception of a scary trip to the Cork hospital when Jimmy had broken his arm.

"How'd you hear about this, uh, thing here?" Maura pressed on, determined to figure out how this was unfolding.

"Niall. He found me at my pub in Cork and persuaded

me to join him. You may have noticed that he can be a very persuasive man."

Maura laughed. "Yeah, I have kind of noticed that!" She slid his mug of tea across the bar. When Aidan reached into his pocket for some change, she waved him off. "On the house." She was already in so deep it wouldn't make a difference. Call it promotional expenses—not that she had any such line item in her budget. All right, call it an investment in the future.

Aidan lifted his mug to her. "Thanks, love." Then he picked up his fiddle case with his other hand and went toward the back, from which ominous noises were emerging.

Chapter 9

In an hour, the old pub was as clean as Maura had ever seen it. She'd even sicced Tim on the bathrooms; he'd started this whole thing, he could do the grunt work. He didn't even complain, and now the loos were better than they once were—still far from what they could be, but they'd have to do. By ten thirty, the regular opening time, there were already a few people waiting outside on the sidewalk, talking to each other. Maura unlocked the door, and as they came in, one asked her, "Is it true? About the music, I mean? Will it be happenin'?"

"Wait and see." She had no better answer to give them, so might as well keep them guessing.

She hadn't noticed Skibbereen garda Sean Murphy waiting behind the others. "Hello, Sean," Maura greeted the young police officer. "What brings you here, business or pleasure?" She wasn't sure which she would prefer. They'd gone out together once—technically, only a half date, since it had been cut short by a call from the gardaí station in Skibbereen. She had the feeling Sean would like to try it again, but she wasn't sure what she wanted: Sean was a nice guy and she enjoyed his company, but that didn't mean she wanted to date him. Going out with him again would probably have half the women in County Cork planning their wedding.

"Shall we walk?" he said.

From his tone, Maura decided that he was in official garda mode. Was there some regulation she didn't know about that she'd already violated? "Sure, I guess. What's up?" she asked as she joined him, after checking that Rose had seen her leaving. He gestured up the low rise toward the church, and they walked side by side until they were a few paces beyond the pub. Sean cleared his throat. "There's a rumor going about that yer plannin' a night of music here tonight."

"Maybe," Maura said cautiously. "I wouldn't say it's exactly planned." When Sean gave her a solemn look, she hurried to explain what had been going on over the past couple of days. "I told Tim to talk to Billy Sheahan, which he did—and then things start happening, and this guy Niall Cronin ups and walks in yesterday afternoon."

"Hold on—you mean *the* Niall Cronin?" Sean asked, surprised.

"Apparently. So you're a fan too? I had never heard of the guy."

"Ah, Maura . . ." Sean shook his head. "He's quite well-known here in Ireland. So what happened next?"

"Well, this Niall comes in asking for Billy, and Tim—that's the student—nearly falls off his chair, he's so excited."

She explained about how the guys had talked all afternoon, then left together. "Then I show up this morning and it seems like they've all decided they're having a thing at the pub tonight."

"A thing?" Sean raised one eyebrow.

"Shoot, I don't know what to call it. A musical event or something."

"You may need a permit for a gathering of unusual size," Sean said, his tone official.

They'd almost reached the church. Maura stopped and said, "But I don't know what's happening! I don't know who's coming, or how many, either musicians or listeners. It still may turn out that no more than three people show up. I just don't know!" She sat down on the low stone wall in front of the church parking lot and glared a challenge at Sean.

He settled next to her. "I see yer problem, Maura, but I wouldn't want things to get out of hand."

"You think I do? How am I supposed to plan for something I don't begin to understand? You tell me. I mean, how far would people come to hear an over-the-hill rocker playing in a small room that's basically a cave?"

Sean's mouth twitched with a suppressed smile. "I hope you've not been callin' Niall Cronin old to his face! There are those would say he changed the course of Irish music in the last years of the twentieth century."

"Yeah, yeah," Maura muttered. "I've already heard that. I do know better than to go around insulting people—if nothing else, it's bad for business. But what is it you want me to do?"

"What you've just done: tell me what's goin' on, so I can keep an eye on things. Do you know what the legal capacity of Sullivan's might be?"

"No, not officially. Mick said something like two hundred people. I'm pretty sure the biggest crowd we've had since I've been here was more like fifty. Why? Do I have to count heads and lock the door if the head count goes too high? Sean, look, I'm not trying to make this hard for you, but this thing has just taken off like crazy since yesterday, and I truly don't know what I'm dealing with. And nobody mentioned permits."

Sean sighed, his eyes on the gas station across the street. "I wish we had more men, but there are few enough as it is to go around in Skibbereen of a Saturday night. I'll ask a patrol to swing by when they can, and you know where to find me if you need assistance, should things get out of hand."

"You think they might?" Maura asked.

"It's been known to happen," Sean said, smiling. "How about I come back with you and talk with Mick and Tim and Niall, just so they know there's someone looking after the place? I'm not assuming there'll be trouble, but I'd rather be ready for it if it happens. Does that suit you?"

"That's fine." Maura smiled at Sean—and wondered if he was looking for a chance to talk with the great Niall Cronin. "You sure you aren't just looking for an autograph? I really wish there was a quickie guide to Irish music for the last twenty or thirty years that I could read fast, so I don't embarrass myself. Again. If I don't watch out, I'll end up insulting any other musicians who show up."

"You'll be grand—just smile and look like yer glad to see them."

"Thanks, Sean. I know you're trying to help. My problem is, I don't know what help I'll need. Every time I think I have a handle on running this place, something else comes up. I'm still trying to figure out if we have enough glasses and whether plugging in a lot of electrical stuff will short out the electricity. Do I have a circuit breaker? Fuses? I don't even know where to look. I'm just hoping Mick or Jimmy does."

"I'd start with the basement, although whoever wired the place might have found that too damp, being so close to the water and all, and put all the connections somewhere else. You could ask at Donovan's Hardware, down the road. They'd likely know who did the work."

"I keep forgetting how small this place is. In Boston, if your power went off, you'd have to call your landlord, and if you were lucky enough to reach him, he'd have to figure out who to call to check it out—if he felt like it. It could take days."

They stood and started walking back toward the pub. "Sean, you're too young to remember the days when there was real music at Sullivan's, aren't you?" Maura asked, recalling that Sean was a year or two younger than she was. "Mick said he was a teenager then, and he's older than you are."

"I never saw it myself, though I've heard others talk about it."

"When I first heard about it, I kind of figured it just faded away because people lost interest. That's why I'm surprised there's so much excitement about the idea now. Or maybe that's just hot air and nothing's going to happen."

"Could be. Or could be something better," Sean said. They'd reached Sullivan's, and Sean opened the door for her. Inside, everyone was still bustling around like ants on an anthill that had been poked with a stick. Billy was settled in his chair with a benevolent expression on his face. He seemed to be enjoying himself immensely.

Maura dragged Sean over to where he sat. "Billy, Sean wants to know what we're planning here, and I told him you'd know best."

"Ah, the young garda, keepin' an eye on us all. Sit, please, so I can look yeh in the eye." He waited until Sean had taken a seat. "What do the young folk call it these days? A gathering of the bands? The word has gone out."

"Excuse me, Mr. Sheahan, but how many people do you expect here this evening?" Sean asked politely, sticking to the point. Maura figured he knew Old Billy well enough to keep him from starting up one of his stories.

"And how am I to know? Back a ways, say, twenty years ago, we'd fill the place wall to wall. Hard to say who's going to come out again. You might do well to talk to young Mick—he's in the back. He's got a better head for the business side of things. Should we have asked yer permission first, me lad? No more than a day ago, we didn't know this was happening."

"I understand that, sir. I'm just hopin' to fend off any trouble before it starts."

"And so you should. Go on now, and talk to Mick." Billy waved his hand at the same moment Mick and Niall appeared in the doorway to the back room. Maura watched with amusement as Sean's eyes lit up at the sight of Niall, although he quashed it quickly. After all, he was the garda here, and he was on duty. He stood up and strode over to where the two men were standing.

Maura kept her eyes on the trio while asking, "Billy, do we have anything to worry about? I mean, I've never seen this place get really crowded, and I have no idea who's likely to show up. Is this going to be"—she fumbled for a music term—"like, heavy rock music? The kind of thing that gets people worked up?"

Billy smiled at her. "No. Even though this won't be a traditional session, the music still draws on the old tunes and some of the instruments."

"Which means it might be kind of sad?" Maura asked.

"Sad, yes. Sometimes funny. Now and again, angry— mostly at the English. Don't borrow trouble, my dear. Let Sean keep an eye on things, but I'm sure it will all work itself out."

"I hope so, Billy. This is all new to me."

Maura saw Sean shake hands with both Mick and Niall, before coming over to say good-bye to her.

"Satisfied?" she asked.

"Fer now. I'll stop by later and, like I said, I'll tell the others at the station what's going on. Those who aren't on duty may come by on their own, once they hear."

"Everyone's welcome, as long as they buy a pint or two. Thanks, Sean, for worrying, and for looking out for us."

"That's my job, Maura. Good luck to you!"

Rose was behind the bar, watching the proceedings with glowing eyes when she wasn't busy serving the customers who came in—who weren't leaving in any hurry. What had they heard? And how?

When he'd gone, Maura turned to Rose. "Should I warn the local restaurants that this is happening? People will want to eat, won't they?" Both a bistro-style restaurant and a take-away place had opened their doors nearby in the past few months and had done good business during the summer season. But Maura had her doubts that they'd be ready for a crowd today—it seemed only right to tell them now, so they could stock up if they needed to.

"It might be a smart thing to do, if you want to stay on their good side," Rose agreed.

"Then I'll do it now, before things get crazy. *If* they get crazy, that is." She went back out the door, turning right this time. The takeaway restaurant was the closer of the two new places. The new owner had retained the old building facing the road, and that now served as a kind of deli and order station, but there was plenty of seating in a new building to the rear, alongside the river and across from Sullivan's. Since it was nearly noon, the place was beginning to fill up.

Inside, Maura leaned across the high glass case. "Is Gerry around?"

The woman making sandwiches nodded toward the rear. "In back. Big doings tonight?"

So she'd already heard. "Looks like it," Maura agreed, then headed back to find the owner. He was talking to a family seated around a table, but smiled when he saw her come in. "Ah, Maura, how are yeh? I hear yer plannin' a do tonight."

"'Planning' might be kind of exaggerated, but it looks like something's happening. I wanted to give you a heads-up in case you needed to stock up, since people may end up here looking for a meal."

"Thanks fer thinking about us. I'll warn the girls. Who's on the ticket?"

"I have no idea. Billy and Mick have cooked this up between them."

Gerry moved a little closer. "There's rumors that Niall Cronin will be playin'."

"He's over there now."

Gerry's eyes lit up. "Oh, that's grand, that is. I'll try to stop in later."

"You should. See you, Gerry." Maura made her way out the front and then crossed the road that led north from the main road, to the bistro. It was a newly built and attractive place, butted against the cliff behind, like Sullivan's, so it kind of spread out along the road. She stepped in and was greeted by more people than she was used to seeing there. Had everyone heard about this event?

She made her way to the bar. "Have you heard about tonight?" she asked the bartender.

"I have. Yer a lucky woman!"

"I don't know about luck, and so far I haven't done much to earn it. Look, I know this seems like a weird question, but in case we run out of room at Sullivan's, will you be able to take the overflow?"

"We surely will, and I'll see to it that we have food on hand for 'em. I should tell you, though, if you get half the musicians whose names I've heard kicked about, no one's going to want to be away from the place fer long."

"You may be right. Wish me luck—sounds like I may need it."

"Ah, you'll be grand. Enjoy the night!"

One more stop, at Sheahan's across the street. The bar there was already full, and the place was noisy. She leaned across the bar and caught the attention of Brian, the owner. "You've heard?" she yelled.

"I have," he said.

"You ready?"

"I am. Question is, are you?"

"I have no idea."

She let him go back to serving drinks and doling out food. Standing on the front steps of the hotel, she looked across at Sullivan's. It still looked the same—save for the growing line of parked cars.

It was barely past noon.

Chapter 10

Inside Sullivan's, controlled chaos reigned. Maura had never seen it so packed at midday, not even on a Saturday. Rose's father, Jimmy, had arrived, and he and Rose were handling the taps. Jimmy was in his element, trading quips with everyone as he pulled pints. He waved when he saw Maura come in.

"This here's the new owner of the place, Maura Donovan," he told anyone who was listening. "She's American, so she hasn't heard all yer stories. I'm betting she'd love to, though. Maura, come 'round behind. Rosie, me love, you go pick up the empties, will you, now?"

"Sure, Da," Rose said, and came around the end of the bar. Maura joined Jimmy behind it. For a moment she was overwhelmed: there were so many people (mainly men, but a few women too) clamoring for a drink—and for her attention. She plastered on a smile and said to the nearest one, "What can I get you?" It took her ten minutes to fill all the requests, and then there was another row behind, and another.

While she waited for pints to settle, she found herself repeating the same brief story over and over. No, she'd never known Old Mick. Yes, she was from America. Boston, in fact, and that usually triggered more questions, along the "do you know" lines. No, she didn't know any Irish bands, old or new, but she'd heard that some of the players might be stopping by later. It seemed that each and every man would launch into a favorite Old Mick story, or speculate on who was around and could be stopping by, or reminisce about the first pub band he'd ever heard.

At about one o'clock Niall Cronin stepped out from the back room, where Maura had been hearing odd snippets of sound issuing from behind closed doors, and there was a momentary hush in the room as people noticed him. Then suddenly the noise was back, louder than before. Niall took it in stride, politely elbowing his way to the bar. "I could use a pint, Maura, love—we're about sorted now, but it's thirsty work."

The crowd seemed evenly split between those who were in awe of the celebrity in their midst and those who wanted to have a word with him or at least shake his hand. Maura figured her stock had risen simply because the great man had called her by name.

"Everything working all right?" she asked as she topped off his pint and set it in front of him.

"Seems so. We'll see. Any others come in, send them to the back, will you?"

"Sure, no problem," Maura said. As if she'd recognize

any of the other players Niall might be referring to. Maybe Tim could help, if he could tear himself away. During a slight lull a short while later, Maura grabbed the chance to take Tim aside. "Tim, you've got to help me out here. If there are going to be all these music people coming in, I won't have a clue who they are. Or where they fit. Can you fill me in on whoever walks in the door?"

"Sure, I'd be happy to. But you can't leave the bar, can you?"

"No, you'll have to come around behind. That's a bonus—I'll show you how to manage the taps and serve at the bar, in case your university career lets you down. It's a handy skill to have."

"If you say so." Tim didn't look convinced, but Maura didn't care. She all but dragged him behind the bar and stationed him in a corner, out of the way of the taps. Rose flashed him a smile but kept pouring. "How should I let you know who's who?"

"You don't have to announce everybody," Maura said, "just give me the lowdown on anybody I should know, so I don't look like an idiot." Which she was, but still.

"Got it. Do yeh want the short history of modern Irish music first?"

"Only if there's time," Maura said to him while smiling at a local man she recognized.

"Right so. Well, if you're tellin' me that you didn't know who Niall Cronin was until he walked in, I can see I've got my work cut out here. Have you ever heard of O'Carolan?"

"No. Look, Tim, assume I grew up on Mars and never heard anything. But keep it simple—we don't have much time, and it's kind of busy, you know."

Tim nodded crisply. "Got it. Okay, here's the basics: old

Irish music was mostly about battles and the like, which the Irish mostly lost. The harp was once the main instrument, and harpers were respected men and treated well, but after 1900 the piano came in big for the upper classes, and in the country they went over to the uilleann pipes. You do know what those are?"

"Kind of like bagpipes but smaller, right?" Maura asked. She nodded at someone across the bar and pushed a waiting pint his way.

"Right. Anyways, most rural music happened in what was called the *clachán*—that's kind of a small group of homes, where the nearby people would gather and sing and dance when their work was done. Most of the bigger gatherings took place based on the agricultural year—you know, sowing, harvest, celebrating the potato digging."

"You're kidding! Irish music was influenced by potatoes?"

Tim grinned. "In a manner of speaking. Then came the famine, when so many people died or left for good, and that killed a lot of the old music as well. They say it was like a silence came over the country, what with how the language fell away as well, and the folklore, and the superstitions."

Maura checked the crowd—and the number of men waiting at the bar for their pints. "This is great stuff, Tim, but can we skip ahead to the heyday of Sullivan's, please?" she said, setting up yet another row of glasses.

Tim sighed; clearly he loved his subject and loved talking about it. "Okay, I'll fast-forward to the seventies: Planxty, with Liam O'Flynn, Christy Moore, Donal Lunny. De Danann out of Galway. The Bothy Band. From the eighties you might know of Clannad—they were a Donegal family, and Enya came out of that. Please tell me you've heard of Enya?"

"Yes, she's kind of hard to miss. Go on."

"Then there was Moving Hearts, one of the first groups to mix traditional music with contemporary rock, but they didn't last long. In the nineties you had Altan, Dervish, Arcady, and some people who went solo, like Martin Hayes, who came from County Clare but left for the States and settled there. Mostly the nineties are known for the commercialization of traditional music."

"So who played at Sullivan's?"

"The Saw Doctors. Glen Hansard, before he got so big. We talked before about the Cranberries. Plenty more you might never have heard of."

"Probably not," Maura agreed. "Are any of them likely to show up here tonight?" Were many of the members of the groups Tim had just mentioned still alive?

"Could be anyone. Plenty of people played with different bands over the years. Plenty more played in recordings behind the bands. Wasn't even fer the money—mainly they'd all help each other out. It wasn't a big community back then, so they all knew each other. And still do, if what's happenin' here is any indication."

Maura reminded herself yet again that Ireland was a very small country. Which right now was a mixed blessing. If this event took off, through word of mouth, and half of the country showed up, they'd be bursting at the seams. It would certainly put the name of the pub out there, and hers as well. It looked like it was too late to stop it now, in any case.

"Okay, Tim, that's great. Now, remind me of who's already here. It's hard to keep everybody straight. And there are more of 'em coming in all the time." Tim listed off a string of names that meant nothing to Maura, so when he finished, she said, "Point them out to me if they come out here again, will you? Oops, here's another one."

A guy with a guitar was standing in the doorway, looking confused; even if Maura couldn't identify the face, she could certainly identify a guitar case. Tim waved him over to the bar. "You've come fer the music, have you?" The man nodded. "It's in the back. But let me introduce you to the owner first—Maura Donovan. If yeh knew the place in the old days, you'll agree that she's a lot prettier than Old Mick was."

The man laughed and extended a hand. "I'm Morrie, and the lad is right."

"Thank you, Morrie. Would you like a pint to take with you to the back room?"

"I never turn down an offer like that," the man said, settling one hip on a bar stool. As Maura filled his pint, she noticed the others in the pub nudging each other and staring. It seemed they knew him, even if she didn't. "How long've yeh been runnin' the place?" he asked as they waited for the pint to settle.

"Six months now. Old Mick was a distant relative, and he left the place to me. It's a long story."

"You'll have to tell it to me someday when there's a bit more time," the man said. He took his waiting pint, grabbed the guitar case, and headed toward the back room.

When he was gone, Maura turned to Tim. "Okay, who is he?"

"That's Morrie O'Keefe. Made his mark playing with the Broken Melons, then went off on his own—has a couple of decent CDs out, not big sellers. He's been a pal of Niall's for years."

It was a scene that replayed many times during the afternoon, Tim feeding her information on the players when he could. Maura lost count and was beginning to wonder how so many people could fit in the back—it reminded her of one of those silly clown cars at the circus, only in reverse. And where on earth would there be room for an audience? Maybe the musicians didn't care; maybe they were playing for each other, as old friends.

Maura supposed she'd find out soon enough.

Chapter 11

There was a slight lull around suppertime, when the local customers reluctantly tore themselves away to go back to their families, promising they'd be back later. Maura wasn't surprised. There were hours left before the sun went down, and a long night to come. Maura decided that since she was the boss, at least in theory, she should get her small staff together and make sure they were on the same page. She ducked into the back room, where Niall and a couple more guys she didn't recognize were shoving equipment and tables around again.

"Mick, can I grab you for a minute?" Maura said loudly, trying to make herself heard over the noise.

Mick had to tear his attention away from the tangle of wiring he was trying to sort out to look at her. "What is it?"

"I want to get you and Jimmy and Rose together and

make sure we're ready for tonight." She smiled at the musicians in the room—or at least, she assumed they were musicians, since most were holding one or another instrument. "If you guys can spare him?"

"Ah, where'd I leave me manners?" Niall said with a smile. "Here we've taken over yer place, and you've never met most of the lads."

"Tim's been trying to help me with names, but it's hard to remember so many new people at once."

For some reason that inspired the group to introduce themselves to her all over again, and she wished desperately that she had name tags to stick on them. But that wasn't going to happen, so she'd just have to muddle along. And as she smiled and nodded, she had to wonder: if Niall was the superstar and the wizard who was pulling this together, where did the others fall in the rankings? Where was the split between leaders and backup? How the heck did the guys figure out how to coordinate what they played, and with who? She had no idea.

"Are more people coming?" she asked, not sure what answer she wanted to hear.

"A few more of me friends said they might be stoppin' by," Niall said.

"Sounds good to me. Mick, just a couple of minutes, please?"

"Do you need me?" Tim piped up from a corner, where Maura hadn't even noticed him. How had he managed to sneak out from behind the bar? Probably she'd been too busy to notice.

"Might as well, Tim. Then you can all get back to . . . whatever it is you're doing."

Mick and Tim reluctantly tore themselves away and trooped out to the front room, not that it was any quieter or more private, so Maura decided to keep going and take everyone into the unused kitchen behind the bar. Jimmy stood in the doorway, keeping one eye on the crowd and one ear in their conversation, with Rose standing beside him. It looked like none of her staff would be going home for dinner.

"What do you need, Maura?" Mick asked. "There's a lot to be done before tonight."

"I know, I know. Look, this is new territory for me. To hear you tell it, we've got half of all the Irish rock superstars either here or expected later today, and God knows how many people coming to hear them. None of us has ever held this kind of event here—yes, Mick, I know you might have seen a few, but you didn't have to manage it. I want to know if we're ready to do this."

"Do we have a choice?" Mick asked.

"It looks like the answer is no, but it's not like we planned for this—it just kind of happened. It's kind of late to reinforce the building, so we'll have to hope everything holds up. How's the electric stuff going, Mick?"

"All good so far. Hell, if that fails in back, these guys can go acoustic by candlelight." He appeared almost happy at the prospect.

"Fire hazard," Maura said absently to no one in particular. "We should have flashlights, just in case. I can run down to the hardware store and pick up some extras."

"I'll do it, Maura," Jimmy said. "Yer the face of the place—you should be up front to welcome yer guests, all of 'em."

"Okay. Or you can send Rose. Take enough cash from

the drawer to cover it. Next, Mick, you said you'd taken care of extra kegs?"

"All set."

"Anyone going to want the hard stuff?"

"A few," Jimmy said. "But the point is to hear the bands, not to get drunk, and we've plenty on hand."

"Good. Somebody keep an eye on the toilets—we don't want them getting jammed up in the middle of everything." Maura wasn't surprised when nobody volunteered for that task. "Okay, I've talked to our neighbors so they know what's going on, as well as the gardaí. Now, how the heck do we handle closing time? Did you tell me about a lock-in, Mick? Or was that Billy?"

"Billy, most likely. He's seen his share. That may be hard to manage. Did Sean Murphy have anything to say about closing time? If not, odds are he'll look the other way, for a one-time event." At least, that was what Maura wanted to believe.

"Let's hope so, because I don't want to think about trying to shove everyone out of here if things are going well. Anybody have anything else to add?"

Tim spoke up. "I'm going to try to keep track of whoever comes in, maybe film some of it if I can, unless you need me for anything else, Maura. I'm not really any use behind the bar, but I can help collect glasses and wash up and the like."

"Thanks, Tim. We may need that. Mick, you're covering the music side of things. Jimmy and I will be serving from both bars, me up front and Jimmy in the back, with Rose's help. Rose, you stick with your dad—I don't want you getting into any situation you can't handle."

"I'll keep an eye on her," Jimmy said.

"Great. That's all I can think of. Are we good?"

"We are," Mick said firmly. "Stop fretting yerself, Maura. It's going to be grand."

Despite his words, Maura wasn't convinced. If she was a more religious person, this would be a good time to pray.

After everyone had gone back to their tasks, Maura waded through the crowd to talk to Billy. "Any surprises?" she asked, leaning close to his ear to be heard over the din.

"Better than I'd hoped," he said. "I only told a coupla friends, and many of us are gettin' on in years, so I wasn't sure if the word would get 'round."

Maura looked around the room. "I think it did, Billy. Of course, I gather that snagging Niall was a big part of that."

"I knew him when he was in knickers—his mother is me second cousin. Always was a nice lad, though."

"Well, whatever you did, thank you. Or maybe I should wait to say thanks until tomorrow morning, if the place is still standing."

"It's lasted this long—and this is what it's meant for."

As Billy greeted another friend, Maura went back to the bar, where Rose was holding her own. "Isn't this amazin'?" the girl said.

"It is. Are you okay with staying?"

Rose smiled broadly. "As if I'd go! Me da will be here to look out for me, if he can drag himself away from the music."

"When will they start, do you think?"

"I can't say, but I've heard it happens when it happens. It's not like this is a band. Just a bunch of guys who like to play. Someone will sit in for a song or two, and then swap out for whoever's willing. You'll see."

"Does your dad play?"

"Everybody plays, just some better than others. Or they sing. What about you?"

"I can carry a tune, barely, but nobody's going to ask for encores. And I don't know the words to most Irish songs, except the corny old stuff."

"After a few pints, no one will care. We'll be charging for the drinks, won't we?"

"Of course we will! Except for the musicians. I've been told that Mick kept the taps flowing for them, no charge. But regular customers should pay."

"Can you afford it?"

"I hope so. I'd bet the patrons will be buying some rounds for the players—isn't that polite? Let's just hope for the best. If this is a flop, we'll go out on a high note, even if we're broke."

The sun began sinking after five, but it was hard to tell because there were so many people blocking the light from the windows. So far there was a bit of space between them, but how much closer would they be before the night was over? Maura wondered. More men than women, no surprise, but more women than Maura had expected. They weren't young, so no doubt they remembered the bands from years ago, and they weren't going to miss this night.

Musicians kept arriving, dragging their instrument cases. Since those were bulky, there was no way they could slip quietly through the crowd, and when someone recognized each of them in turn, that slowed their progress toward the back room even more. Maura calculated the mean time of transit through the room as at least ten minutes. Of course, often they stopped to pick up a pint on their way, chat to a few people, and introduce themselves to Maura. She met a Danny, a Liam, a Connor, and a few others, but she never managed to catch their last names—not that they would have rung any bells for her anyway, in spite of Tim's coaching. Maybe Tim would have notes, or pictures. She was going to have to adopt a more Irish attitude: it would all come right in the morning. However it had come about, he had walked into a rare and wonderful opportunity, and he must be over the moon. Maura wondered if he realized what his simple quest had started.

The excitement ramped up gradually, after darkness had fallen. Maura, Jimmy, and Rose were kept busy doling out pints and picking up the empty glasses. At close to nine, a series of electronic shrieks and squeals came from the back, where Maura had left the door between the two rooms wide open, followed by sounds even Maura could recognize as guitar chords. What else could she hear? No keyboard, apparently. That caterwauling sound, she had learned, came from an uilleann pipe. A small drum set, she guessed. Banjo? Definitely guitars, both electric and acoustic. The music emerged in a gradual way: what started out as random sounds finally blended into something with a recognizable tune and structure. And then the voices joined in.

Maura looked at the crowd in the front room—the late-comers who hadn't made it to the back. The music drifted out, muted in volume but still clear. The talk in the front stilled as everyone began paying attention, looking rapt in the uncertain light. Maybe half of them were already mouthing the words to familiar songs.

And it went on. The crowd grew to as much as the room could, and most people had smiles on their faces. People flowed between the two rooms, and every now and then

Maura would look out the front window to see a garda car slide by, but there was no need for their assistance. The crowd wasn't looking for trouble. Most people were kind of middle-aged and were reliving their memories. As Billy had suggested, the younger people had stayed with their own kind, in flashier places in Skibbereen. At Sullivan's Rose might have been the youngest in the room.

After a long time she came out briefly from behind the bar to stand by the front door and take in the whole scene. The front room was dark, but golden light spilled from the back room, as though the music had a color, drawing people toward it. Maybe Maura couldn't remember anything about Niall Cronin, but she wouldn't forget him now. And after a couple of hours, she was beginning to believe in the magic of it all.

Mick was leaning against the doorjamb between the two rooms; he noticed her watching and gave her a warm smile, and she returned it. She felt rather than heard a quiet rapping on the front door and turned to see Sean Murphy on the other side. She opened the door enough to let him slip in; nobody else seemed to notice a garda in their midst.

"How's it going?" he said into her ear.

"Great. Amazing, in fact. I can't tell you how many guys are back there playing, but don't they sound wonderful?"

"That they do. No problems?"

"None that I've noticed. Of course, I haven't been looking for them, but so far everyone seems very . . . happy, I guess. I'm glad I'm here to see it."

"It's something special, I'd say. I only wanted to stop by and make sure you and yer lot were all right."

"Do we have to close soon?" Maura hadn't looked at her watch in hours, apparently: she was surprised to see it was now past midnight. "If I go in there now and try to shut the music down, I might cause a riot."

Sean took in the crowd. Those in the front room were fairly calm; those in the back were cheering at the end of each song, but with affection. "I'll drive by in another hour or so. Spread the word that's leaving time and you should have no trouble."

"Thanks, Sean. Wish you could have been here to hear more of it."

"You sound like you've been won over."

"Maybe I have."

"Then I'll come next time. Good night."

She watched him leave before she realized he'd said "next time." Would there be a next time? Maybe there would, if the pub hadn't gone belly-up handing out free pints to all the musicians tonight. Yet she had a feeling they'd be fine.

She conveyed Sean's hint to Jimmy, then went toward the back to tell Mick as well. In the doorway she took a look at the musicians left onstage. They looked drunk, but not with liquor: more like drunk on the music. How often did these guys get to play together, without all the bright lights and glitz? This must have been how they'd all started, in one place or another, and they looked glad to be back again. They looked like they belonged.

She leaned toward Mick. "Sean wants us to clear the place out in another hour. Does that work?"

"I think so. These guys have been at it for ages, and I think they're about ready to pack it up. I'll have a word with them."

"Thanks, Mick." Maura went back out front, where the crowd was already beginning to thin.

Jimmy asked, "Last round?" Maura nodded. Some fifteen minutes short of Sean's deadline, the patrons had trickled away, leaving only a hard-core few of the band members packing away their gear in the back.

"You guys were terrific," Maura said to the musicians, and she meant it.

"Ah, darlin'," Niall said, "we were just messing about, but I'm glad you liked it. Old Mick would be happy."

"Where are you headed now?" she asked.

"We'll find a place, no worries. Let me know if you've a mind to do this again. I'd forgotten how good it felt."

"I will. Thanks for coming, and for bringing everyone else with you."

"That wasn't me, love—that was the magic of the place." Niall turned away, and Maura went back to the front, in time to see Jimmy leaving with Rose. "Good night!" she called out. She wondered briefly where Tim had gone. She looked around at the darkened pub. At least Jimmy had done a fair job of tidying up. It might look worse in the morning, but not as bad as it might have.

She wasn't sure what to do next. She was exhausted, and even the late open on Sunday wasn't going to help much. She had to be here: people would want to talk about tonight's event, and if she had any hope of continuing it, she should be front and center to talk it up. But she didn't want to move. It was as if the lingering notes of the music and the voices still hung in the air, making the dark, shabby place look somehow more . . . she couldn't think of a good word. More than it had been the day before, at least.

Mick came in, carrying a bunch of used glasses. "You're still here?"

"I can't seem to tell my feet to move. Thanks for making this work, Mick. I wouldn't have believed it, but it really was something special. Even if there's never another one, I'm glad this happened."

"Go home, get some sleep. We can talk in the morning."

"Shoot, we should clear out the cash register," Maura said suddenly. "I can't believe I didn't think about that. I wouldn't want to leave it here—this place is too easy to get in and out of." She popped open the drawer and stared in amazement at the rumpled stacks of bills and the piles of coins. "Mick, look at this," she said, almost reverently. "I don't think I've seen this much *total* since I got here."

"You going to count it or just admire it?" Mick came up behind her and peered over her shoulder.

"Shut up—I'm enjoying the moment. I'd better get it to the bank ASAP, but I'm guessing it's a little late for that right now. What do I do with it? Take it home? Stick it under a floorboard?" She'd heard that Ireland was safe, but no way was she going to risk losing this pile of cash.

"The banks won't be open tomorrow, on a Sunday. Would you rather I took it with me?" Mick said.

She turned to look at him. Did she trust him? Maybe. Probably. "Promise you won't be on the first flight to Spain in the morning?"

He smiled. "Tempting, innit? You'll have to trust me on that."

She grabbed a plastic bag from under the bar and stuffed the bills into it; the coins could wait. Then she thrust the bag toward Mick. "Here. Take it home."

He looked startled; had he been joking about hanging on to it? "You don't want to count it?"

"No," Maura said firmly. "Either I trust you or I don't. So if you skim off a few bills, it'll be on your conscience. Right now all I want to do is go home and go to sleep."

"Right so." Mick folded the bag carefully and stuffed it into his jacket's inner pocket.

"You'll close up?" Maura asked.

"I will. Safe home."

"You too."

Chapter 12

The next morning Maura slept in and awoke to sunshine. She stretched luxuriously in bed. The night had been wonderful. Surprising. Hard to explain, even to herself. She was no stranger to big events back in Boston bars, often loud, busy evenings that spilled over into the wee hours (and often ended in a fight, especially if a local sports team lost, which meant it was time to duck the flying fists and bottles). But she'd never been part of an event in a pub that was so happy, and focused only on the music, not even an advertised event—just a bunch of old guys getting together and playing songs they all knew, and people who'd come from who-knew-where to fill the place and listen. And had left happy. Had it been a onetime thing, or could she do it every month or so, with the same results? She didn't know. It was risky to mess with magic, she was finding. Everything had come together this time, but there were no guarantees that they could re-create it. She'd have to talk to Billy and Mick and Jimmy to see how it compared to the old events and ask what they thought about doing it again. But no rush. Right now she just wanted to wallow in the good memories.

Finally Maura climbed out of bed, threw on some old sweats, and went down the stairs to make herself some coffee. When it was ready she filled a mug and opened her front door, stepping outside to see what kind of day it was. She could hear the tolling of a church bell; it had to be the one at the church in Drinagh, because that one was on a hill only a few miles away, and the sound carried if the wind was right. She wouldn't stop by to see Bridget this morning, because Mick often came by to pick up his grandmother to take her to Mass in Leap, or one or another of the neighbors would give her a ride and bring her home again.

Maura shivered in the morning air and went back inside, closing the door firmly behind her. As she finished a second cup of coffee, along with brown bread (Bridget's) spread with the black currant jelly she had become addicted to recently, she realized that somehow in the last twenty-four hours she seemed to have made a decision: she was planning a future at Sullivan's. Six months earlier she had stumbled into Leap, still aching from the loss of her grandmother (her only family), made worse by the loss of the rented apartment she and Gran had shared (the only home she had ever known), and clueless about what the heck she was doing in Ireland. Gran had told her to go, and Maura had had no better ideas. No plan, no purpose.

Now here she was with a house of her own and a

business, likewise her own. It was mind-boggling. In the beginning she had been cautious about committing herself to anything, and she hadn't wanted to make any changes to Sullivan's because she didn't know if she was going to stay. She'd also wanted to give people time to get to know her, an ongoing process but one that seemed to have been the right move—at least now they knew she wasn't one of those infamous obnoxious Americans who thought they knew how everything should be done and shoved it down their throats. If anything, Maura was going backward: reviving a tradition that people seemed to have missed, even if they hadn't realized it, and would be happy to have back again. Of course, Old Mick had created it in a different time, and there was no guarantee that it would work now, but if last night was any indication, it was worth a try.

Suddenly she wanted to get moving, to go back to the pub and see how things looked in the clear light of morning. To count the cash they'd collected and see if they'd made any money after she paid the Guinness distributor and overtime for her staff. They'd worked hard last night and they all deserved it. Had she been careless, handing the cash off to Mick? She didn't think so. She had to have faith in someone sometime, and he'd done nothing to shake her trust in him. In fact he'd proved plenty of times that he was trustworthy and dependable. Besides, if he took off with the cash, he'd earn Bridget's wrath, and she was pretty sure he didn't want that.

Maura took a quick shower, dressed, and drove the few miles into the village. It was, not surprisingly, quiet—she knew there'd be a brief flurry of traffic before the noon Mass, but otherwise there were few cars on the road. She unlocked the front door and stepped into the pub, stopping on the threshold for a moment and listening . . . for what? Trying to catch any echoes of the previous night's music? *Don't be daft, Maura,* she chided herself. She liked the word "daft"—it was one her grandmother had used often. Anyway, the room held no echoes. Considering how many people had been in the place the night before, it was reasonably tidy, with only a few glasses on the bar waiting to be washed. She reminded herself to thank Jimmy again for taking care of that. He had seemed more committed to making the event work than she'd ever seen him. Maybe he was finally over his snit about not inheriting a share of the pub. And Mick had been a rock throughout, managing the music side of things. She couldn't have done that, but under his watchful eye all the equipment had worked and the musicians had all played nicely with each other—in both senses of the word. Maura was looking forward to comments from the townspeople today, for surely they'd come by to contribute their two cents. Or however much that was in euros.

She drifted toward the back room, which was a bit less tidy, but then, the musicians hadn't cleared out until late. Mick had said he'd oversee this end of things. She couldn't complain—whatever mess there was could be cleaned up quickly, and she didn't mind doing her own washing up. She walked into the room, picking up glasses and trash as she went, but when she reached the far end and turned, she stopped. In one of the banquettes that lined the rear wall, someone was apparently sleeping. Maybe Mick hadn't had the heart to wake him, or maybe he'd been forgotten by the crowd and left behind to sleep it off.

Maura walked closer, then stopped again, her happy mood disappearing like air from a leaky balloon. Even from a few feet away it was clear this guy wasn't going to wake up again—ever. Nobody turned that shade of gray and lived to tell about it. And his half-open, blindly staring eyes confirmed it.

Worse, she recognized him: it was the man who'd come in Friday afternoon, Aidan something, the first one to show up at Niall's invitation to join the fun. From her position a few feet away, Maura could see no obvious signs of injury. Maybe he'd had a heart attack or a stroke. But when? If it had happened during the music, why had nobody noticed last night? There had been so many people coming and going . . .

All she knew was that he was dead. In her pub. Was this some sort of punishment from the gods for thinking maybe the place had turned a corner and might have a future? Ha! No wonder most of the country seemed permanently depressed, if this was what a brief glimpse of good luck brought about.

Now what? Maura's mind reeled. For one brief, hysterical moment she thought about disposing of the body herself, but that was a ridiculous idea. First of all, she had no idea what to do with it. Him. Sure, she could toss him into the harbor or pitch him into a handy bog, but how was she supposed to haul a body—and not a lightweight one, from the looks of him—out of the building and across a major road? Nope, not working. Bury him up the hill behind the pub? She owned the land, and nobody had touched it in decades, so who would notice?

Oh, come on, Maura. You're a law-abiding citizen and a respectable business owner. You can't go around hiding corpses just to make your life easier. She went back to the front, where she'd left her bag behind the bar, pulled out her mobile phone, and called the garda station, asking for Sean Murphy, though she doubted he'd be in yet.

Turned out, he was. "Maura, hello. How're you feeling this morning?" he said cheerily when he answered.

"You're in early, after last night. Anyway, I was feeling pretty good until I got to Sullivan's. I have a problem."

"Oh, no. And what would that be? Somebody rifled the cash drawer? Vandalism?"

"Uh, neither of those. There's a dead man in the back room."

"Oh." Sean was silent for a moment, and Maura could almost hear him shifting gears, from friend to serious official. "Do you know the deceased?"

"Only his first name—Aidan. He was one of the musicians, a friend of Niall's. He came with a fiddle case." Niall would know his name. But she had no idea where to find Niall.

"Yer sure he's dead?"

"I haven't touched him, but I'm pretty damn sure."

"I'll be over in ten minutes. Don't touch anything. Don't let anyone else in. Are you all right?"

Nice of him to worry about her. "I'll manage. I'll wait for you in the front, Sean."

Maura sat on a stool in front of the bar, watching the street, where little was happening. Restless, she stood up again and went around behind the bar to make some more coffee. No doubt some people would think a stiff drink would be the right strategy for dealing with an unexpected body, but she didn't work that way. She hoped the poor man had died of natural causes. She had no reason to think anything else, did she? On the other hand, maybe this was the universe reminding her that her luck just didn't work that way. She'd had a great night last night, but now she had to pay the price? When the coffee was ready she went back to sit on the stool and sipped slowly, waiting for Sean.

What message was the universe trying to send her? It was certainly mixed. On the one hand, she'd been gifted with some extraordinary blessings over the past few months, as she reminded herself: a house, a car, even a business had all pretty much fallen into her lap. A friendship with Bridget, who had known her grandmother. On the other hand, she seemed to be paying for it with a lot of unwanted trouble, even though she wasn't responsible for any of it. Still, how much would the locals take before they started shunning her as bad luck?

Sean pulled up within the promised ten minutes and parked directly in front of Sullivan's. Maura went to open the door for him and let him step past her inside before locking it again.

"How are yeh, Maura?" he asked anxiously, and for a moment Maura considered bursting into tears and throwing herself into his arms. Weren't police supposed to be prepared for that?

She stifled the urge. It would only embarrass both of them, and besides, she almost never cried. "I'm okay. Better than that guy Aidan, anyway." She nodded toward the back.

"Before I take a look . . . what time did yeh lock up last night?"

"I left about one, I think. Mick was still here, but all the musicians in back had left before that, as far as we could tell. Mick said he'd close up—you can confirm that with him. The front door was locked when I arrived this morning. I haven't checked the back doors, but I'm not even sure they lock, and just about anybody could have come and gone that way."

"Right so. You said you recognized the, uh, deceased?"

"Aidan Crowley." Now that the initial shock had worn off, Maura was proud that she had managed to remember his full name. "I talked to him a couple of times, mostly stuff like, 'Would you like some tea?' But you saw how it was last night."

He nodded. "And you haven't disturbed anything?"

"I picked up a couple of glasses from the back, before I noticed the guy. That's it."

"Leave them aside for now. I'd best go take a look at the man. You don't need to come with me."

"I'm coming," Maura said tersely, and she followed Sean into the back room.

"Were the lights on when you came in?" he said.

"No, I turned them on. This room is pretty dark, and I wanted to see what had to be done."

"When did you first see the deceased?"

"I was over there by the stage"—she pointed—"and when I turned around I noticed him, kind of tucked in the corner there. I went to see if he was just sleeping it off, but when I got closer it was pretty clear he wasn't."

Sean walked carefully toward where the man was slumped against the back wall. He spent a couple of minutes examining him closely, without touching him, before saying, "I'll wait for the rest of the team before disturbing him. Most likely he'll have some identification on him, with his address and all, but I'll let them look for it."

"He said he lived in Cork. He is dead, right? Not just passed out, or in a coma?"

"Yes, Maura, he is dead. I'm sorry. Excuse me." Sean turned away to call the station, then explained the circumstances. He ended with, "I'll stay here with the owner until you arrive." He signed off and turned to Maura. "The sergeant will be over shortly, and he'll alert the medical folk."

"I know. I've been through this before. Should we wait out front? Can I get you some coffee?"

Sean wavered between protocol and an obvious desire for coffee. In the end he said, "I'd be glad of a cup, thanks."

"Coming up."

Maura was happy to have something to do, some way to keep her hands busy. She didn't want to think beyond the next step. "Hey, should I try to call Mick and Jimmy? I'm not sure when they'll be coming in." She handed Sean a mug of coffee.

"We'll be needing to talk to them, Mick in particular, since he was the last one here, right?"

Maura nodded. "Yes—Jimmy left before me."

Sean went on, "I don't want anyone else coming into the building just yet, not until the sergeant's been over the scene." He sipped his hot coffee, his brow furrowed.

"What?" Maura demanded.

"I was just thinkin' . . . How many people would you guess were here last night?"

"We weren't counting. A couple of hundred, easy, although there was a lot of coming and going, so they weren't all here at the same time."

"Had they all left before you went home?"

"Yes, like I said. The musicians too. I wouldn't walk out with people still in the pub. I'm sure the place was empty, except for Mick and me. Mick was going to clean up in back before he left."

"And he would have noticed a dead man?"

Maura looked more closely at Sean, whose expression was serious. "Are you joking? Of course he would have."

"Or he could have let him in after you'd gone."

"I guess. Or the guy could have snuck in through the other doors back there. There are two of them—they open onto the balcony from outside. Maybe he was looking to rob the place after our big night. You'd know better than I would if there's ever been a problem with theft here at Sullivan's, but I'd guess there was never enough money on hand before to make it worth the effort, until last night."

Maura realized she'd started to become more trusting since she'd left Boston. From what she'd seen, here in Leap nobody locked much of anything. The church was open to all comers any time of day, whether or not there was a priest on-site. More than once she'd heard the clerks at the few shops in town say, "Just leave the money on the counter." She herself locked the front door of Sullivan's out of habit, and because she didn't want anybody helping themselves to her liquor—although she'd rather they walk through a door than smash a window to get at it. The night before had been a special case: she had no real idea how much money they'd taken in, but it was mostly cash, and it was a lot more than usual. That was why she'd wanted to get it out of the pub and let Mick take it home. Had she let herself be lulled into a false sense of security? Well, she'd know for sure if Mick failed to show up for work this morning, but she really didn't think he'd run out on her. And it seemed very unlikely to her that Aidan had come back to the pub to rob it and just happened to die in his sleep.

"Was there any money missing?" Sean asked.

Maura shook her head. "No. I thought it would be stupid to leave it here, so I gave it to Mick to take home. I haven't even looked in the cash drawer yet, but there were only some coins in there."

Sean shrugged. "Do you have a number for Mick?"

"Just his mobile—that's how I usually reach him."

"And an address?"

Maura stared blankly at him. "Uh, no. I've never needed it. I pay him in cash, and I've never had to mail anything to him. I'm sure you can find it better than I can."

"So you don't know where he lives?"

"No, I don't. And I don't know where Jimmy and Rose live either, although it must be within walking distance, because Rose doesn't have a car. I think Jimmy does." Of course "walking distance" around here could be miles, easily. Not much help.

"Billy Sheahan—he lives down at the end, does he not?"

"Yes, he does, and has for years. But if you're wondering if he heard anything, I doubt it. You know how thick these walls are. Maybe if somebody stopped in front of Billy's door and had a big argument he'd notice, but not otherwise. He left long before I did last night, anyway." Maura couldn't even remember if she'd seen him in the back room while the music was playing or if he'd enjoyed the music from his seat in the front all night.

"Did yeh see anyone on the street when you left?"

"Not a soul. No other lights on either, except the streetlights."

Sean paused, then finally said, "I can't think of any more questions. I guess we'll just wait for the others."

Maura set down her mug carefully before looking at Sean. "I hate to ask, but do you think the guy was killed?"

"I couldn't say, Maura. Could be he had some sort of medical condition. There's no obvious cause, but I'm not the one to decide. We'll be treating it as a suspicious death until we know more."

"Really? Because I thought that as the first officer to arrive, if you decided there was no crime involved, you'd just jump to the next step and call for the ME to pick up, uh, Aidan." It seemed unkind to call the man a "body" when he'd been breathing only hours before.

"If he'd died in his bed you'd be right," Sean answered. "But he's a stranger, and he's been found somewhere he shouldn't be, so far as I know. I'm just being careful. Don't be alarmed."

"Yet," Maura muttered glumly. Sean didn't respond.

Chapter 13

The next representative of the Skibbereen gardaí—Sean's sergeant—arrived a few minutes later.

Mick arrived at the same time as the second garda and looked appropriately startled to see a police presence in front of the pub. Maura watched through the window as he gestured and pointed and seemed to argue with the uniformed officer; he looked inside and spotted her, then cocked his head, as if asking, "What the hell?"

"Can Mick come in?" Maura asked Sean.

"Of course. I want a word with him." Sean unlocked the door to let Mick and the sergeant in, then locked the door behind them once again. Up close Maura recognized the sergeant, although she couldn't recall having had a conversation with him.

"It's Maura Donovan, isn't it?" the sergeant asked. "I'm Sergeant Tony Regan—I recall we've met before."

"Right. Sorry to call you out on a Sunday."

Sean and Sergeant Regan stepped away and conferred briefly, while Mick looked a question at Maura and she hastily whispered, "Tell you in a minute." When the gardaí returned, the sergeant said, "I'd like to examine the scene with Murphy first, if you don't mind. Wait here." They disappeared into the back room.

Mick went around the bar and started a cup of coffee for himself. "You all right, Maura?" he asked, watching the coffee drip from the machine. "The garda said you found a dead man in the back. Did you recognize the poor sod?"

"I did, actually." Suddenly Maura remembered the hours Mick had spent in conversation with Aidan and the others on Friday. She added, a little more gently, "It's that fiddler, Aidan Crowley. Niall's friend." Maura watched Mick's face change.

"Aidan Crowley? Bugger."

"Who was he?" Maura asked. "I mean, he wasn't as famous as Niall, right?" Maybe someone had told her before, but it had flown right out of her head.

"Nah, Aidan Crowley used to be a sideman for some of the bands, but he never seemed to connect with the right one at the right time."

"From what little I saw of him, he wasn't young."

"Are yeh askin' if he was old enough for a heart attack? Or maybe if he just wore out after all those years of drugs and rock and roll?"

"Well, I guess that's what I want to know. Won't the gardaí want to?"

"Could be."

"Mick, you didn't happen to offer the guy a place to crash for the night, did you?"

He turned to her. "The thought crossed my mind, but no one asked. I can't tell you where he or any of the others scattered to."

Maura sighed. "I told Sean that you locked up after I went home. Hadn't everybody cleared out by the end? Did you check the back room after I left?"

"Of course I did," Mick said. "Checked the doors too—I know we haven't always bothered, but some of the boys left their heavy stuff here for the night, and I didn't want that disappearing. All the doors were locked. I turned off everything that would turn off, and then I left by the front."

"You check the bathrooms too?"

"I did. Maura, I swear there was no one in the building when I left, unless yeh count Old Billy down in his flat at the other end of the building."

"So how did this guy get in?"

"I can't tell yeh. Although we both know it wouldn't be hard to get into this place, if yeh really wanted to."

Maura made a mental note to fix that, but this wasn't the time. "So if no one was here when you left, Aidan must've come back after you'd locked up. Why do you think he'd have done that?" Had he come back here for one last hurrah with the boys? She hoped fervently that the postmortem would show that his heart had given out or something in his brain had given way—although he looked no more than sixty, which was young for either.

Mick startled her when he said, "Yer not thinking he came in to rob the place, are yeh?"

"Could be," Maura said, "but if it was the money he was after, the coins are still here."

"Maybe he was just looking for a place to sleep."

"I thought that for about three seconds. Even if he had broken in to rob us, he never left the building, right? Maybe the strain of breaking in was too much for him and he had to lie down and rest." Maura realized she was being snide, and that wouldn't go over well with the gardaí. She'd have to watch her tongue. "Doesn't make much sense, does it?"

"No, it does not."

Sergeant Regan and Sean reappeared. "We've found a wallet," the sergeant said. "Like you said, the man's name was—"

"Aidan Crowley." Mick finished his sentence. "He first came by on the Friday, from Cork city, he said, and met up with Niall Cronin here. He was part of the music last night. Do you know yet how he died?"

Sergeant Regan shook his head. "Inconclusive," he said, apparently relishing the word. "We'll need a postmortem, to be sure. Nolan, is it?" he went on. Mick nodded. "Miss Donovan says you locked up last night. Was the man in the building when you left?"

"He was not," Mick said firmly.

"Might you have been the worse for drink? It sounds as though it was a long night."

"I'd had a glass or two, but I was managing the equipment for the show so I needed a clear head. There was no one left in the building when I locked up, and I'll swear an oath on it."

"And you have no knowledge of how this man might have come to be lyin' dead in the back room?"

Maura watched the exchange and was beginning to wonder if there was some hostility between Mick and the sergeant. As far as she knew, Mick had never had any problems with the law, but then, she didn't know a lot about his history.

"Who invited the performers?" the sergeant added, addressing Mick rather than Maura.

"Some people put the word out, is all," Mick told him. "Nothing so formal as an invitation. You know how that happens."

"Do any of the people who performed here live nearby?"

Mick shrugged. "I can't say."

"So no one knew this Crowley would be here last night?"

Maura was growing impatient. She had a business to run, and there was a dead man in the back of the house. "What are you getting at? You don't know how he died, so why are you asking these questions? Why ask Mick?"

"Maura," Sean began, in an apparent attempt to sound soothing, "we're only doin' our job. Since we can't say how the man died, we have to treat the death as unexplained until we find out."

"Which will take an autopsy, right? So when are your people going to get him out of here to do that? And can I open for business?"

The sergeant and Sean exchanged a glance, and finally the sergeant shrugged and addressed Maura. "Might be we should treat this as a crime scene until we know more, but it sounds like there was so much going on last night that we'd be swamped with information and no way to know what's important. You had a couple of hundred people tramping through here, I'd wager, and half of them in the back room at any one time. It'd take all the forensic lads in the whole country to sort through the mess. So I'd say, go ahead and open."

Maura felt a surge of relief. "Thank you! Look, if it helps, I can close off the back room. We don't generally use it anyway—I'll just say it's off-limits for now. We'll wait until we hear from you to open it up again. Fair enough?"

"That'd be grand, thank you," the sergeant said, clearly relieved at the compromise. "I'll wait outside for the van, Murphy."

"Oh, one last thing: can you please take Aidan out the side door, please?" Maura asked. "Seems like it sends the wrong message to have you take a body out the front door." In any case, if all went well, poor Aidan would be removed while Mass was going on and most people wouldn't notice.

"I think we can manage that."

Once the sergeant departed, Sean, Mick, and Maura were left alone in the pub, which suddenly seemed a bit darker and shabbier than it had earlier. "Interesting morning," Maura said, her voiced edged with sarcasm. "Anybody need more coffee?"

"Please," Mick said.

"None for me," Sean said.

Maura set about making more coffee, then turned back to Sean. "So you really don't know how he died?"

"I can't say."

"Can't or won't?"

"Doesn't matter—the outcome's the same," Sean told her, giving nothing away. "Tell me, Maura, who else besides you two has a key to the place?"

"Jimmy Sweeney, and his daughter, Rose. Maybe Billy

Sheahan—heck, for all I know the key to his door fits all the doors in the place. It's an old building. I can't say who else Old Mick might have given a key, for one reason or another. Does it matter?"

"It might. The dead man had a key in his pocket that opens yer back door."

Chapter 14

Sean's statement left Maura speechless. She knew that security in the building was a joke, but she'd never had any reason to use the back doors—she'd only learned about them when Mick had pointed them out before the event. She wouldn't even recognize a key for them if she had one. Had Old Mick had others? She should check the drawers both in the pub and back at her house to see if there were any more kicking around. But that was kind of shutting the barn door after the horse was long gone.

In any case, if Aidan had had a key for some mysterious reason and had let himself in, either for some illegal purpose or just to crash for a few hours, that still didn't shed any light on how he'd died.

She checked her watch: past eleven. Almost Leap's "rush hour," if the people attending Mass constituted traffic. Maura knew it was the only time that the big parking lot in front of the church was anywhere near filled, and even then, not every week. She would normally open at twelve thirty, the legal time, and after the night's festivities, she expected something of a flood when Mass was over today. How long would it take for news of Aidan Crowley's death to spread and draw still more in?

Maura realized they'd all been silent for a couple of minutes, apparently lost in their own thoughts. But time was passing. "So, Sean, we'll open as usual?"

"Yes, as Sergeant Regan said. As soon as the deceased is gone."

"Mick, is there anything we need to do to get ready? Thanks for leaving the place in good shape." Well, except for a body. "I would have hated facing cleanup this morning."

Mick didn't comment. He said, "I've got to check the kegs—I think I'll need to swap one out, and better sooner than later." He vanished behind the bar to the stairs that led to the basement, where the kegs were kept.

"Fine," she called out as he went.

Maura saw an unmarked van pull up in front of Sullivan's, and Sean perked up. "That'll be the coroner. Thanks for the coffee, Maura. I'll let you know what we find out."

"Thanks, Sean," Maura said to his retreating back as he rushed out the door to join the sergeant. She stayed where she was on the bar stool. She hoped—oh, how she hoped—that the man had died a natural death. But she also should be prepared for bad news on that front, and she'd better sort out what she remembered from the night before while it was still fresh, although she wasn't sure if the gardaí would want any more information than she'd already given them. But she was troubled by the man's death, and by the lack of information on how he'd died. If it was a medical condition—the best option—the case would be closed almost before it started. But could it have been something like a drug overdose, something that wouldn't be obvious? She really wasn't sure about the role drugs played in this quiet corner of West Cork. Drugs she'd seen plenty of back in Boston, but she hadn't noticed any signs of them in the pub last night, even in the bathrooms—or any other time, for that matter. No sweet scent of weed, no discarded vials or baggies or syringes— she'd seen lots of those in her time working in bars. Of course, she'd heard that there were new party drugs popping up all the time, and their signs might not be obvious. Would Rose know? Or Jimmy? What about Tim? Still, Aidan hadn't looked like the type to use party drugs. If anything, maybe he'd taken something just to give him a boost for the session last night, and it had been too much for him. Maybe she was willfully blind, but she wanted to believe that the people who had shown up the night before, most of them middle-aged, had truly just come for the music. Maybe she really did hope that in coming to Ireland she'd stepped into a simpler way of life. She knew she didn't want to be disillusioned.

The transfer of the body was accomplished quickly, and she watched as the van made a U-turn and headed back toward Cork and the university hospital where the morgue was. Sean gave her a quick salute through the window, then he and the sergeant departed in their respective cars, Sean following the coroner, the sergeant headed back to Skibbereen. The street directly in front of Sullivan's was empty again, save for the church-bound traffic.

Rose and Jimmy Sweeney came in shortly before twelve.

"Amazin' last night, wasn't it?" Jimmy said, still riding high. "I remember some of the lads, I do, from back in my younger days. Rosie here, her lot don't have the same kind of experience, like. It's all on the YouTube now."

"Did you enjoy it, Rose?" Maura asked, stalling. She hadn't had time to figure out how she was going to tell them what had happened, though she knew she had to tell them something.

"I did. It's nice to see all the old people enjoyin' themselves," Rose said, struggling to keep a straight face. Jimmy made a rude noise but didn't say anything. "And the musicians! They were older still—'tis a wonder they were still standing at the end of the evening."

Not all of them were. Maura took a deep breath. "There was a little problem here, after we closed up."

"And what would that be?" Jimmy asked, turning to stare at Maura, troubled by her tone.

There was no way to sugarcoat it. "It seems that one of the musicians came in last night after Mick had locked up and left. He, uh, died in the back room. I found him this morning."

Her bald statement brought incredulous stares from Jimmy and Rose. Finally Jimmy managed to choke out, "Who?"

Maura watched his face as she answered, "Aidan Crowley."

Jimmy's expression gave nothing away. "I think I've heard the name, but I wouldn't know him to his face. Is he still . . . ?"

"No. I called the gardaí, and they took him to Cork for a postmortem. They said we could open, but I promised we wouldn't use the back room again until they said we could. Rose, are you okay with being here today, after . . . ?"

"Sure. I'm sorry he's dead, and that he died here, but I didn't know him. And I guess I won't. What happened?"

"I don't know. The gardaí couldn't say. Nothing obvious. Keep your fingers crossed that it was natural causes." Maura thought about mentioning the key, but decided it might be smart to hold that back. If the gardaí wanted to mention it to Jimmy, let them talk to him themselves.

"Who else knows about the dead fella?" Jimmy demanded.

"Mick. Now you and Rose. Nobody else has been by. So if someone comes in talking about the death, ask them how they found out, will you? The coroner's van was out front here, but not for long. I don't know how many people will have seen it, but it's not marked." It occurred to Maura that she should talk with Tim. He'd been part of the group talking to Aidan Crowley on Friday night, and possibly last night. She hadn't mentioned Tim to the gardaí, but there was no need to unless the death was . . . not natural. She still shied away from putting that idea into words, even in her thoughts. "Rose, was Tim still here when you left?"

"If he was, he was in the back. I never saw him leave, but I left with me da well short of midnight. I didn't talk with him much, we were that busy. But he was having a grand time watching all the old ones play in the back."

Nervously Maura checked her watch again: nearly opening time. If it hadn't been for poor Aidan, she would have been looking forward to opening today, to hear what people had thought of the night's event and to begin to get a sense of whether it was worth doing again or even making a regular thing. It had been good, hadn't it? Was it ruined now, for good?

At twelve thirty she sighed and told Jimmy, "We might as well open up." He walked over and unlocked the door. Billy was already there waiting, his face turned to the sun, and Maura was reminded of Bridget, who sought the sun's rays in the same way. Old bones seeking warmth. "Come in, Billy, and I'll get the fire going," Maura said.

Billy stepped into the room, then stopped, studying everyone's face. "What's wrong?"

Maura sighed. Was the man fey? At least there was no one else around to overhear. "I found Aidan Crowley dead in the back room this morning."

Billy automatically crossed himself. "What was it took him?" he asked.

It took Maura a moment to work out what Billy meant: Aidan had been taken from life by something—or someone. "We don't know for sure yet. The gardaí have been and gone, and Sean Murphy said he'd let us know what happened, after the postmortem. Did you talk to Aidan last night?"

"I did, but not for long. He was one of the regulars, long ago. Never stood out, but you could count on him. Was it his bad heart?"

"He had a heart problem?" Maura asked, surprised and immediately relieved. A heart problem was a legitimate— if sad—reason for him to have passed away peacefully. Nothing to do with her or Sullivan's.

"He was born with a weak heart, which kept him from any heavy work. Never stood in the way of his music, but he seldom had two pennies to rub together. Poor man. Most people who knew the man would know of it, but not likely a stranger."

"Did he have any particular friends? Or did he come with someone last night?"

"I can't say. He was a friend of Niall's, of course, but there were so many people crowded in here, I couldn't see my own feet. It was a great night, right enough. Good to hear the old sounds in this place."

"It was," Maura agreed. "Look, I know it's a long shot, but do you have any idea where Aidan was staying?" Assuming, of course, he hadn't sneaked into Sullivan's on Friday night as well and found a corner to sleep in without Maura's knowledge.

"That I don't," Billy replied.

"You ready for yer pint now, Billy?" Rose asked.

Billy settled himself heavily in his chair, while Maura set to work building a small turf fire. "After such sad news, I'm in sore need of one, love. Thank you fer askin'."

Maura finished laying the fire, then stood up and dusted off her hands. "Will we be seeing the players here again today?"

"Not to play, I'll wager, but they might stop by to see how the folks liked it."

"Do most of them live around here, or did they have to travel to get here?" Maura asked.

"Some of both, I'm guessing. Ah, Rose, a thousand thanks." Billy accepted the brimming pint that Rose held out to him.

Maura went back behind the bar, but looked up when a shadow crossed in front of her window. It was Niall Cronin, who opened the door and stepped in just as Maura's mobile phone started ringing in her pocket. She checked the display: Sean. Did she want to answer it? She could pretend she hadn't heard it and delay what might well be bad news just a little longer. But in the end she turned her back on the room and hit the button.

"Sean? You have something?"

"I do. Yer man did die of a heart attack . . ." *Just like Billy said,* Maura thought, relieved. But Sean was still talking. "Signs point to it being someone's hands around his neck that brought it on. The bruises didn't show right off."

"Oh, no," Maura said without thinking. "Can you tell me anything more?"

"No time now, and little to add. I'll be back in a bit. Try to keep things quiet, will you?"

"Of course. No one's here yet. Well, Billy is, and Niall just came in, but that's all."

"I'm sorry, Maura. I'll see you later."

"Good-bye, Sean," Maura said to a dead phone. She slipped it into her pocket and turned to face the others. Her eyes flickered to Niall, who was standing indecisively in the middle of the room, as if trying to decide whether to stay or to go. The others were watching her, waiting for an update. She shook her head, not daring to say anything more.

Then she turned to Niall and summoned up a professional smile. "Good morning to you. Everyone had a great time last night. Can I get you something now?"

Niall finally came over to the bar and sat on a stool. "Have you seen Aidan Crowley?"

Chapter 15

Maura struggled to keep her face neutral, but she was pretty sure she wasn't fooling anyone. So much for saying nothing. She couldn't lie to Niall.

"Why do you ask?" she said cautiously.

She half expected Niall to come back with some remark amounting to "It's not yer business," but he surprised her by saying, "I didn't want to leave without askin' if he was headed back to Cork city and needed the lift." Niall sensed something was wrong. He leaned against the bar and faced her squarely. "Has he gotten himself in trouble, then?"

Maura looked at the others around the room, but they offered no help; this was up to her. "I'm so sorry to have to tell you this, Niall, since I know you were old friends, but Aidan's dead. I found him here this morning, in the back."

The color left Niall's face. "How?" he said, his voice rough.

"It looks like a heart attack, but we don't know anything for sure."

"Poor man. Never caught a break in his life." Niall dropped onto a bar stool. "I could do with a coffee, maybe with a drop of something in it? It's not every day that a man loses one of his oldest friends like this with no warnin'."

"I'll do it," Rose murmured and set about messing with coffee and mugs.

Lucky Rose, with something to do, Maura thought. She was at a loss: she barely knew Niall, and Aidan even less, beyond exchanging a handful of sentences, and she sucked at playing the sympathetic listener, even if it was part of her job description. "Listen, Niall, do you know if Aidan has family who should be contacted? The gardaí will want to know."

Niall shook his head. "Once I might have been able to tell you—I think he has a sister somewhere. But we've been out of touch for years. It was only by chance that I ran into him in Cork city the other day, and we got to talkin', and I persuaded him to come down fer last night's do. Damn, this is not the way things should have ended."

Niall looked sincerely shaken. Rose added a splash of whiskey to his coffee mug and slid it wordlessly across the bar. Niall grabbed it and swallowed half at once, then set it down again.

Maura debated mentioning that the death wasn't quite natural, but decided it wasn't her place—let the gardaí tell him, if they wanted to. "Did he join in the playing last night?" Maura asked. "I didn't have much chance to listen in the back."

"We all took our turn. Even the young lads. I didn't take note of when Aidan sat in, but he was part of it."

"Look, do you have any idea why he would have been in the pub here after we'd closed?" she asked. "Did Aidan have any problem with any of the musicians here last night?"

Niall was shaking his head before she'd even finished speaking. "He hadn't seen the lads fer years, decades even. If he had any troubles, he brought them with him. As fer the other thing, though, many's the time we used to bed down here, upstairs or wherever we could find a bit of open floor. Old Mick didn't mind—he gave those of us who played regular the keys to the place, although that was more like his stamp of approval, for any of us could have found our way in without." He fell silent, staring into his dark coffee.

At least now she had an explanation for the key in Aidan's pocket: he had gotten it either from Old Mick himself or from someone else who'd played at Sullivan's all those years ago.

Maura looked up to see several people standing outside, reluctant to come in. Most likely someone had in fact seen the coroner's van and was now spreading the word about a death at Sullivan's. How long would it take them to put a name to the dead man? They nudged each other and nodded toward the bar inside. Clearly they recognized Niall, but weren't sure whether to bother him. Maura leaned forward. "Niall, do you feel up to talking with your fans, or would you rather go somewhere more private?"

He looked up at her then. "Give me a bit to get myself together first."

"Come sit with me by the fire, Niall," Billy said. "They'll leave you alone 'til yer ready."

"Thanks, Billy." Niall stood up and joined Billy in the corner next to the fireplace, and they settled themselves there, Niall with his back to the room. That emboldened the people to come into the pub, leaning on the bar to order their pints but sneaking the occasional glance at the two men in the corner, although they maintained a respectful distance.

Maura gestured to Mick and Jimmy to follow her, while Rose was serving the new customers. They retreated to the hall next to the closed doors that led to the back room. "We need a story to give out," Maura said in a low voice. "Suggestions?"

"The news'll come out soon enough," Mick said. "We might as well tell people that it was Aidan and he died here last night, and let them decide if they want to stay."

"If Niall stays, I'm betting they will as well," Jimmy added.

"What about the rest of the musicians?" Maura asked. "If Niall decided to stop by, they may too. A lot of them knew Aidan, right?" Maura's phone rang in her pocket, and when she fished it out she recognized Sean's number again. She held up a finger to Mick and Jimmy, then turned and walked into the far corner before answering. She looked quickly around to be sure that no patrons could hear her. "Sean? Is there something new?"

Sean came straight to the point. "I'm looking fer Niall Cronin, and fer Timothy Reilly as well."

"Niall's right here. I haven't seen Timothy today. Uh, Sean, how much can I tell the people who come in today?"

"Tell whoever comes in that Aidan Crowley is dead, and it looks like it was his heart. It still might have been an accident, and no one meant to kill him. But don't say more than you have to. Can you keep Niall Cronin there?" Sean asked.

"I don't think he's in any hurry. He seems kind of upset.

He came looking for Aidan, wondering if he needed a ride back to Cork."

"Well, keep him there. I'll need a word with him."

"Are you coming back now?"

"I am."

Maura thought for a moment. "Look, are you going to have to round up everybody and interview them one at a time? I hate to sound cold, but that would be lousy for business here. And there's no place here to do it, unless you use the back room."

"I understand yer concern, Maura. Truth be told, it might be best if we kept this low-key—people might be more willing to talk to us. Just sit in the pub and chat with 'em—less formal than an interview."

"Can you do that? I mean, just sit here and talk?"

"It's not the way we'd choose to do it, but given the circumstances it might be the best. I'll see yeh in an hour, no more, Maura."

"Thanks, Sean." It was kind of an unusual interview strategy, but she agreed that the informal setting, combined with a few pints, might loosen some tongues. And given how many people had passed through Sullivan's the night before—and how small the Skibbereen police force was—it might be the best chance to get any real information while it was still fresh. Bringing in gardaí from other stations would probably slow down the process, which wasn't good—not that there were many other stations, or men to pull from them. And then individual interviews could take a week, and a lot of the people would be gone long before that. This was the best chance.

She ended the call, then turned to Mick and Jimmy, who didn't pretend they hadn't been listening. "Our story is that

Aidan died of a heart attack, which is true anyway. It just might not be the whole truth. Sean says he's leaving the morgue now, so he'll be here in an hour or so. Until then, we should listen to what everyone who was here last night has to say. Don't ask questions, just let people talk, and pay attention. Sound good?"

"Gettin' this group to talk will be easy, especially with a pint or two in them," Jimmy said. "Should we offer a free round on account of Aidan?"

The suggestion made sense, even if it meant saying good-bye to a chunk of the day's profits. "Good idea. But one round only, please—we can't afford more than that. Let's go."

"I'll explain to Rosie," Jimmy said, leading the way.

The church crowd started trickling in a half hour later; more followed a while after that, likely after first going home or to the hotel for Sunday dinner. By midafternoon the place was packed. Sean had come in and kind of set up shop sometime earlier while Maura wasn't watching, and she'd been careful to let him go about his official business, although he wasn't wearing a uniform. As she had guessed, he was doing informal interviews. When she had time to think, Maura wondered why Tim hadn't shown his face yet. Niall hadn't left; in fact, he had settled himself on a stool in the center of the bar and was holding forth to any-one who would listen, and there was no shortage of eager ears. Niall still looked sad, and the snatches of conversa-tion that Maura heard revolved around the days when Aidan and Niall had crossed paths while playing in Dub-lin. She hoped that Mick was keeping up with who said what; Maura was having trouble following all the talk, but then, she didn't know half the people there.

She brought Billy a fresh pint when he was alone for a brief moment. She set it on the table, then dropped into the chair next to him.

"How're yeh doing, Maura?" Billy asked softly.

She considered for a moment. She felt sad, mostly. A bit angry. Some self-pity over how an otherwise extraordinary event had gotten messed up. Worried about what might come next. Finally she said, "Okay, I think. How close do you think Niall and Aidan were, really?"

"Back in the day, I'd say they were mates. But it has been a long time, decades even, since they'd gotten together. People do drift apart." Billy studied Maura's face. "I see young Murphy's come in," he said, nodding toward the opposite corner. "He's doin' more listenin' than talkin'."

"Yeah, he told me he was coming," Maura said. "He figured this was the best way to get information. Besides, rounding up and interviewing everyone who showed up last night would be a nightmare, even if it's possible."

"Smart lad, that one. He's right."

"Do you have any idea who might have had something against Aidan?"

"I'm flattered that yer askin', but I hadn't seen the man in years. He was never a harsh man, nor much of a fighter—the heart, yeh know."

"I know, you told me. And Sean confirmed it. Any idea why he would have come back here after closing?"

"Looking for a place to kip for a bit? Old Mick used to let the players stay on. Maybe he didn't want to ask you, seein' as you don't know how it was back then. I dunno. Keep talking to folk and see what comes out of their mouths." Billy looked up to see another group of men coming in the door.

Maura recognized a couple of them as musicians from the night before.

"I'd better get back to work," she said. "Let me know if you hear anything interesting." She was about to add "or tell Sean" but realized that the odds of Old Billy navigating his way all the way across the room to where Sean sat were slim to none. But if Sean was as smart as Billy thought, he'd find his way to Billy soon enough.

There was a slight lull at about four, and Maura slipped into the chair opposite Sean, setting a mug of tea in front of him. "You look like you can use this."

"That I can. I've been talking fer hours."

"Have you learned anything new?"

He shook his head. "I'll be all night writing down what I think I heard, and I may have missed a lot, but I still don't see that we've made much progress."

"Poor man!" Maura laughed. "There's a lot of paperwork back home for me too, so don't feel too sorry for yourself. And you should talk to Billy—he's paying attention. Has anybody said anything that leads you to think—" She stopped when Sean fixed her with a stern glare. "To think they think there's anything unexpected about this?" she finished carefully.

"I can't say."

She'd expected him to say that. She looked around the crowded room. "This may take quite a while. Will you be staying all evening?"

"Sergeant Regan will be coming in soon, and I'll go back to the station and try to set down what I've heard. There'll be the regular meeting in the mornin', and I'll call you after and let you know where we are by then. Keep talking with your lot here, will ya? They might see something differently than I do, knowing more of the people and all, and they might have heard something new durin' the day today."

"I'll do that." Of course, she would have done it even if Sean hadn't asked. "Unless, of course, you guys have it all wrapped up by then."

Sean smiled. "Hope lives on. Thanks fer the tea. Now, go on about yer business, so I can do mine."

Maura stood up. "Okay, then, I will."

She joined Rose behind the bar and then realized again that she hadn't seen Tim all day. His absence now was a little strange. Maybe he'd been spooked when he heard about Aidan's death. "Have you seen or talked to Tim today?" she asked Rose.

"That I haven't, and I've been worried about him. You'd think he'd be all over this—all these idols of his together talkin' about the past, not carin' who's listenin'. Maybe I should run over to the Keohanes' house and see if he's all right?," Rose volunteered eagerly. "If yeh can spare me, that is."

The crowd was manageable, at least temporarily, and there might not be another opportunity for Rose. "If you move fast," Maura said. "I have a feeling it's going to be a busy night, and I'll need you here. Tell Tim that Niall is here—that might bring him."

"I will. See yeh in a bit." Rose all but ran out the front door. Maura watched her through the window and saw Rose crossing the street before heading down to the Keohanes' house below the road.

She turned to find Niall leaning on the bar, minus the entourage he'd had all day. "A pint?" Maura asked.

"Please," he said.

Maura started the pint, then looked up to see Rose returning with a rather bedraggled Tim. The last time she had seen Tim, the night before, he hadn't appeared to be drunk, but he certainly looked hungover now. Rose all but dragged him toward the bar.

"Well, Tim, looks like you must have had quite a night." Maura greeted him. "Did you get what you wanted?"

"I don't know. Could I get a cup of coffee?"

"I'll get it," Rose said quickly.

Tim settled himself on a stool without even noticing who his near neighbor was. Niall took pity on him. "Yeh should be pleased with yerself, after what yeh started."

Tim focused slowly, then recognized Niall. "Maybe I should have left well enough alone."

That was an odd comment, Maura thought. He'd been so eager only the day before. What had happened?

Niall appeared taken aback. "Why are yeh sayin' that? I thought it was a grand evening. Haven't seen the like for quite a while. Were yeh disappointed?"

"No. It's just—it wasn't what I expected. None of it. Excuse me." He stood up abruptly and bolted for the bathroom. Maura hoped he made it in time before he lost whatever he'd had to eat that day. And why was he still drunk this long after the event had ended?

She looked at Rose, but Rose looked as bewildered as she felt.

Niall had an odd half smile on his face. "Looks like he was pretty much hammered, eh? Not much experience with hard partying, that one. He'll learn."

Tim came back, still pale around the gills. "Sorry about

that. I didn't mean to say yeh didn't do a great job last night, Maura. It's just that it wasn't what I thought it would be. That's on me. And yeh were wonderful . . . Niall."

Maura glanced at Rose. "Did you tell him . . . ?"

Rose shook her head. "I hadn't the chance."

Tim blinked. "Tell me what?"

"Tim, I'm sorry to say that Aidan Crowley is dead. I found him here when I opened up."

Tim turned even paler than he had been before and dashed back toward the toilets.

Chapter 16

The night dragged on and on. Tim remained in hiding for a while, then slunk back into the room and sat in a dark corner, looking miserable. Rose volunteered to go to the takeaway place and bring back some food for Maura, Mick, Jimmy, and Sean, and even Tim, although she had to know he might not have much of an appetite. *What is his problem?* Maura wondered. He wasn't talking to anyone at the pub—not Rose, not even the music semi-stars who had wandered in. Despite Aidan Crowley's untimely death, Tim should have been in his element, collecting a wealth of material for his project as well as a unique perspective on how music worked in this corner of Ireland. And yet now he was missing more opportunities—why?

Niall had hung around too, graciously fielding questions from others who came in and worked up the courage to talk with him. When he was briefly alone, Maura went over and said, "No music tonight?"

Niall looked at her curiously. "I'd say it's not the right thing fer now. Wouldn't you?"

"I agree, but I wasn't sure what local customs are."

"Did you say yer from Boston? Surely there's enough Irish there to carry on the old customs."

"I guess. I didn't pay much attention, and I think a lot of it was aimed at tourists, and it wasn't really authentic. So why no music to honor one of your, uh, fallen comrades?"

"Because we don't know the story. When we do, then we'll honor him."

Niall thinks there is a story? That's odd. "I hope it will be soon."

Niall looked around him. "Seems to be doing yer business no harm."

Maura was stung by his comment, though it was true. "Not my preferred way to make money," she said sharply.

Niall ducked his head. "Fair enough. My apologies."

"Accepted," she replied with a sigh. "So tell me, were you and Aidan close?"

"Twenty years ago, I'd have said yes—as well as I knew any of me mates. Most of us who played with one band or another have run into each other now and again. Or used to. A lot have left the music behind now." Niall took another long draw of his pint. He glanced around; most people had returned to their own conversations, with only the occasional glance his way. "Aidan and I, we go way back. Like so many lads back then, we started playin' together before we left school. He had some talent, back then. We must've been part of, oh, three or four bands, but he and I were the only ones who stuck with it."

"How far did he go?"

"He did a demo album or two that got some attention, but somehow something always went wrong. The recording company folded or the gigs stopped coming or yet another band member dropped out. Never his fault, exactly—he showed up and did his part, but he had lousy luck."

"You two didn't stick together?"

"Not after the first coupla years. Not that we had a falling-out, but we ended up going in different directions, kinda. He kept on with the fiddle. A lot of bands then, and even now, still hung on to the old Celtic sound, so he found work often enough."

"Did he get into drink or drugs?"

"Yeh know about his heart?" When Maura nodded, Niall said, "He knew he couldn't do that kinda thing. But he also couldn't do much heavy work, and that was most of what was available then, to a lad with little education. Again, he was dealt a bad hand. He tried, truly, but he never caught a break."

"Did you keep in touch with him?"

"Now and again. I mean, the man knew me when, if yeh hear what I'm sayin'. I could be meself with him, not some aging idol." Niall leaned back on the bar stool. "I hadn't seen Aidan in ten years or more, until I came upon him in that pub the other day. Do yeh know Cork?"

"Only the bus station."

"What, yer chained to this place?"

"More or less," Maura answered, but without resentment. "I'm not much of a sightseer. And I've got a business to run."

Niall glanced around again, and Maura interrupted him

142

before he could comment. "I know, it's kind of a dump, but I can only do so much at once. I'm working on it."

Niall smiled. "I was going to say, there are a lot of good memories here, soaked into these old walls. You'd do well to tap into that if yeh can. You've a good start, with this weekend."

"Yeah, except for Aidan."

"There is that," Niall conceded. "But I'd be surprised if that kept people away, if you play yer cards right."

"How so?" Maura asked.

"A fair number of people remember the music here. Old Billy recalls it all. Mick there was a starry-eyed kid, and that's another piece of the picture. You can use that. You could make it work. If yeh want."

"Would you come back? To play, I mean?" Maura challenged him.

"I might do. We'll see."

And then another group came over and drew Niall away.

Maura didn't have the heart to throw people out until past closing time, but she hoped the gardaí would look the other way once again, considering the circumstances. Still, it startled her to see Sean Murphy outside her door when she finally shooed a few stragglers away. She hadn't even seen him leave, or seen his sergeant arrive. "Coming to cite me for keeping late hours, Sean?" she asked, smiling.

"I'm off duty, at least fer now."

"Are you coming in?"

"I will. Actually, I was looking for that young lad over there." Sean nodded toward Tim, sunk in misery in the corner. Even Rose had given up trying to cheer him up, and

Maura had sent her home a few hours earlier. She had gone without protest.

"You haven't talked with him yet?" Maura asked.

"I hadn't the time earlier in the day. I heard he was staying at Ellen Keohane's place, but when I stopped by there on my way here earlier she told me she hadn't heard a sound from him all day. I wondered if he'd packed it in and gone back to Dublin, but his car was still there."

"Rose went over and dragged him out of his room and over here this afternoon," Maura told him, "but he's been moping ever since. Which kind of surprised me, because he was so excited about the research possibilities on the music the last couple of days. But so far the only thing he's researched tonight is the bottom of a glass."

"Is he sober now, do you think?"

"Ask him. But if you're off duty, shouldn't you wait until tomorrow to talk to him?"

"Maybe yer right. It's been a long day. Could yeh do me a pint?"

"Coming up."

Mick emerged from the cellar stairs and greeted Sean, then turned to Maura. "We'll be needing to reorder in the morning—we're running low."

"I'm not surprised. Can we get a fast delivery?"

"I'll see what I can do." Mick sat a couple of seats down from Sean at the bar. "Since yer already there, could yeh fix me a coffee?"

"Sure, why not? At least then I'll feel useful."

Mick ignored her dig. "Anythin' new on Crowley's death, Sean?"

Sean shot a quick glance at Tim in the corner. "Keep it down, will yeh?"

Mick followed Sean's glance. "So yeh haven't told . . . the whole story yet?"

Sean shook his head. "I want to see what people would say without it. But there's too many people who don't know enough. Sure, they were here. Sure, they saw Aidan play. Some of them saw the man leave as well, through the front door. None of them saw him come back in after."

"Have you located any of Aidan's relatives?"

"Not yet."

Maura pushed the pint and the mug of coffee across the bar, then came around and sat on the other side of Sean. "You did talk to Billy?"

"Of course I did. The man knows everybody in the county. And his eyesight is as keen as it ever was. He saw nothing out of the ordinary here last night. He did see a lot of familiar faces from the past, but that gets us no nearer to the truth. And, yes, he told me who I should tell, from what's left of the family, if I can locate them."

"So now what?" asked Mick.

"We'll be meeting at the station in the mornin' to go over what we've got. You'll go on about yer business."

"Sounds like you need a computer program to sort this all out," Maura said.

"Are yeh volunteerin'?"

She raised both her hands. "Not me! I don't own a computer, and I don't want one. I'm just saying that you've got a lot of information, and you need to see where it overlaps."

"I'll raise the point at the meeting tomorrow." Sean

drained his pint and stood up. "Thanks for the drink." He slid a couple of euro coins across the bar. Maura wrestled with whether to slide them back, or whether a free drink might violate some garda rule she didn't know about. "No doubt I'll be seein' yeh tomorrow," he said.

When Sean had left, Maura and Mick were left alone—except for Tim, quiet as a mouse, sunk in gloom in the corner. "Hey, Tim, we're closing now," Maura called out to him.

He raised his head slowly to look at her, his eyes dim. "Oh. Sorry. I didn't notice. I'll get out of yer way." He stood up stiffly, but at least he appeared steady on his feet once he made it to upright. And he wasn't driving, just walking across the empty Sunday street. Maura couldn't recall serving him more than one or two pints since he'd come in, hours earlier, so he must be sober. "You okay, Tim?"

"Yeah, sure, fine." His tone suggested anything but.

Mick looked at her with a question in his eyes. "You go ahead," Maura told him. "I'll close up."

Mick didn't argue. "See yeh tomorrow evening, then," he said. "Unless of course yeh'd like me to open?"

Maura thought for a moment. "You know, I'd like it if you would. And you've still got last night's take at home, right? I need to get that, plus today's, to the bank in Skibbereen in the morning, so I'll stop by here and get it from you. We can work out the rest of the hours tomorrow, okay?"

"No worries. I'll be here early. Good night, Maura."

He slipped out into the dark, leaving Maura and Tim alone in the half-dark pub. "Tim, what's going on?" Maura said quietly.

"Nothing. Not. A. Thing," he said firmly.

"I don't believe you. On Friday and Saturday you were in here practically jumping up and down with excitement. Now you look like your dog died. But on the other hand, you could have left, gone back to Dublin. Why are you still here?"

"Why do yeh care?" Tim glared at her with bleary eyes.

Maura took a moment to think about that. "Because you showed up here and started something, and I'm grateful to you for that."

"Yeah, and are yeh grateful for ending up with a body in the back?"

"And is that your fault?" Maura demanded.

Tim straightened his back and looked her in the eye. "How do yeh know it wasn't my fault?"

Uh-oh. "Did you talk to Aidan Crowley last night? Maybe get into some kind of argument?"

"No. Well, not exactly."

It had been a very long day, and Maura was tired. "Tim, stop playing games. I don't feel like guessing. Did something happen between you last night or not? Did you know him?"

Tim took a deep breath. "I only met him on the Friday, but I was wondering if he wasn't mebbe my father."

She hadn't expected that. "I think you're going to have to explain." She debated about offering him something to drink, but settled for, "Will coffee help? Did you manage to eat earlier? I could probably scrounge up something."

"Coffee'd be grand."

Maura started two cups of coffee. She was pretty sure she'd need it as much as he did. When they were ready she presented him with one, then sat down next to him. "Okay, talk. What makes you think Aidan was your father?"

Tim sighed again, and Maura wanted to shake him to get the words out. It was late, she was tired, and if he had something to say, couldn't he just spit it out? Finally he started speaking, sounding less like a college boy than he had before. "I was raised by me mother, in Dublin. She never mentioned me father. When I got old enough to wonder about him, she refused to say anything. Except she called him a bastard, and worse. Never told her family who he was either, and there wasn't anybody else to ask. She had a sister she might have been close to then, but she lit out for Australia years ago, and I didn't think she'd answer me mail or e-mail. Anyways, me ma got married a few years later, had me sisters, and refused to talk about it at all, even when I kept nagging. It was *my* father, wasn't it? Didn't I have a right to know? Finally I guess she thought she'd better say somethin', if only to shut me up. She told me he was some guy she'd met, a musician, at an event she'd gone to with a girlfriend when she lived in Clonakilty, growin' up. And that was all she'd say. She kind of hinted she might not have known his name, and that was her excuse for keepin' her mouth shut—she was ashamed of that night."

Tim swallowed some coffee and cleared his throat. "Not much to work with, eh? I did the math so I knew more or less when she'd have run into the man, then I looked up what bands were big then. I mean, big enough for her to make a special effort to go hear them a few towns over. But there were so many . . . Seems like every town spawned its own band or three, and they all kept movin' around, and they'd swap players. And then there were the sidemen, who didn't belong to any group but ended up playing for a lot of 'em."

"Do you know the girlfriend?" Maura asked.

"Nah, Ma said they drifted apart years ago, and she never told me her name. Anyway, then me mother died last year, of the cancer. And before yeh ask, she didn't leave some handy letter behind tellin' me all the facts. But with her gone, I really wanted to find me father if I could, so I studied music at uni, thinkin' it might get me closer to him somehow."

"So what did you hope to find, just showing up here the way you did?"

Tim slumped in his chair, looking drained. "I don't know. I was running out of ideas, and I had a fortnight free before term starts, and I truly was curious about how this place just kind of happened to become an important place for the music. I mean, what I told you about the research I was doin', that part was true. So here I am. I figured I'd run into a few old guys and we'd talk fer a while, and maybe I'd get some more names—who hung out with who in the day—and I'd go back to uni and write it up and call it an oral history. I told a couple of people what I was looking for, and I guess they told a couple of people, and then Old Billy stepped in and last night just . . . happened. Like it used to do. I never expected anything more. Certainly not that someone would die."

"Nobody did, I'm pretty sure," Maura said tartly. "So how'd you expect to flush out the man who might be your father? And what made you think it was Aidan Crowley?"

"I'd run into the name, now and again. Sometimes along with Niall's, sometimes with other bands. But the more I read, the more people I talked to, the more it seemed like he'd been in the right place at the right time. He never made it big, so he played a lot of the smaller places in West Cork, where me ma could have . . . seen him. So when he first came by on the Friday, I told him I wanted to talk to him—I never mentioned why. He put me off then, and I thought it was because he was playing and getting reacquainted with his old mates, and he couldn't be bothered. But I kept after him, and finally last night he said I should meet him after the pub shut down. So I did—outside, partway up the hill overlooking the stream. He was alive when I left him there, I swear."

And outside, not inside, if Tim was telling the truth. At least that explained why she and Mick hadn't seen anyone in the pub when they had closed: Tim and Aidan would've been outside then. Except Aidan *had* used the key to come back in later. With someone else? "What time was this?"

"One thirty, mebbe?" Tim said.

"You never came back into the building?" Maura asked, just to be sure.

"No. It was locked up, wasn't it? So we sat up there and talked, and I worked my way around to who he might have . . . been with at the right time, and he laughed and said he couldn't remember much of anything from those days. I showed him a picture of my mother and he said he didn't know her. It's not that I wanted anything from him, like money or a big 'welcome to the family, my boy.' I just wanted to know."

Was that enough motive for throttling Aidan? "And he blew you off. Did you get mad at him?"

"No! I mean, I realized how daft I must look, cornering strangers and asking, 'Are you me da?' And I didn't think he was lying—I think he really didn't remember. So I just said thank you and went back to the Keohanes' place, and that's the whole of it."

"So why were you so hungover all day?"

"I had a bottle back in me room, didn't I? After talking with Aidan, I finished it, which is not something I do much. I really don't have any other ideas for looking for my father, and maybe it's time I give it up and move on. I was feeling pretty sorry for meself, if yeh want to know the truth. Then Rose dragged me out of bed today. I didn't want to come over, but I figured I'd better—it might get me out of my funk. Then you tell me Aidan's dead. Is it any wonder I've been drinking?"

No, thought Maura, *it isn't,* but she wasn't about to tell him that. "Look, Tim, you've got to tell all this to the gardaí. Don't just cut and run, because Sean Murphy already wants to talk to you. If nothing else, it sounds like you were probably the last person to see Aidan alive." *Not counting whoever might've assaulted him.* Maura kept that thought silent.

Tim hung his head. "I know. I will, in the morning. Will that do?"

"That's fair enough. You're in no shape to go anywhere right now. You can talk to Sean Murphy tomorrow, early. Deal?"

"Yeah. Thanks, Maura."

She escorted Tim to the door and watched him cross the street. Then she locked the door behind her and headed home.

Chapter 17

A man died at Sullivan's.

That thought slammed into Maura's head when she woke up Monday morning after a short and restless night. She lay in bed worrying while the sun came up. Why had Aidan Crowley died at Sullivan's? Was it going to affect her business? It seemed kind of heartless to worry about that, but she couldn't help it. It would help if the gardaí could settle the question of Aidan's death. The one thing they knew for sure was that Aidan's heart had given out. But had someone frightened him to death? The bruises on his neck hinted at that, but who could say that had made the difference? Maybe it was just Aidan's time. She made a mental note to call Sean and have him talk with Tim ASAP. Assuming Tim hadn't run for Dublin already or disappeared entirely.

Did she believe Tim's story? Maybe. Maura could understand from her own life wanting to know who your parents were and where you came from. Of course, there was a slim possibility that Tim was obsessed with the man who had knocked up his mother, and had come seeking revenge. But that didn't match what she'd seen of Tim, who seemed anything but aggressive. He was sweet. Kind of innocent. Even Rose seemed more mature. Maura had to keep reminding herself that Tim was only a few years younger than she was, closer still in age to Sean. Of course, it wasn't exactly comparing apples to apples: Tim was a student, while Sean was a garda, trained to solve—or even stop—crimes and keep the peace, not that it was a difficult job around here. Not like in Boston. Anyway, Sean had a very different set of responsibilities.

Maura wondered just how the Skibbereen gardaí were going to handle this case. Sean had told her once that most crimes in this part of Cork were committed by people already known to the gardaí and were solved quickly. But Aidan Crowley wasn't a local, so if there was a crime here, nobody even knew who the likely suspects would be or where to find them. Maura had to admit that the simplest course for everybody—gardaí, Aidan's friends, Maura and her staff—would be to call it a heart attack and be done. Not a crime.

What a mess. Maybe she should go talk to Bridget. She'd missed seeing her the past couple of days and was kind of curious about what news had filtered to Bridget through her own network of friends and what she thought about it. Having decided on a plan, Maura got up and showered and fixed herself some breakfast.

She was glad that Mick would be opening the pub this morning. Not that she expected any more unpleasant surprises today, but she figured she really would need the help. Mick had kind of a reassuring presence—he didn't get rattled by problems, he just fixed them quietly. Jimmy, on the other hand, was a schmoozer. He'd talk with anybody, and while sometimes he lost sight of business, Maura had to admit she was beginning to realize how making customers feel welcome played a part in keeping them coming back again and again. That was something she had to work on herself, because she wasn't usually a warm and chatty person. People in her past had told her she didn't smile enough. Maybe if she ever found the time she should check out other local pubs and see who stood behind that bar and how they handled things.

Breakfast eaten, she checked her watch: still early. She decided that before visiting Bridget she should try to call Sean, in case he got sucked into his morning meeting. She was relieved when he answered.

"Good mornin', Maura. Why so early? No new problems down the pub?"

"None that I know of—I'm still at home. But I wanted to tell you that I talked with Tim Reilly last night, after closing, and I think you need to hear what he has to say."

"Ah." Sean didn't ask dumb questions, like "what?" or "why?" He simply thought for a moment. "We've a conference on at ten, but I could be over to Keohanes' well before that. Will it be important to hear him before the meeting?"

"I think so. For what it's worth, I don't think he had anything to do with Aidan Crowley's death. But you can decide for yourself."

"Thanks, Maura. I'll see you after."

There, that was her good deed for the day. She grabbed a raincoat to head down to Bridget's—after the early glimpse of sun, the clouds had started rolling in.

As usual, Bridget was up, and two fresh loaves of brown bread were already cooling on her pine table when Maura walked in.

"Ah, there you are, Maura." Bridget greeted her when she let herself in. "I wondered if you'd stop by today, what with all the fuss at the pub."

"Is that what you're calling it? Fuss?" It seemed a mild term for a dead body, but Maura realized she was glad that Bridget wasn't upset.

"Sit. Help yerself to the bread, and the tea's almost ready." Maura obediently sat and sliced herself a piece of the warm bread and began to butter it. Bridget set a mug of tea in front of her, then settled herself on the chair next to hers. "I don't mean to belittle the poor man's passing, but he wasn't one of ours, was he?"

"From around here, you mean? Not that I've heard. Is it better if he's a stranger?"

"Just different, I'd say. Poor soul. Is there any family to be found?"

"Sean's looking into it. The only person who seems to have known him is Niall, and he says they lost touch years ago."

"What's the man like?"

"Who, Niall? Why? Were you a fan of his?"

"Who wasn't, twenty years ago? You couldn't turn on a radio without hearing his voice."

Maura smiled to herself. It was hard to imagine the graying middle-aged man she'd been talking to as a rock idol, but that was what people kept telling her. Maybe the standards in Ireland were different. Of course, U2 seemed to have hit it big on both sides of the Atlantic—and Bono had to be about the same age as Niall. Was Niall ever in their league? The only kind of music her grandmother had played on her old plastic radio in their kitchen in Boston had been what Maura now recognized as traditional Irish.

"Weren't there any women performers then, Bridget? Because all the guys who showed up on Saturday were, well, guys. And so were most of the people who came to hear them. I mean, I've heard of the Cranberries—they have a female singer, don't they? What about Sinéad O'Connor?"

"I'm not the one you should be askin', love. But I'm guessing performin' was a hard life then, and still is. I mean, the men, they can bed down anywhere there's space—a bed, a chair, even the floor. But a woman couldn't do that, not the same way."

"I hadn't thought of that."

"And if yeh look in the stores, I'm told, yeh'll see that there are more women playin' the traditional music, not the newer stuff. And singin' it too."

"Huh. Thanks, Bridget. That's interesting. This is still new to me."

"Was it a good crowd?"

"I'd say so—we filled the place, and we were busy all night. What did Mick tell you?"

"That it was like he remembered it, and it made him happy. Will yeh keep on with it?"

"I don't know. I would have said yes, probably, until I found Aidan. Now I'm not sure how people would feel about it. I'll see how it goes today."

"Ah, sure and his death is a sad thing, but it's the music that matters, and it's been missed around here. Let things settle a bit—yeh don't have to decide today."

"I'd like to find out more about how Aidan died before I decide anything." She debated about telling Bridget about the bruises on Aidan's neck, and Tim's unexpected announcement, but decided that it would only upset her.

"And that's as it should be."

"Did you hear from Mick about the death?"

"That I didn't. He knows I have trouble hearing the phone. But anywise, he's afraid of unsettling me, he is, so he might say nothing at all. It's kind of him, but I don't need to be cosseted."

"He's pretty closemouthed in general, isn't he?"

"He's a good lad."

Maura noted that Bridget hadn't answered her question, exactly. Mick never talked about himself. Was there a reason? Some dark secret? Or maybe he simply had nothing to tell. But she'd seen his eyes light up when the bands came back, so she suspected there was something hiding behind his usually calm face. Was it worth digging for?

Maura drained her mug. "I'd better get going. Mick's opening today, but we may still be busy just answering everyone's questions. Although it felt like half of the county passed through Sullivan's yesterday, just to hear the news from us. And Sean may be coming by too."

"He's a steady boy, that one."

"Yeah," Maura agreed amiably. "Thanks for the bread and tea. I'll see myself out."

It was just past ten when Maura arrived at Sullivan's. Everything looked peaceful. She walked in to find Mick talking with their distributor about swapping out kegs. It crossed her mind that as the owner, maybe she should step in and demand the distributor talk with her, but it seemed kind of dumb to upset what had been working fine until now. If she was going to start throwing her weight around, she could pick her times more carefully. Besides, she was glad she didn't have to wrestle the darn things: she could if she had to, but they were heavy and hard to handle, so it was nice to have someone else do it.

When the man had left, Mick turned to her. "That's one problem solved. How're yeh doin' this morning?"

"Okay. I stopped by for a cup of tea with Bridget. I think she's ticked off that you didn't give her all the juicy gossip about Aidan's death yourself."

Mick's mouth twitched. "Better than the telly, are we?" Then his expression sobered. "Did yeh hear anything useful out of Tim last night?"

"I think he has some information that the gardaí can use." She didn't think the details about Tim's parentage were hers to share. "I called Sean earlier, and he said he'd talk to Tim this morning, and then he's got a meeting at the station, so we probably won't hear anything new for a while. You don't know anything else, do you?"

"I've had no news at all since we left last night."

"You'll be here all day today? You don't have other plans?" *What does Mick do when he isn't working here?* She'd never asked directly.

"I may go see Granny and fill her ear, since she wants to hear the news. Jimmy'll be in, and Rose as well. We can send her home if we don't need the help."

"It might be good if Rose is here if Tim comes in after talking to the gardaí."

"Fair enough. Shall we open?" Mick asked.

"I want to run to the bank first. I get nervous with a lot of money sitting around. You did bring Saturday's haul, right?"

"Nah, I'm sitting on a beach in Ibiza right now," Mick answered. "Yes, of course I did." He handed her the bundle of bills, held together with a rubber band.

"That looks nice," Maura said. "Would you mind getting the rest out of the till and counting it, while I count this?" She knew Sunday's take had been far less than Saturday's but suspected it was still well above average. She started counting. When she was finished, she started counting again. Finally she said, "Wow."

"That would be good, then?" Mick asked, his eyes on the bills he was counting.

Maura was still trying to wrap her head around the total. "That would be *great*. This is more than we've made in months. Maybe ever, in one night. Or week. How much from yesterday?"

Mick squared up the stack of bills and named a figure that was over half of Saturday's income. "Good enough fer yeh?"

"It's . . . amazing." Maura felt a spurt of joy: the music had worked its magic. Then a stab of dismay: could it ever be the same, after Aidan? "I am going to take this straight to the bank, right now. For all I know, the roof is about to fall on my head, and I want to know the money's safe. I'll try to be back before Sean gets here."

"I'll take care of the place. See yeh," Mick replied.

Maura retrieved her car and drove carefully to Skibbereen. Maybe she was being superstitious, but she didn't want to have an accident and have the car burst into flames, destroying all that hard-earned money. She was still stunned. Even if it never happened again, Saturday night's session (and Sunday's overflow) had together brought in enough money to see Sullivan's through the quiet winter season and up to next year's tourist season. She would survive her first year at the place, with change left over. Maybe she could even think about replacing a couple of pieces of ratty furniture.

Happy fantasies occupied Maura as she drove the seven miles to Skibbereen, made her deposit at the bank—smiling—and drove back to Leap.

Maybe things might actually work out after this.

Chapter 18

By the time Sean finally arrived it was late in the afternoon, although Maura had been so rushed that she hadn't noticed the time. As she had told Bridget, there were more curious people who wanted to hear about the music and the death, which apparently made an appealing combination. It was fairly quiet when Sean walked in, during the lull between the lunch crowd and the predinner crowd. He looked tired.

"Hey, Sean," Maura said when he came over and leaned against the bar. "You look like you could use a coffee."

"Could yeh make it a tea, please?" He settled himself on a stool.

"Coming up." She filled a pot with hot water from the coffee machine's spout, added a pair of Barry's tea bags, and set it down to steep before turning back to talk to him. "So, did you talk with Tim?"

"Couldn't find him," Sean said. "This morning, I checked at the Keohanes' where he's been stayin', and Ellen let me in. His things are there, but there's no sign of him. Hasn't come back either, or so she says—I was just over there again."

"Damn," Maura said, more to herself than to Sean. "He promised he'd talk to you. Maybe he went on a long walk to clear his head and got lost." Not that city boy Tim had seemed like much of a hiker to her.

"I hadn't the time to hunt for him earlier, what with the meeting at the station this mornin'. I thought I'd stop by and see if he's here."

"I haven't seen him yet today. How'd the meeting go, if you can tell me?"

Sean glanced around the room, assessing the crowd, which was made up of Old Billy, chatting volubly to a stranger, and a small group of thirtyish guys near the front window, talking about sports. Apparently he decided it was safe to talk. "We've learned a bit more about Aidan Crowley, not all of it good."

"Really? Like what?"

"Well, he's lived in Cork city or thereabouts the last few years. But he's been all over. We've had no luck finding his family, since we don't know where he came from. Doesn't seem to have had a fixed address. We don't know if he was employed. It's a wonder Niall stumbled on him when he did. Have you seen Niall today?"

"No, I haven't. Hold on." Maura turned to ask Mick, who was swabbing off tables and seeing to the fire. "Do you know if Niall's gone back to Dublin for good, or if he's planning to come in today?"

"He didn't tell me, no surprise, but the feelin' I had was that he wanted to stay around to see how this thing with Aidan plays out—I think he feels guilty for drawin' him in."

"Do you know where he's staying?" Maura asked.

"No. Maybe in Glandore? I didn't ask, and he didn't share it with me."

Maura turned back to Sean. "Sorry, we don't know. But I'd agree with Mick—he didn't seem to be in any hurry to move on or to get back home. Do you need to talk to him again?"

"We've had his information, and there's no cause to look for him. But if he should come back, I'd like a word."

"Sure." Maura pushed the teapot, along with a mug, sugar, and milk, across the bar to Sean. "There you go."

"Ta, Maura." Sean hesitated a moment before going on, "I'd rather hear it from him, of course, but could yeh give me the heart of what it was Tim told yeh last night?"

Maura wondered if Tim would be offended or angry if she shared his secret. But then, she owed no loyalty to Tim, and she trusted Sean's discretion. Plus her business was in the middle of the mess. She came out from behind the bar. "Let's sit over there, where it's more private." She gestured toward a table in the far corner, away from the sports fans. Sean picked up his mug of tea and followed her.

When they were settled Maura said quietly, "Tim says he's the result of a one-night stand his mother had with a musician, but she never named names, and now she can't. Tim did some math and some research and decided Aidan was a possibility, so they met out back after the pub closed

Saturday night, to talk. Tim said that Aidan denied knowing his mother—well, more like he couldn't remember those days at all, which isn't exactly denying it, but he simply didn't know. I think Tim was hurt—he'd probably gotten his hopes up. But he swears that he left Aidan alive and well, outside the building."

"Did yeh believe him?" Sean asked in the same low tone.

"I think so. He seems like kind of a lost kid—his mother's gone now, and he wants to figure out who he is. I don't think he wanted anything like money or a public announcement from Aidan, he just wanted to know."

"Which he didn't get. Did Tim seem angry last night, when you talked to him?"

"No, more like sad."

Sean digested that before saying, "It wouldn't have taken much to bring on Aidan's heart attack. Even a threat from a strong young man could have been enough. And maybe Tim panicked after and ran off, so didn't see where Aidan went. He could have made his way inside, before . . ."

"I get it," Maura said quickly. "But I have trouble seeing Tim attacking anyone. Was Aidan's neck badly bruised?"

"Are you asking how strong a man it would have taken? Or how long the man kept his hold? Truth is, it wouldn't have taken much force. We need to find Tim," Sean said. "Would Rose know anything about his whereabouts?"

"You can ask her, assuming it's okay with Jimmy—I don't know what your rules for interrogating underage kids are around here."

Sean looked startled by Maura's implication, and then he smiled. "It's just a few questions, Maura. Is she here?"

"She was in this morning, but may have run home to put something on for Jimmy's dinner. She'll be back. I told her we might need her, if people keep coming in."

"I'll look out for her, then."

Maura leaned her elbows on the table. "Sean, what happens next? I mean, you guys have talked to everyone who you know was here on Saturday, and any outsiders they could name. You've done some digging into Aidan's past. Have you found out more about him, things you can't tell me? You said not everything was good in his background. What did you mean by that? And how did you find out? I don't know how this works here."

Sean smiled. "It's not like those *CSI* shows they've got on the telly, but we can ring one of our pals in Cork and ask for the odd favor now and then—like a file on Aidan Crowley, if there is one. Still, it doesn't appear in seconds. We'll have more information today. But the Cork gardaí did admit a file existed fer the man."

"What about tracking down other people—the rest of the roving musicians? Can you check credit card use or track mobile phones to see who was here?"

Sean laughed outright. "Not without a lot of paperwork to justify it all, and by then whoever it was might be in Africa for all we knew. We start with the smallest circle, sort of—who was here, who saw what. If that doesn't give us the results we want, we make the circle a bit larger. I'll give you that this is an odd situation, since people seem to have come from all over to hear the music, but we've completed what I'd call the first circle. Now we'll move beyond that. It takes time. I know yer worried about people staying away from Sullivan's, but we're doin' our best."

"I know. I wasn't criticizing. But when I find a body, I take it kind of personally."

"So yeh should. And pray that it won't happen again."

Rose walked in and looked startled to see Sean and Maura together in the corner. She made a point of avoiding them after that, trying to seem busy behind the bar.

Troubled by Rose's odd behavior, Maura stood up. "Excuse me, Sean—I need to talk to Rose for a minute." When she reached the bar she leaned across and asked, "What's going on?"

The whites of Rose's eyes flashed as she said innocently, "What do yeh mean?"

"You know what I mean. I'll get right to it: do you know where Tim is?"

Now Rose looked down at the glass in her hand, one she was polishing for the fifth time. "I might. Is he in trouble?"

"I don't know. Sean needs to talk to him."

"You mean, about his ma and Aidan?"

"Wait—when did he tell you about that?"

Rose looked away. "Just now, before I came in. He rang me on my mobile and asked if we could talk face to face."

So he was somewhere nearby, Maura realized. "Did he tell you he didn't hurt Aidan?"

Now Rose looked her in the eye. "Yes, and I believe him. He's not like that."

It was clear that Rose really did want to believe that, and it more or less matched what Maura thought too, but she wasn't about to give that away. "So where is he?"

"He was thinkin' he might go back to Dublin, but I told him he needed to see this thing here through. Maybe

166

Aidan wasn't . . . who Tim thought he was, but Tim was here late that night and might have seen or heard somethin' without knowin' it. So he didn't go."

"I'm glad to hear that. Where is he?" Maura repeated.

"Will he get in trouble?" Rose shot back.

"I don't think so. Look, please tell Sean where to find him, will you? Sean's a friend. He just wants to ask Tim some questions. Tell Sean where Tim is, or call Tim and tell him to meet Sean here or somewhere else. It'll be fine, I promise." Maura hoped she was telling Rose the truth, but she did trust Sean to be fair.

Rose stared her down for a long moment, then nodded. "All right, then, but I'll hold yeh to it." She came out from behind the bar and went over and plunked herself in the chair across from Sean Murphy, who looked startled by her abrupt arrival. Maura debated joining them but decided that this was Rose's responsibility; let her act like an adult and be treated as one, without Maura hovering. Besides, she had customers to deal with, and the rest of her staff seemed to have vanished for the moment.

Maura watched from a distance as Sean listened patiently to Rose. He nodded several times and asked a question or two, then both of them stood up and went out the front door, leaving Maura feeling just a bit annoyed at being left out. She sighed. It was not her problem, and she'd hear the results soon enough. In the meantime, the crowd was growing again, with the talk split between the music and the death of Aidan Crowley, and she eavesdropped when she could.

It was a half hour later when Sean and Rose returned, without Tim. Sean looked a bit grim, and Rose appeared to be fighting tears. She didn't look at Sean before walking stiffly around the bar and serving the next person who asked.

Sean followed more slowly and came up to the bar.

"What happened?" Maura asked quietly.

"The man wasn't there, where he told Rose he'd be. Where she'd met with him only an hour or two before."

"You think he ran?"

Sean shook his head. "There were signs of a struggle, and we found his mobile under a shrub."

Maura did not like what she was hearing. "Did you check at Ellen's?"

"Of course. No one's seen him. And his vehicle is still parked there."

"Where was he supposed to be?"

"You know the old slate factory, down by the harbor?" Sean asked.

"I've seen it. It's locked up, isn't it?"

"It has been, for years, but that doesn't mean someone can't get in. Tim told Rose he went there to think things through. He wasn't exactly hiding; he only wanted to be alone fer a bit. And he'd left all his gear behind at Ellen's, so it doesn't look like he meant to flee."

"So the big question is, who found him there?"

Sean nodded. "Someone who didn't exactly wish him well."

Maura swallowed a couple of words that weren't appropriate for the setting, no matter how strongly she felt. "What now?"

"I've got to report this to the station as a suspicious disappearance, since he knew that the gardaí want to question him and he's nowhere to be found. But the circumstances tell me that he didn't leave of his own choice. So we'll start a search. Rose, there, she's upset, no doubt. It seems she really took to the young man."

"But she's not in any trouble, is she? I mean, she didn't know where he was, earlier."

"Until he called her on his mobile and told her."

Not good. "But she tried to get him to come here and talk to you."

"So she says, but we have only her word for that. Maybe the two of them are conspiring to get Tim away from here. I'm sorry, Maura, I've got to go. Keep an eye on Rose." Sean stood up, but as he reached the door, a nondescript car pulled up outside Sullivan's. The passenger door opened, and Tim Reilly fell—or was pushed—out. He'd barely hit the pavement when the car sped away toward the east and Tim scrambled to his feet and watched the car disappear.

When he turned toward the pub, he found himself face-to-face with Sean Murphy, who said, "I'd like a word with yeh, Mr. Reilly."

Chapter 19

As soon as Sean led Tim into the pub, Rose intercepted them. "Tim, are yeh all right? I was that worried! Whatever happened with yeh?"

Before Tim could open his mouth, Maura stepped up. The rest of the customers in the room watched the exchange with interest, but Maura wasn't offering free entertainment, nor did she want Sean dragging Tim off to the garda station without a chance to collect himself. "Sean, why don't you and Tim go back to your table. Tim, you look like you could use a coffee. Rose, will you get that for him?"

Sean, Tim, and Rose all did as she had ordered. *Maybe I'm getting the hang of being in charge,* Maura thought. While Sean and Tim sat, Maura stationed herself between their table and the small crowd, who finally took the hint and turned back to their pints and their conversations, although Maura was sure they were listening. Oh, well, with luck they'd stick around a bit longer and order another pint, just to see what all the excitement was about.

Rose delivered the coffee to Tim and a fresh cup of tea to Sean. Maura was surprised when Sean gestured to Maura to join them. She scanned the room: Jimmy was still enjoying his dinner at home, it seemed, but Mick was in, and he and Rose could handle things for a bit. Maura sat at the table, prepared to listen to Tim's story.

Sean pulled out a small notepad. "All right, then. Start from the beginning, if yeh will."

"Are yeh arrestin' me?" Tim demanded.

"Nothing like that, Tim," Sean reassured him.

Maura interrupted. "Before you start—Tim, I'm sorry, but when Rose and Sean couldn't find you, I told Sean what you'd told me last night. I thought it might help. So Sean knows the basic details."

Tim looked relieved. "No worries. I'm not the only boy who grew up without a father, where I come from." He turned to Sean. "Look, everything I've said about my uni research into this place's music history—that's all true. But I guess I also thought my nosing around it might flush a few of the old players out of the woods, so to speak. And it did."

"And I thank you for that, Tim—it was a great turnout," Maura said. Sean glared at her for interrupting again.

Tim didn't seem to notice and went on, "Like I told Maura, Ma said me father was a musician, and Aidan was on me short list. But it was so much more crowded than I'd expected—there was no way to have a proper conversation with anyone. That's why I asked Aidan to meet me after the pub closed, and he told me to meet him out back."

Aidan knew the place that well? Maura wondered. Well, he *had* had a key to the place on him, so it seemed likely. But she didn't interrupt.

"And what time was that?" Sean asked, in his professional voice.

Tim's eyes darted at Maura. "Just past closing, which was pretty far after hours. Maybe one o'clock? Or later? I wasn't looking at the time—I just went out and waited for him. Anyways, we sat outside, and I told Aidan me story, and he said that there were a lot of girls back in the day and he couldn't remember the half of them. I was disappointed, sure, but I guess I wasn't really surprised. Then he said he was shattered, so that was the end of it. I went back to me room and I guess he came in here."

"Did yeh see anyone else about?" Sean asked.

Tim gave a short laugh. "Have you not seen this place in the middle of the night? I might've seen a dog, up toward the church. The rest of the village was locked up tight."

"I didn't see anyone either when I left after closing," Maura added.

"Go on, then," Sean said to Tim.

"So like I said, I went to me room and was feelin' a bit low and sorry for meself, so I drank myself to sleep. Yesterday I was still hangin', as you saw me here. This mornin' I woke up with the sun and felt like the walls were closing in on me, and I didn't want to have to talk to anyone, so I started walkin' down along the shore."

"That woulda been when I first went looking for yeh," Sean said.

"Could be. Anyways, out by the water it was quiet, except

for a lot of birds. I found this old building, where I'd be out of sight, and settled meself inside."

The old slate factory, Maura thought.

Tim went on, "I sat there for a while, tryin' to sort things out, I guess. Maybe I'd pinned all me hopes on Aidan. Or maybe seein' him and the others had showed me how hopeless it was. I had nothing to go on, and I can't spend all my time runnin' around the country lookin' for middle-aged musicians and saying, 'Are you me da?' like an eejit. Maybe if Ma didn't want me to know, she had her reasons. Maybe it wasn't a musician at all, or she'd been attacked, or it was a boy from her village and she wanted to build the story up. Or maybe she was drunk or high and really didn't know. Too late to tell now."

"Then you called Rose," Maura said bluntly, earning another glare from Sean. "Why?"

"I was thinkin' that if I was goin' back to Dublin, I'd want to say good-bye to her. After Rose left I was sittin' there lookin' at the water and thinkin' it was time I just gave this up and go on with me life back in Dublin. And then this fella shows up."

Maura knew the place he was talking about. While there was a path of sorts, no one would just happen to be strolling along it, since it didn't lead anywhere. It was also not visible from much of anywhere, other than the water. So whoever the man was, he had to have followed Tim there, because he couldn't have found it on his own.

"Did yeh recognize this man?" Sean asked.

Tim shook his head. "I don't think so. But you saw how packed the place was on Saturday night, and how dark. He could have been there but I might never have seen his face. And I wasn't in any shape to notice faces on Sunday."

"And yeh didn't see him hanging around, after yeh met with Aidan?"

"No. Like I said, I didn't see a soul then."

Sean made another note. "All right, then. What did the man look like?"

Tim squinted, trying to picture him. "Maybe late thirties? Short hair, hard to tell the color. Heavier than me, but not too tall. Kind of weasely, if you know what I mean. Ordinary clothes."

"What happened when he came upon yeh?"

"That's when things got strange. I didn't like his looks, so I stood up. Then he says, 'Where is it?' And I go, 'Where is what?' And he says, 'Crowley's stuff.' And I say, 'I don't know what yer talkin' about.' Except he didn't believe me, I guess. He says, 'Word's out that Crowley's dead, and it's not at his place, so it's got to be somewhere here. How'd he get here?' I told him, 'The bus, mebbe?' The big guy says, 'No car?' And I say, 'How would I know?' And then he gets angry and grabs me by the front of me jacket. I tried to fight him off—I mean, it was broad daylight and we were standin' on the shore where anybody could see, and he wants to get into it right there? But he was stronger than me, and he kind of dragged me back to where he'd parked his car. And I'm yellin' at him, 'What do you want? I don't know anything!' I don't think he believed me."

"Did he physically assault yeh?" Sean said formally.

"He hit me a time or two, mostly to scare me, I think, but then he kind of gave up. Most likely he figured it out that I really didn't know anythin', and it wasn't worth beatin' me to a bloody pulp as I still wouldn't know any more. So he shoved me in his car and drove back here and dumped me out, like yeh saw."

Maura felt chilled. The stranger sounded like a thug, and she hadn't seen many of those around Leap or in Skibbereen. Was he local? Had he been at Sullivan's? Tim didn't look like he'd been hurt by his attacker, but things could have been much worse. Why had the man let him go?

"Why didn't he just leave you where you were?" Maura jumped in. "I mean, then he could have gotten away without anybody even noticing."

"Maura," Sean cautioned her. Then he turned to Tim. "What she said. Why'd he bring yeh back here?"

"Bugger if I know," Tim admitted. "Maybe he felt sorry for me. I mean, whoever he was, he didn't stand to gain anything by roughing up an eejit like me. And he didn't really hurt me. More like put the fear in me. But I really had no clue what he was talking about, and I still don't."

"He never said what he was lookin' fer?" Sean asked.

Tim shook his head vigorously. "Believe me, if I'd known anything, I woulda told him."

"Let's think this through, then," Sean said. "You left Aidan here, alive, yeh say, sometime past one o'clock. Maura comes in about nine hours later and finds him dead in the back room here. Sometime in between, it looks like someone laid hands on him. We know he had a bad heart, so if he was confronted by the same man who took yeh off, he might have died before his attacker got anythin' from him. So what was he lookin' fer?"

"Aidan's fiddle!" Maura interrupted, which brought a

stern look from Sean. "When he came in on Friday, looking for Niall, he had a case with him. But I don't remember seeing it near him on Sunday."

"We haven't found it," Sean said, almost to himself. He looked at Maura. "We should look more thoroughly in yer back room," he said, standing up.

Maura stood up too. "Let's go." They went over to the bar, where Mick and Rose were dispensing pints.

"What's up?" Mick asked.

"It's possible that Aidan left something here," Sean said. "Yeh didn't happen to find the odd fiddle case or any other lost items when yeh cleared out the back after the music, did yeh?"

"No, but I haven't done a full cleanup in there, since we weren't planning on using the room right away, and your lot wanted us to stay clear of it," Mick said.

"Can you and Rose handle things while we look around?" Maura asked.

"Sure. Jimmy'll be in any minute. I take it yeh don't have anything for me to say to our customers as have seen young Tim here dumped on the doorstep?"

Those customers were obviously all but drooling with curiosity. "Not just yet," Sean said. "Thanks, Mick."

Maura, Sean, and Tim went to the back, where Maura opened the door to the room and turned on the lights. Damn, it was dark in there. There were few windows, and the sun was low. The wattage of the lights were good for a party, bad for a search. But at least the surfaces were clear—and there was no fiddle case in plain sight. She pulled the door shut behind her, to keep out nosy customers. "Any instructions?"

"If yeh find anythin' interestin', try not to touch it, will yeh?" Sean said.

"Got it," she replied. "I'll take this end. Tim, why don't you check out the balcony? Aidan might have planned to sleep up there."

"I'll take the stage and behind," Sean said.

They split up. Maura wished she'd thought to bring a flashlight—it was so dim that she couldn't see into the corners. She hadn't spent much time back here, and she hadn't realized how unappealing it could be. But the event on Saturday had transformed it, making it come alive. She'd have to think about that.

She could hear Tim banging around over her head, though apart from tables and chairs, there were few places to conceal anything up there. All the electronic equipment had been shifted downstairs to the stage area, and that was where Sean was poking around now. At her end, the surface of the bar was bare and relatively clean, so she went around behind. There were a couple of unwashed glasses in the sink, but otherwise Mick had done a good job—she'd give him a B plus for his efforts. Nothing against the wall but a small refrigerator, which wasn't even plugged in at the moment—she checked inside it, just in case. Empty. Shelves along the wall held only what they were supposed to—bottles and glasses— and wouldn't conceal a fiddle case anyway. She turned to face the bar. Sink, a couple of kegs underneath. No luck there.

But there was a low shelf that ran just under the bar for its entire length. She felt along it, and in one corner she felt something bulky and rounded. She pulled her hand out. "Sean, I might have something," she called out.

Sean hurried over. Maura pointed under the bar. "There."

Sean knelt down for a better look. "You have a cloth or something?"

She was confused for a moment before she figured out what he meant. "You're seriously thinking about fingerprints?" Maura stifled a laugh. "What, you don't carry latex gloves at all times?"

Sean looked exasperated and held out a hand. "Cloth, please?"

Maura found a relatively clean bar rag under the sink. At least it was dry. She handed it to him.

Sean covered his hand and reached under the bar. He pulled out what was unmistakably a fiddle case—covered in battered brown leatherette, with a few odd stickers attached. Holding it by its worn handle, Sean set it on top of the bar.

"Is this the one yeh saw?" Sean asked Maura, as Tim came up to join them.

"The stickers look right. No ID on it?" Tim said.

"Not on the outside."

"You going to open it?" Maura demanded.

Without answering, Sean released the latch on the case and laid the cover back. Inside was a fiddle, as battered as its case, a bow—and a roll of euros over an inch thick.

Chapter 20

"I'll take that to the station now," Sean said crisply. He shut the lid with a snap, then looked confused momentarily as he realized he had nowhere to put it, and nothing to carry it in.

"Do you need a bag?" Maura asked. "We've got trash—uh, bin bags, if that helps."

"It would do," Sean said. Maura went through the door between the two bars and retrieved a new bag, ignoring the sudden lull in conversation as half the people in the pub, including Mick, turned to look at her, eager for news. She avoided their looks and returned to the back room, handing the bag to Sean, who slipped the fiddle case gingerly into it, then tied it off.

"So you think that guy was looking for Aidan's dosh but

he couldn't find the fiddle case?" Tim asked. When Maura looked blank, Tim explained, "That money in there."

"That'd be my guess," Sean said.

"I'm surprised the guy didn't find it before, if he was in here with Aidan," Maura said. "But maybe he wasn't looking for an old fiddle. And that shelf isn't easy to see unless you know it's there. How much cash do you think there is?"

"I'm not about to count it out now," Sean said firmly. "I'm goin' to take this back to the station and let our boys there examine it officially. But I'd agree it must've been what the man was looking for. Question is, how did he know Aidan had it?"

"Aidan withdrew his life savings and this guy saw him pocket the cash?" Maura suggested. "He stole it from the guy? Or he was planning to settle a debt, but changed his mind? Who knows. Maybe he just hated banks and liked to carry it with him. Or maybe it's all fivers and really isn't as much as it looks."

"We'll see," Sean said. "Thanks, Maura. Tim, stay around Leap will yeh, just 'til we sort this out?"

Tim nodded. "I will. Maura, yeh won't mind if I hang around here fer a bit, will yeh? It's been a hard day, and I'd feel better bein' around a lot of people, after this mornin'."

No doubt Rose's sympathetic attentions would also help, at least in part. "Sure," said Maura.

Sean added, "I guess you can talk about getting dragged off by that fella. Anyways, everyone in the pub saw you get dumped outside, didn't they? Mebbe someone will have recognized the car or the man. But keep quiet about the money in the case."

"Right so," Tim agreed readily.

Sean turned and marched out of the room and then out the front door of the building, carefully carrying the fiddle case wrapped in plastic.

Maura and Tim went back to the front room. "What was that about?" Mick asked.

"Hang on, Mick—I'll explain in a minute," Maura told him in a low voice. All eyes in the front room had looked up eagerly, hungry for information. Maura sighed again—it was beginning to be a habit. No way were they going to be able to ignore what had just happened, when they had disappeared behind closed doors with a garda, who had emerged carrying an unidentified plastic-wrapped bundle. Besides, maybe somebody had seen or heard something that could be useful. She slid behind the bar, then she turned to the waiting patrons. "All right, if you guys will buy a pint we'll tell you the story."

Rose had sidled as far as she could toward the end of the bar to be closer to Tim, who looked both scared and excited to be the center of attention. If he wanted to talk about looking for his lost father, that was up to him—he could just say he had been interviewing Aidan, for example. Which was true, although Maura wasn't sure how much information he'd managed to gather, or even how hard he'd tried. In fact, she wasn't sure how much he really cared about that project he claimed he was working on. Was finding his father the main reason he'd come here and started the ball rolling?

No, she decided. Maybe that had been part of it, Maura thought, but somehow Tim had tapped into something bigger. She'd seen it: Tim had planted the seed, but Old Billy had somehow sent the word out through his nonelectronic low-tech network, and the results had been amazing. Look at the people who had shown up—they'd included an old rocker who people kept telling Maura had been big news in his heyday. Maybe he was a bit past his prime, but he was still plugged in enough that he'd heard the news and cared enough to show up at the door. And that had drawn Aidan in. And Aidan had brought something with him that wasn't part of the music, and he'd died for it.

Jimmy Sweeney came in about six and sent Rose home. She was reluctant to go, but Tim was telling his story for the fifth or tenth time to a group of men in one corner of the room, and while he raised a hand to wave good-bye to Rose, he made no move to join her. Maybe it was for the best, Maura thought. Better Rose shouldn't pin her hopes on a student from Dublin, which was kind of a long way away, practically speaking.

Jimmy, his attention focused on the row of pints in progress lined up in front of him on the bar, spoke out of the side of his mouth to Maura. "You've stirred the pot, right enough."

"Things kind of took off. Think it's a good thing?"

"The music, yeh mean? Maybe. Or it may all blow away again."

Jimmy was a pessimist, Maura reflected. Of course, he'd seen a lot of people come and go in his time at Sullivan's, so he might know better than she would. "Is there any place in Skibbereen that has this kind of thing?"

Jimmy leaned against the bar to look at her. "Nah, although there's a couple of clubs now, opened in the past year or two. But a different crowd there, younger—not likely to stop in here. The hotel in Rosscarbery books some events, but not in the off-season, and things are a bit more posh there. Bandon, maybe. Cork city, though I don't get up that way much, so I wouldn't know what's on."

Maura checked out the room. Mick and Jimmy had things under control at the bar, so maybe she should go mingle, find out what people were actually talking about. She realized that she hadn't talked to Billy at all—he'd slipped in while they'd all been distracted hunting for Aidan's fiddle, and she'd been busy ever since. He'd probably take himself home before too long, so she should talk to him first—if she could pry him away from his circle of admirers, who seemed to be hanging on every word. She didn't recognize the group, so they weren't from Leap. But they didn't look like tourists either. From Skibbereen, maybe.

"You guys all set?" she asked, approaching the group.

"Ah, Maura, have yeh met these fine lads from the town?" Billy asked, beaming. When Maura shook her head, he proceeded to introduce the circle to Maura, who smiled and nodded and wondered if she'd ever remember even their first names. "Maura's the new owner here at Sullivan's, and a fine job she's makin' of it. Not that she's any Mick Sullivan—she's a lot prettier!"

Billy's joke brought a laugh from the group. Maura smiled back and hoped she wasn't blushing.

Billy seemed to pick up on her reason for coming over, for he said, "Can I have a word with this lovely lady without yeh oafs butting in? Go get yerselves another pint."

To Maura's surprise, the men complied, and they even went to the bar for the suggested pint. Maura dropped into a chair next to Billy's. "How's it going?" she asked.

"They're after tellin' me that this is better than the telly. A mysterious death, a nice young boy roughed up, the gardaí on hand, big-name bands thrown into the mix. What more could they want?"

"I'm glad they're having fun, even if I didn't exactly plan it. I'd be happy if we could get the first part sorted out at least. Do you think the whole music thing worked? I'm sure you've heard plenty about it. Will Aidan's . . . passing"—Maura found she was reluctant to call it anything stronger—"mess things up?"

"Nah," Billy said, waving a dismissive hand. "It'll only add to the mystery of it all. It'll spread the story even more. The gardaí will sort things out, soon enough."

"I hope so."

Billy recognized her intent. "I think I've told yeh, the place—the Sullivan's that was—has been missed. It filled a need, but then it just kinda slipped away. Mick was a great friend, may God rest his soul, but he kinda let things go toward the end."

"Would people take me seriously, if I try to bring it back?" Maura asked. "I mean, I'm an outsider, and a woman, and I'm kinda young, so I don't have the right kind of history. Or was this weekend a onetime thing?"

"It's not you that's bringin' 'em in—not that yeh aren't a part of it, of course—but it's the music. Yer walking a fine line, I'd say. It's not music for the young ones, and they've their own places to go. You want the ones who remember the way it was."

Hard to market nostalgia for something she'd never seen. Maura debated telling Billy about the money they'd found in the fiddle case, but Sean had asked her not to say anything about that. Besides, they were surrounded by people who shouldn't know that bit of information. Then she realized that Billy's earlier entourage had returned and were hovering, respectfully, to reclaim their places in the circle. One of them held two pints and offered one up to Billy. "I'll let you sit down again, boys," she said, getting to her feet. "Great to have you here."

Business held steady until closing time, unusual for a Monday night. Toward the end Tim came over and dropped onto a stool in front of the bar. Maura thought he looked more settled than he had earlier—but who wouldn't be unsettled by being kidnapped and threatened by a stranger in this peaceful area?

"Can I get you anything, Tim?" Maura asked.

"A coffee, please. Everyone in the place has been buying me pints all evening and I think me kidneys are floatin'. I'm glad I don't have to drive anywhere."

"Did you learn anything helpful?"

"About me mystery attacker? Or the long music history at Sullivan's?" He smiled.

"Either one."

"No one seems to have recognized the car, more's the pity. But you'll be glad to know that everyone loved the music, and they're still talking about it. The general opinion is that Aidan's death was a shame, but nothing worse."

Maura presented him with a mug of coffee. "How much longer do you think you'll be around?"

"I don't have to be back in Dublin fer a week or two, and I'd like to talk with more of the others who remember the past—Billy's given me some more names. The man's memory is deadly, isn't it?"

Maura hoped that "deadly" meant something good, because she hadn't heard it before. "He is. He's like an institution here, and he's definitely the keeper of memories. Listen, uh . . ." Maura stopped, unsure how to go about talking to Tim about Rose. She felt kind of responsible for her, since Rose had no mother. "About Rose . . ." She swallowed. "I hope you're not just looking for a little fun. She's kind of young, you know."

Tim smiled into his coffee, then looked up at Maura. "I like Rose, and I know she's been lookin' out fer me, and I'm glad of it. But I wouldn't promise her anything I can't give her, yeh know? And I think she knows that."

"All right," Maura said. "Just be careful—or I'll have to sic Jimmy on you. And I'd bet he fights dirty."

"I hear yeh. Thanks, Maura." Tim drained his coffee and stood up, reasonably steadily. "I think I'll go back across the road now, but I'll be stoppin' by tomorrow. I hear some of the musicians might be planning some kind of memorial to Aidan. He was one of their own, if not lately. I'd like to see that."

That was the first Maura had heard of that, but it seemed like a good idea. She said good night to Tim and watched him make his way across the street, glad to see him look both ways.

And then Sean Murphy's car pulled up.

Chapter 21

Maura checked her watch: just past closing time, not late enough to be a problem. She figured Sean's arrival would probably clear out the last lingering patrons. They looked up as Sean came in, but when he clearly had no announcement for them, they started fumbling in their pockets for their keys.

Sean made straight for the bar. Mick was the first to speak. "Any news?"

Sean shook his head. "None to speak of."

Maura turned to Mick. "You and Jimmy might as well go home—I can handle the cleanup."

Mick looked at her for a moment without speaking, then collected his jacket and made for the door, Jimmy on his heels. The last of the patrons went out the door, leaving her alone with Sean.

"You really haven't learned anything?" Maura asked as she mopped off the top of the bar.

"A bit. The Cork file arrived. The money came to a coupla thousand euros. A lot for a man like Aidan Crowley to be carrying around with him, but hardly a fortune."

"Still no relatives for him?"

"Not a one. Crowley lived at three different addresses in the past ten years, and not a soul at any of them remembers the man. He'd been on the dole a time or two, but not currently."

"Nothing more useful in that file?" Maura asked.

"There were suggestions that Crowley had been involved on the fringes of the drug trade in the city. He had to have had some income. But no arrests, just suspicions."

"Have you talked to Niall about him?"

"I did the other day, but I haven't followed up with the man yet. I've been phoning Cork half the afternoon. I'd run over there meself, but I don't know the neighborhoods, and I wouldn't be welcome there. The Cork gardaí don't want to trouble themselves—seems Aidan Crowley doesn't make the cut for them, and I can't say I'm surprised. We don't know if he'd seen a doctor about his heart anytime recently, but it seems like it was a condition he'd had since he was a child—the coroner said she was surprised he'd lasted this long. They're content to call it a natural death."

"I'm sorry. It must be frustrating for you."

"Have yeh learned anything new here?"

"I don't think so. After you left, Tim was a really popular guy, so maybe he picked up something from someone here."

"I'll talk to him again. Putting this investigation aside, it may be that Tim is better off, knowin' that Crowley's not his da. Lets him hang on to a few dreams about who it might be, I guess. You told me yeh never knew yer own father?"

Maura was surprised by the personal question, although they'd talked about it on their one, interrupted dinner date. "Yeah. He died when I was too young to know him, and I was raised by my gran."

"And yer mother?"

"Took off. Not the maternal type, I guess. Never heard from her again—if Gran did, she didn't tell me. So I guess I can understand Tim wanting to find someone to claim as his own. Although, like you said, maybe he'd rather hold on to a nice fantasy than be stuck with a down-and-out loser for a father." At least her father, who'd died in a construction site accident, had been a decent and hardworking man. "What about you? You don't talk about your family much. You come from around here?"

"I do. Both parents alive and well. Five brothers and sisters, scattered all over—the youngest sister's at uni in Cork. Me da's still running dry stock in his pastures, and me ma worked in a real estate office before that business went bust."

"Dry stock—what's that?" Maura asked.

"Cattle. Steers, not milk cows. At least people are still looking for good Irish beef."

"There are cows down the lane past my house, but I don't know whose they are or even what kind. They're probably milk cows, since they have udders."

Sean smiled, clearly amused. "That would be a good indication."

"So what happens next? About Aidan, I mean," Maura asked.

Sean rubbed his hands over his face. "Wait for the rest of the reports from Cork. Keep talking to anyone else who comes forward. Truth be told, there's not that much more to be done, and not much interest in doin' it."

"Have you been looking for the guy who grabbed Tim?" Maura pressed, although she wasn't even sure why it mattered to her.

Sean shook his head. "Not much to work with there. Twenty people, including yerself, saw Tim get pushed out of a car. He was a bit distracted so he couldn't tell us much about it. What description the others gave of the car comes down to a two-door or four-door sedan that was golden brownish red, unless it was gray. Not new, not old. Do yeh have anything to add?"

Maura shook her head. "No. I only saw it through the window, and I didn't even notice it until Tim fell out onto the street."

"No surprises there, then. There was a man driving it, clear enough, but no one seems to recall if he had hair or glasses or even a nose. We've Tim's description of him, of course, but no one's added to it."

"Think he'll be back?"

Sean shrugged. "Hard to say. If it's the money he's after, he doesn't know we have it, unless you or Tim has spread it around. If it's drug money, he may decide to cut his losses. He's been drawing too much attention to himself. So that's where it rests, then," Sean said. He stood up. "I should let yeh get home—you've had a long day." He hesitated, looking suddenly nervous, and looked around the empty pub. "Uh, there's a show on at the hotel in Rosscarbery week after next, a comic who's been on the telly. I was wondering if yeh'd like to go? I'd need to see to tickets."

Ah. Maura had been wondering if he'd get around to asking her out again. Their first date had been nice enough, but it had been cut short by a police call, and he hadn't tried again, until now. Sure, she was a modern woman and could have asked him, but she'd been on the fence about that. No doubt Sean had a number of local lovelies pursuing him; employed, healthy young men were scarce in Ireland, especially rural Ireland.

Now here he was in front of her, asking her out again. She liked Sean—he was a decent guy. She certainly trusted him. But did she want to go out with him? Maura felt like she was standing on a tightrope: if she said no now, that might end it for good. If she said yes . . . "Sure, I'd love to go. Sounds like fun," Maura said. "Tell me which day and I'll make sure somebody can cover here."

"Brilliant," Sean said, looking relieved.

Maura quickly changed the subject. "Oh, by the way, somebody said that Niall and his crowd might be planning some kind of memorial thing for Aidan, since a lot of them knew him—have you heard about that? Nothing's been set up yet, but it might be like Saturday's thing." Only sadder. Or maybe not: she'd seen wakes in Boston that were anything but sad. "When I know when it's going to be, let me know if I need to ask you guys to keep an eye on things—I have no idea how big this thing might be. Or you might want to come yourself and see who else shows up. Maybe out of uniform?" Oops, that almost sounded like she was inviting him to come, as a guest rather than a garda. *Well, why not?*

"I hear what yer sayin'," Sean said. "I've always fancied goin' undercover. I'll see yeh tomorrow, then. Safe home."

"You too." She watched as he left, then she came out from behind the bar to take one last pass through the back room. Nothing seemed out of place, but this time she walked up the stairs to the balcony and checked the back and side doors to make sure they were locked. She hadn't had the time to ask about getting the locks replaced, but it was probably pointless—a strong man leaning against either door would open it.

She went back down the stairs, turned off the lights, and shut the door to the back room firmly behind her. In the front room she collected the last few glasses and set them behind the bar. She gathered up the last euros from the top of the bar and put them in the cash drawer. A respectable take, although nothing like the past weekend. But if the pub's income held at anything like this level, she wouldn't complain.

And then she took the money out again. The way things were going at the moment, she figured it would be safer with her than in the pub. She closed and locked the drawer, turned off the lights, and went home.

In the morning, Maura counted the cash she'd brought home and filled out a deposit slip, then sat at her kitchen table eating breakfast and dreaming, something she rarely did. When she'd arrived she'd done all the necessary things to set up a bank account for the business in her own name, but she admitted to herself that she was kind of sloppy about balancing the checkbook regularly, and she hadn't even thought about working out the overall income and expenses for the pub until recently, once the first six months had passed. She wondered yet again whether there were any business taxes in Ireland and told herself to find out before she faced a nasty surprise. Soon. Once the tourist season was over for the year. Mostly she'd been operating month to month, giving Mick and Jimmy and Rose their hourly wages in cash, and paying the distributors and the power bill. But she really had no idea what kind of a profit they were making, and she had been kind of afraid to find out. At least there had always been some money in the bank—she hadn't scraped bottom or bounced any checks—but that was as much as she could say. But now? Saturday's music had brought in an amazing crowd, and the income had given her enough to tide the business over for months—more than she'd ever expected or hoped for. Even the past few days had added to the total. When all the dust settled, she'd think hard about trying to keep it going—with the help of some people who knew something about who was who in music these days, because she certainly didn't. Would Mick know? He'd recognized most of the older guys who had showed up, but would he know the new crop? Who else could she ask? Maybe in the dead of winter things would be slow, and she could do some basic research, see if she could get Sullivan's listed in tourist brochures, stuff like that . . . Maura had never planned to run her own business and hadn't exactly prepared for it. Yet maybe it didn't matter: so far the best promotional route she'd seen here was word of mouth, and that she couldn't control anyway beyond doing what everyone said Old Mick had done: offer music and drink and the people would come. Now she'd seen it herself.

She decided to make another quick trip to the bank in Skibbereen and deposit the previous day's take, which was still larger than average. She didn't like having that much money just sitting around. But that would mean no time to stop by and talk with Bridget this morning, not if she had to make a trip into Skibbereen before she opened the pub. Not that it was any great hardship to go there: she really liked the town, and from what she'd seen, it was a busy place, with lots of people on the streets at any time of day—women shopping, school kids coming and going, trucks delivering stuff. At least she finally felt comfortable navigating her car through the one-way streets, and she knew where to park.

After she had taken care of the bank business, Maura stopped on the sidewalk outside and took an informal count of the drinking establishments that she could see from where she stood. There was the big hotel down at the end, of course, which had a bar and a nice restaurant. The Eldon Hotel was smaller and closer to the center; it also had a bar, famous—or infamous?—for sending Michael Collins off to his death. A few more places also served food (still a back-burner idea for Sullivan's, but she couldn't reject it completely yet). It was tempting to think of taking a bit of time to explore her competition, but she had a pub to run. This early in the morning the other pubs in town wouldn't be open anyway. She needed to see them at their busiest times, but of course that was when she was busiest at Sullivan's too. Maybe after their recent busyness died down a bit she could sneak away. On the other hand, if the music thing took off, she wouldn't need to check out her competitors because she'd have as much business as she could handle. She hoped.

Maura was still counting pubs as she drove back: nothing

between Skibbereen and Leap, but in Leap there was not only Sullivan's but also the old inn—Sheahan's—and the new bistro, both of which also served food. She really was going to have to find something to distinguish Sullivan's if she wanted to stay in the game—but without going quite as far as the relatively new Motorcycle Café up the road toward the church.

When she got close to Sullivan's, Maura was surprised to see lights already on inside. Mick opened the front door before she could get her keys out.

"What're you doing here?" she demanded.

"There's been a robbery. The cash drawer's been emptied."

"No, it hasn't—I took the money out last night and took it to the bank this morning. I just got back from Skib."

"Well, that's a relief," Mick said. "But someone still broke in—the side door was forced open."

Without replying, Maura went through to the back room and up the stairs. Yes, the side door was still hanging open, its lock useless. She'd been right about that much, unfortunately. "It's still early—how'd you find out?"

"A mate of mine saw from the street that the door was open and rang my mobile. You locked up last night, right?"

"I did, and I checked all the doors. And took the cash just in case, thank goodness. You know what this means?"

"I'd think whoever was after Aidan's money is still looking for it."

"Exactly." They stared at each other for a moment. Finally Maura said, "The good news is, he doesn't know that the gardaí have it. The bad news is, he's clearly getting more and more desperate, if he's broken in. I need to tell Sean."

"And what will he be able to do?" Mick demanded. "You know they've no men to spare. Do we stand guard at night?"

"Shoot, I don't know, Mick! I thought this part of the country was supposed to be so peaceful. Sean and the gardaí need to know, if only so they can file some kind of report."

"It *is* quiet—that's why my mate noticed the door. People here look out for one another. This man must be from away."

"Well, duh. No one here recognized him when he was skulking around after Aidan or stalking and threatening Tim." She rummaged in her bag for her mobile. "I'm calling Sean."

When Maura reached him and outlined the situation, Sean promised to be there in ten minutes, and he lived up to his promise. He stalked into the pub, looking grim. After he'd greeted Mick he turned to Maura. "What time did yeh leave last night?"

"About ten minutes after you did. And, yes, I checked all the doors. They were locked, so whoever it was had to break in. That's a crime, right? I took the money from the cash drawer home with me last night and put it in the bank this morning."

"It is a crime, Maura," Sean said. "Mick, when did yeh get the call this morning?"

"About nine. Though the break-in could have happened at any time between, while it was dark, couldn't it?"

"Right. So it seems our man is still in search of Aidan's money."

"That's about what we decided. What do we do now, Sean?" Maura asked.

"What would the man do next?" Sean said, almost to himself. "The money wasn't on Aidan. Our man has looked here, twice, with no luck. Or mebbe not—the man might have panicked when Aidan died and left without looking for what he had come for the first time. So he had to come back, right? Aidan had no car to search, since yeh say he took the bus."

"We should warn Niall," Maura said suddenly. "The man may go looking for him next, thinking that Aidan could have stashed the money with him, if he saw them together at all. Which we can't say he didn't."

"Do yeh know where he's stayin'?"

"No. He never said."

"Try the hotel at Glandore," Mick volunteered. "There's lots of big-name folk who pass through there. Hadn't yeh checked before?"

"We've only a small force, and it's only me that's doing the interviews," Sean told him, sounding a bit defensive. "I'll be needin' to talk to Niall."

"You haven't already?" Maura asked, surprised.

Sean looked embarrassed. "There was never the time, what with all the other interviews, and he didn't seem to be goin' anywhere."

Maura wondered if that was the whole story. Had Sean been scared to talk to a former rock star? "Can we open as usual?" she asked. She was getting tired of having to ask that question.

"If yer askin', will we be sending a team of investigators armed with colored powders and brushes and sprays to gather evidence from yer door, the answer to that is no, as yeh well know. Go ahead and open. And before yeh ask again, don't worry about trying to keep this one quiet. Better not to hide it—yeh can tell folk whoever broke in was lookin' fer money, with no luck. The more people on the lookout, the safer yeh'll be. Not that it's likely the man'll be back, if he's already checked this place again and found nothin'."

"Got it. I'll tell Jimmy and Rose too. Do you think Tim is safe?"

"The man let him go once, and there's nothing more to be had from him. But tell Tim to take no chances. If I can find Niall, I'll ask him if he can get in touch with the other players and alert them as well. I wish there were more to be done, Maura."

"It's not your fault, Sean." Was it hers, for listening to young Tim and getting her hopes up for a bit more income for the place? If she hadn't let this music session go forward, none of this would have happened. But how could she have known?

Chapter 22

Tim came in just after noon, cursing. "They've trashed me car!" he protested, looking like an angry little boy.

"What? Who?" Maura asked, startled.

"I don't know who! Probably the man that grabbed me. She's an old banger I borrowed off a friend so I could come down here, but it runs. Me friend is going to have me head. Why'd he have to slash all the seats?"

"Probably looking for . . . something," Maura said cautiously, eyeing the others in the room, who, she knew, were all listening eagerly, even if they didn't look toward Tim.

"Yeah, well, they didn't find the 'something' 'cuz I don't have it." He dropped heavily onto a bar stool. "Bejaysus, I never should have come here. I coulda done plenty of research on the Web and talked to a few of the local fellas in Dublin. If it hadn't been for . . . yeh know, I woulda done just that."

This talking in circles is getting annoying, Maura thought. "Did you talk to anyone about the, uh, something, while you were here yesterday?"

"No. Yer garda friend told me not to, and I didn't."

"Have you talked with the gardaí about your car?"

"What's the point? What could they do? It'll be on me to get it fixed. But I wish this would end."

So did Maura. "Do you happen to know where Niall is?" she asked, changing the subject.

Tim shook his head. "He's still around somewhere, I think, but I haven't seen him since Sunday. Have you tried the hotels?"

"Sean has. Now we're thinking that the person who was looking for that something might decide to look for Niall and his car, in case Niall gave Aidan a lift at any point. He might guess that Aidan thought the something would be safe in Niall's car."

"I hadn't even thought of that, I was that upset. Can we warn him?"

"Only if we can find him. Sean's looking for him. Can I get you something?"

"Is Rose here?" he asked plaintively, no doubt hoping for a more sympathetic ear.

"She'll be in later. Coffee?"

"Sure, fine," Tim said, then lapsed into glum silence.

Poor Tim—nothing was working out the way he'd wanted. She hoped Rose could cheer him up, because she didn't have the time to try. She'd never seen so many people in Sullivan's on a Tuesday.

Sean called her mobile later in the afternoon. "Can yeh talk?" he asked.

Maura took her phone and retreated to the back room, which looked grimy and bleak to her at the moment. "Now I can. Have you got something?"

"I found Niall, at that new hotel in Glandore. Anything new at Sullivan's?"

"It's pretty busy, for a Tuesday, but I haven't heard anything interesting except that Tim says his car was trashed, probably by our mystery man searching for the money."

"Ah. I'll be sure to check that Niall's car is safely parked in the garage at his hotel and no one's been near it."

"So what happens now? Did you talk to Niall?"

"I did, but he couldn't shed any light. Though he did mention that he might stop in at Sullivan's later."

Maura wasn't sure how she felt about that. Having a star, even a faded one, hanging around the bar was certainly good for business, but he seemed to bring trouble. But to be fair, it wasn't his fault, any more than it was hers. "Do you think he knows anything about the break-in?"

"I can't say, but it felt wrong to ask when we know so little."

Or it may be Sean is indeed just a bit starstruck and couldn't bring himself to interrogate Niall Cronin, as she had already guessed.

"Look, I've got to go," Sean said. "I might stop in later meself."

"See you then." Maura hung up and went back to the bar.

Several hours later, a sudden lull in pub conversation made Maura look up to see Niall at the door. He looked tired, and older than he had when she first saw him. Or maybe the bright daylight was unkind to him; put him onstage making music and he looked far younger than she knew him to be.

He nodded to several of the men in the pub, but crossed directly to the bar. "A pint, please."

"Coming up." Maura started a glass. "I'm surprised you're still around. The past few days must've been hard."

He smiled ruefully. "What, yeh think I lead a glamorous life in the big city? Not lately. Now and then someone sets up one of those reunion shows—I hate 'em, but they pay the bills. Or some eager journalist with a Sunday column to fill or, God save us, a blog post to write, rings me up and tells me he's doin' another damn 'where are they now' bit and what'm I up to these days?"

Maura decided she might as well be blunt. "What *are* you up to these days?"

"Mostly keepin' my accountant honest so I get all me royalties. Sounds grand, doesn't it? My last wife left me two years ago. I live in a simple house in a simple village an hour from Dublin, and me car's eight years old."

"No kids?"

"Grown and out on their own."

"No music?"

He cocked his head at Maura, curious. "Do yeh care about the music?"

Maura smiled as she topped off his pint. "To tell the truth, I'm clueless about music. But it seems to me that it was a big part of your life once, and I can't imagine you'd just kind of stop cold turkey." She slid the filled pint across the bar.

He smiled into it. "Yer right. I write a few songs now and then, for other people. But I've no desire to go back to the life. Surely you've seen those sad shows where the old bands are practically using walkers to stand on the stage as they trot out the old audience pleasers? I played with a lot of 'em, and I don't want to be one of them. If yer worried about me, I get by."

"And Aidan? Where did he fit?"

"Are yeh planning to write an article about me? Or Aidan, God rest his soul?"

Maura laughed. "I'm not a writer. And aren't pub owners supposed to be good at keeping their mouth shut and listening? But I've got a personal interest, since I'm the one who found Aidan's body, remember?"

"Sure, and it must've been a sad thing for yeh," Niall said.

"It was," she replied. Maura briefly considered her options. After all, there was some slim possibility that Niall could have been involved in Aidan's death. She didn't really believe that; still, she opted to be discreet. "The postmortem showed that his heart gave out." Which was true. It didn't account for the bruises, but she wasn't going to mention those.

"Which wouldn't surprise anyone who knew Aidan. You know something different?" Niall said. The words hung in the air between them.

"I've still got questions," Maura finally replied.

Niall took a long draw of his pint before answering. "You asked how we met up this last time. Word went out that there was something on at Sullivan's. Talk about a 'blast from the past.'" Niall made air quotes at the corny phrase. "I had no other plans, so I decided to check it out. I stopped in Cork on the way down, and I went to a pub there where the players used to hang out. I hadn't been there for years—I don't spend much time in Cork. I'd forgotten, or maybe I never knew, that Aidan lived somewhere about. But I walked into the pub and there he was, large as life, sittin' on a stool at the bar. So I sat myself down next to him and we got to talkin', catching up, like, and I asked if he'd heard about what was goin' on at Sullivan's, and he said he had. I told him I was goin' that way and offered him a lift. He turned me down—said he had some business to take care of but he'd see me here later. That's all."

"Did you know where he was staying around here?"

"No. I knew there'd be little problem finding a place this time of year, but I'd heard about the new hotel so I rang ahead. I would've shared with Aidan, because from the look of him he hadn't much money, but I never had the chance. He might have planned all along to bed down here for the night—Mick Sullivan was easy about that, back in the heyday. Hell, Mick encouraged it—he always said if he let some of us go out in the state we were in, we'd be dead on the road by mornin'. Of course, the floor wasn't so hard in those days." Niall smiled at the memory.

"Did you have a key from Mick?" Maura asked.

"I did, and so did Aidan—it was a sign that you were one of the insiders, that Mick approved of you. That meant something then."

"You think I should get some air mattresses, if we keep doing this?" Maura asked, only half joking.

"Will you keep on with it?" Niall asked, looking her in the eye.

Was it important to him? she wondered. "I might. A week ago I had no idea that this place was famous for its music. Heck, a year ago I barely knew this village existed, and I never knew Mick Sullivan. But then Tim walked in, talking about the music, and Billy Sheahan confirmed it, and suddenly all these people like you start showing up. Which was great, of course, but it's not like I organized anything. Could I keep it going, or was this a onetime thing that could never happen again?"

"I'm not the one to ask—I've a lousy head for business—but there was always something special about this place. I fer one have missed it, and I know there'd be others." He leaned forward. "Listen," he began in a lower voice.

"Hold that thought," Maura said as she saw Rose come in, followed by her father, Jimmy. She came out from behind the bar and intercepted her, while Jimmy went around behind the bar. "Hey, Rose, Tim's here and he seems kind of depressed. Do you mind trying to cheer him up a bit?"

"Why, Maura, whatever do yeh mean?" Rose dimpled. "Sure and I'd do that without yer askin'. But it looks busy again. I see *he's* here again." She tipped her head toward Niall at the bar. Maura noticed that Niall was no longer alone there—a couple of the other men had approached him and they were now all lost in conversation, and Jimmy was leaning on the bar, listening eagerly.

How had she ended up in the middle of all this? Maura wondered as Rose went off to stow her things and say hello to Tim. Old rock stars, young lovers, dead bodies—nothing in her past had prepared her for any of this. What was next?

Chapter 23

By six that evening Maura was starving, and the crowd showed no signs of shrinking. She wondered wistfully what it would be like if the place was always this full. Tim seemed to have perked up a bit, and now he was back in interview mode as some more of Niall's friends drifted in. Most of the Sullivan's regulars—even the ones who seldom smiled—looked happy to be part of whatever was happening.

"I'm going to run over to the takeaway and get something to eat," Maura told Rose. "Do you mind staying late?"

"Of course not. It's rare that we see this kind of evening."

"Thank you. You want anything?"

"I'll go later, and me da can look after himself. But don't be long—it's mad busy, isn't it?"

"It is." Maura grabbed her jacket and her wallet and

went out the front, turning right toward the takeaway place on the corner. Inside she had to wait a few minutes in line to place her order, and she decided she deserved a break, so she went into the newly built room at the back and snagged a small table, one that gave her a view of the back end of Sullivan's.

That part was kind of a hodgepodge of additions and sheds and even a small stand-alone building up behind, which someone had told her had once housed a butcher's shop. It was a bit hard to imagine, but she'd seen stranger things since she'd arrived. There was a corner at the back, with a low stone wall perpendicular to it, which must have been where Tim said he and Aidan had met. Could someone have seen them together? She looked around her. The new addition where she sat had a great view, but it would've been long closed by that time of night. There was line of sight from the northbound road that ran along the narrow river, but it was hard to imagine anyone looking for people behind a building, especially after dark: it was a tricky curve with a stop sign at the end of it, and drivers had to pay attention. There was nothing up the hill except trees. So who could've seen Tim and Aidan?

Someone who had been following Aidan—that was the only real possibility. He could have been lurking outside Sullivan's, although someone would have noticed a stranger hanging around where he shouldn't have been. As Mick had said earlier, people looked out for each other here. Or the man could have been *in* Sullivan's, blending with the crowd. But wouldn't Aidan have noticed him? Unless Aidan hadn't known him, Maura reminded herself. Maybe he'd been a stranger, who knew Aidan wouldn't recognize him. But at least two hundred people had passed through

Sullivan's over the course of the evening, and there was no way to identify all of them.

Which left her nowhere. How had Aidan come by that much money at all? From all she'd heard, he'd been barely scraping by. Niall would've mentioned something by now if he'd made him a big loan. So why would someone have followed Aidan to Leap? She could think of only one answer: the money wasn't Aidan's. And it might not have belonged to the other man either; he might have been sent to collect it and to bring it back to . . . who? Maybe the guy hadn't known about Aidan's weak heart, and his threat had been enough to bring on the fatal heart attack. Which had left him with a body but without the money he really wanted to find. The unknown man had been desperate enough to break into Sullivan's looking for the money— money that she and Sean had already found—then go after Tim, and then Tim's car, and he would probably go after Niall's as well, except that was protected in an upscale garage in the next town.

Would the man try again? Or would he give up the search and go slinking back to wherever he had come from?

Maura looked down to discover she'd finished her meal while she was thinking. She needed to get back to the pub, where it promised to be another busy night. At least now she had some more questions to ask Sean if he came by later. She gathered up her trash and headed back to Sullivan's. Inside, the noise level had ratcheted up a notch. Niall was still at the bar, holding court for his admirers. He might claim he was out of the game now, but it sure looked to Maura like he was enjoying the attention. She waded through the crowd to join Rose behind the bar, nodding to Niall along the way. "How're you doing, Rose?"

"I'm grand. Isn't this wonderful? Do yeh mind if we open up the back for the overflow? If any more come in, the walls may start bulging out."

Maura thought for a moment. "I think the gardaí have done all they want to do back there," she said. She was pretty sure there was nothing more hidden after being thoroughly searched by more than one person, and the gardaí couldn't object. "Sure, why not? It's a bit cold, but a few bodies should take care of that fast. I never thought we'd need to use that room."

"Yeh do now," Rose said, her eyes on the row of pints lined up in front of her.

Maura filled a few more orders, then asked Rose, "Why are you enjoying it so much, Rose? I mean, you're too young to remember all these old guys. Is it just because it's busier here than usual?"

"Sure and I know their names and the songs, don't I? And Tim's been filling me in on the history. I never knew this place was so famous!"

Maura laughed. "Me either. What's your dad say about it?"

"We haven't talked much, but he seems to be havin' a wonderful time talking with all the musicians."

Maura handed over the pints Rose had poured before asking, "Will Tim be going on with his research?"

"Seems like," Rose replied. "I told him this was something special, that it might never happen again and he'd be an eejit to waste what he's got. Maybe he can find someone to publish it or he could go on the radio with the story."

Tim must have cheered up at that, even if it was only Rose's wishful thinking, Maura thought. It helped having Rose to spur him on.

It was near closing time when Maura saw Sean come in, out of uniform. Rose had gone home a couple of hours earlier, but Maura, Jimmy, and Mick had been kept busy by the shifting crowd. To Maura's surprise, Niall had stayed for most of the evening. As he was packing up to go, he had snagged Maura. "I need to talk with yeh about something. Do yeh have a minute?"

Maura had a pretty good idea what he might want to talk about. "Sure. Do you want to go into the back? It's emptied out now."

"It's not a secret thing, or won't be fer long, but I thought it might be only fair to ask you."

"Okay," Maura said. She led him to the back room, now empty of patrons, shadowy, and dim. "What is it?"

"The boys and me, we were thinkin' of wakin' Aidan, and we'd like to do it here on Saturday, if yer willin'."

She'd guessed right. "I think that's a great idea. What would you need?"

Niall smiled, and Maura caught a flash of what kind of appeal he must have had when he was a star. "This space, fer starters. And a glass to drink his health. I can do the rest. Thank you, Maura Donovan. Fer bringin' this place back and bringin' us all together once again. It's been too long."

Maura didn't know what to say. It seemed wrong to claim that the whole thing had just kind of happened and she'd gone with the flow. "I'm glad I was part of it—it really was special."

He smiled. "It was that. So we're on for Saturday night,

fer the wake? We'll talk before then." And he turned and was gone.

Maura followed him out more slowly, strangely moved by what Niall had said. And by what he wanted to do for Aidan. The front room had cleared out while they had been talking, and Sean was one of the few left. When he saw Maura, he nodded back toward the back room, and Mick was quick to notice. "We'll close up out here, if you two need to talk," Mick said.

"Thanks, Mick. See you tomorrow."

Maura led the way to the back room once again, followed by Sean. Almost by reflex Maura collected the empty glasses scattered around, placing them together on the bar to wash in the morning. Then she joined Sean at a table against the back wall. "What's up?"

"I haven't much to add. Still no family for Aidan, and the coroner's ready to release the body, but there's no one to release it to."

Maura hadn't even considered that. "If you don't find anyone, where does he go?"

"In the normal course of things, he'd be cremated and the ashes held in case someone comes forward. But we're not there yet."

"Sean, there might be a better idea." Maura hesitated, trying to sort out her thoughts. "Maybe you saw Niall leaving just now. He asked if he and his friends could hold a wake for Aidan here on Saturday night. They might be able to scrape up enough to bury him properly."

"It's kind of Niall, and if someone could put it to him that Aidan needs buryin' . . ."

"Someone like me, you mean?" Maura smiled.

Sean smiled back. "Could be," he said. "You two seem to be close these days."

"Yeah, right—me and the rock star! But at least he asked me nicely. Anyway, I was thinking about the guy who broke in here, who I'm guessing is the same guy who attacked Tim and who scared Aidan to death."

"Go on," Sean said.

Maura outlined her thoughts for him about the guy who was looking for Aidan's money.

Sean was following closely. "Yer worried the man won't give up? So what're yeh thinkin'?"

"That the guy is just a thug who reports to someone else, so it's not his decision to make. Look, I grew up in a city that had its share of creepy characters and violence, so I'm not stupid. But I don't know how things work around here. I can't believe I'm saying this, but what can you tell me about gangs and drugs in Cork?"

"How long've yeh got?" Sean parried.

"Just the short form, please. I'm not planning to go into the business," Maura said. When Sean looked bewildered, she added, "Joke!"

"Right so," Sean said. "Why do yeh bring it up at all?"

"I'm wondering if that money of Aidan's was related to drugs somehow. It's the only reason I can think of for why he was carrying so much cash."

Sean stared at her, his expression a mix of surprise and amusement. "Yer sure yeh don't want to join the gardaí? Because I think we're on the same page with this. I won't try to tell yeh there are no gangs nor drug distributors in Ireland, or even in County Cork. There's problems in the cities, like Dublin, of course, and Limerick. But the gangs of Cork city try to keep a low profile so as to keep the gardaí out of the mix. That may be balanced by the fact that so much of the coast in West Cork is poorly patrolled, so smugglers can get away with a lot. A lot passes through the county, if you get my meaning."

"What kind of smuggling?" Maura asked.

"Cannabis and cocaine, is what. A lot of it. We try to stay on top of it, but yeh know how few officers we have."

"Do you think it's a big problem?"

"It's a problem everywhere, but this part of the country is more a conduit than a market. Which is not to say that there aren't users hereabouts. Have yeh seen anyone who yeh'd suspect?"

Maura laughed. "Heck, no. You know how few customers we usually have—before this past week. We know most of the regulars. If somebody was trying to deal, we'd notice."

"That's good to know," Sean said thoughtfully. "Trouble is, there's been a lot of strangers in town for this music thing of yours, and if word went out to the musicians, the dealers could have heard as well, maybe seen an opportunity."

"That sucks," Maura said. She thought of asking Niall if he knew anything about drugs. But she didn't want to insult him, and she didn't want to prompt Sean to ask the same kind of question. "Well, all I can say is that I haven't seen anyone who looks like a shifty drug dealer, this weekend or after, but I haven't seen a lot of Irish ones, so I can't really be sure."

"Would yeh know a Boston one?"

"I might. You had to know who to stay away from back there. Remember, I grew up in Whitey Bulger's backyard."

When Sean looked blankly at her, Maura explained, "Big South Boston crime boss? Had quite a few people killed? Hid in plain sight for years? Oh, never mind. But he was from an Irish family, you know, and so were quite a few of the people he ran with."

They fell silent for a moment, chewing over their own thoughts. It was Sean who stood up first. "You've given me something to think about, Maura. I'll ask around at the station, maybe check with the Cork city gardaí. Be careful, will yeh?"

"I know, I know. Keep my eyes open, don't take any chances. I certainly don't want to see anyone get hurt." *Anyone else,* she corrected herself.

At the door Sean turned. "About that show—does a week Wednesday suit?"

"Oh, right, the comedian. Sure, that'll work. Thanks for asking me, Sean."

"I'll be after gettin' tickets, then. Safe home, Maura."

Maura followed Sean out of the back room and saw Mick leaving with a backward wave. She went around turning off the last lights. Much as she hated to admit it, she was nervous. Drug dealers, here? Maybe in the six months she'd spent in Ireland she'd let her guard down, but in the time she'd been running the pub she'd seen only a handful of drunks and nobody she suspected of taking drugs. Smugglers along the coast made sense, but she hoped the deliveries kept right on going to Cork city or Dublin or even England without stopping in Leap.

She realized that she was happily ignorant of the state of crime in County Cork—and that had been her choice. Back in Southie, she'd grown up with the stories of Whitey

Bulger and his gang. Violence had been a regular part of her life there, and she'd learned how to avoid it, mostly by keeping her head down and trying to stay invisible. Apparently she'd hoped that Ireland was different—cleaner, more innocent, more peaceful. But cities were cities. If Aidan had been involved with something illegal in Cork city, the trouble could well have followed him to her tiny village here. She was going to have to get her head out of the sand and find out what it was.

She was glad to see that someone had fixed the side door, even if it was really only for show. She'd worry about fixing the cash drawer tomorrow. She locked all the doors carefully and headed for home.

Chapter 24

Maura spent another restless night. After growing up in a city, in a neighborhood that boasted its share of shady characters and a few outright criminals, it had taken her a while to get used to living in a small cottage on a hill in West Cork. It was dark at night; it was quiet, except for the occasional complaint from a cow or sheep. She still fought the need to lock the door every time she left, although she had nothing to steal and there were few people around anyway. Plus she had a friend on the police force. But an unfamiliar noise was an unfamiliar noise, whoever or whatever made it, and she admitted to herself that she was sometimes nervous.

Was there drug dealing at Sullivan's? It seemed unlikely—but then, so did an unexplained death. Under its quiet surface, rural Ireland had a lot going on, and it wasn't all good.

Maybe a chat with Bridget would cheer her up. Maura took a quick shower, dressed, and ambled down the lane to Bridget's house. Bridget opened the door quickly when she knocked.

"*Fáilte, a Mhaire!* Come in. I've been wonderin' when yeh'd come and tell me all the news. Help yerself to a cup of tea—it's ready in the pot there."

When she was settled with a cup of tea and a piece of Bridget's brown bread with butter, Maura said, "How much have you heard from Mick?"

"Ah, the boy never tells me anything! Thinks it'll upset me. Like I've never heard bad news in my eighty-some years. There's been talk of nothing else fer days, what with the music and that poor man dyin'. I'm told the gardaí have been keepin' busy around yer place. What does yer young garda think?"

"Sean? He's not exactly mine, you know. Anyway, he's looking into it. Has Mick told you about the other things that have been happening?"

Bridget made tsking noises when Maura talked, and when Maura wrapped up her story, Bridget said, "It's worryin', right enough. Any one of those things could be the work of some unhappy local fella, lookin' fer easy money. But comin' all together? I believe yer right—there's somebody else from outside. Yer bein' careful, aren't yeh?"

"I try, but I realized I'm kind of out of practice. Look, I've always heard that musicians attract . . . problems, so I guess I shouldn't be surprised. And I've seen the inside of enough bars in Boston to know what goes on. I just wasn't prepared for this, not here."

"Yer talkin' about the drugs, are yeh not?"

Even Bridget knew, up here in her country cottage on a lonely hillside? "Yes, I am. What do you know about drugs? Wait, *why* do you know about drugs?"

Bridget smiled, if a bit sadly. "Ah, Maura, I may be old and I may live in the country, but I'm not stupid nor daft. I listen to the radio, and I watch the telly. It's not the world I grew up in—back then drink was the only problem, and a serious one at that for some people. But this other stuff . . . It's no surprise to me that a lot comes in from the sea around here. There's plenty of coastline, much of it beyond the sight of any houses. And too few gardaí—plus I've heard they might be layin' off some and closin' stations because the country can't afford so many. So anyone with a fast boat could make good money haulin' stuff, and no one the wiser. Maybe like you I'd hoped that it hopped right over West Cork and went straight to Dublin. I should know better, at my age."

"Bridget, I think you're amazing to keep up with all this. And you've pretty much nailed the situation, as Sean described it to me. But it hurts that it's landed on my doorstep."

"Is that what yeh think happened with poor Aidan? The drugs, I mean?" Bridget asked.

"I'm starting to think so. I mean, I want to think someone from Cork followed him for . . . something he had. But the person is still around and he's still looking. I don't know which would be worse: him refusing to give up until he gets what he's looking for, and hurting more people along the way, or him giving up and going back to wherever he came from, and the rest of us never knowing what really happened."

"Ah, Maura, yeh've got yerself a fine puzzle, haven't yeh? Is Sean Murphy up to the task, do yeh think?"

"I hope so. I mean, he's smart and he works hard. But I can't say if this whole drug thing is out of his league altogether."

"Is the boy smart enough to ask for help if he needs it?"

"I think so. I don't think he's looking just to make a name for himself. If he needs to call in the big guns, I'd bet he will."

"Do yeh like the lad?"

Maura considered playing dumb, but she knew what Bridget was asking. "I don't know, Bridget. I don't know how I feel about him. Sean's a good guy, like I said. But to tell the truth, sometimes he seems kind of young to me, even though we're close to the same age. Or maybe I mean I feel old around him—I feel like I've seen a lot more than he has, even though that's not his fault. And take Tim Reilly. You haven't met him, but he seems younger than Sean even, although they're only a couple of years apart. But Tim just doesn't act grown up yet. He and Rose hit it off well, but she's wiser than he is sometimes, and she's years younger than him."

"What a muddle it all is," Bridget said, smiling. "Well, there's no rush, now, is there? Such things often work themselves out for the best."

"I hope so!" Maura said. "I'd better be going. The one good thing about all this trouble is that business has been up for days now, and we need the whole staff there. And the crowds may last through the weekend."

"You go to work, dear. You can tell me all about it when yeh have the time. *Ádh mór ort!*"

Maura stopped at the door. "What does that mean?"

"Good luck to yeh!"

Tim was waiting when Maura arrived at Sullivan's, and

he looked less depressed than he had for days. "Hi, Maura," he said. "Sorry to bother yeh so early, but I figured that I'm runnin' out of time to collect what I need for my studies, and I'd better get on it before I lose me chance."

Maura unlocked the front door and led him in. "So you're going to keep going with it?"

"I think so. I mean, I've learned a lot, and I've talked to a load of people, so I've got stuff nobody else does. It'd be a shame to waste it. And even if Aidan didn't turn out to be . . . yeh know . . . a lot of the guys have said they'd stick around or come back to hold a session in his honor, so maybe I can talk to them again. Funny how they remember him after all these years. Could I trouble yeh fer a coffee?"

"No problem." Maura busied herself with the coffee machine, marveling at how resilient Tim was. He'd lost the hope of a father, he'd been involved in a death investigation, he'd been kidnapped, and he'd struck up a relationship of sorts with Rose, all in the space of a few days. Now he was planning to get back to his studies and use all of this. Maura smiled, trying to picture what his adviser would say when he presented his plans. If that was the way things worked—she had little experience with American higher education and none at all with the Irish kind.

"There you go." She slid the coffee across the bar. "What does Rose think about all this?"

"Oh, she's been a big help—she's the one who told me I should go on with it."

"Do you need more information?" Maura asked.

"Well, maybe. I have to sit down and figure out what I've already got. But I'll stick around through Saturday, if that's when the tribute will be—that could be really special. Hey,

I'd almost forgotten—I took pictures on my mobile of the event last Saturday. I thought I'd lost it when that man came at me, but the gardaí found it and gave it back to me. The photos're kinda small, but I can upload them to my laptop and identify who's who. And I can e-mail yeh a set—maybe yeh can print them out and put them up on the walls, with all these others." He waved around at the walls crammed with curling photos, business cards, and notes, some of which dated back years or even decades.

Maura looked blankly at him, having neither a laptop nor a phone that took pictures. Nor any need for either.

Tim must have noticed. "Here, I'll show yeh." He pulled out his mobile phone and punched some buttons, then handed it to Maura. "See, I was takin' pictures from the back of the room, and from the balcony, once the players got rollin'. Even did a few short videos. Hang on, I'll show yeh Aidan on the stage." He took the phone back and scrolled through a few pictures until he found what he was looking for. "There, playing with Niall. He looks like he's having a grand time, doesn't he?"

Maura had to agree. The two men were smiling at each other like the old mates they were. "I'm glad he had that moment, at least." She looked through the next few pictures, which showed the stage from different angles, before handing it back.

"Maybe I could get it blown up, like, for the do on Saturday." He looked at the screen, rotating the phone and scrolling back and forth. And then he went still. "Oh, shite," he whispered.

"What is it?"

Tim turned the phone to face Maura. "That's him, on

221

the left, in the back of the room. That's the guy who grabbed me. He was there!"

Maura leaned in closer to study the man Tim was pointing to. A stocky thirtysomething, his hair buzzed, dressed in nondescript brownish clothes—and staring intently at the stage. "You're sure? He doesn't look familiar to me, but there were a lot of people there that night."

Tim nodded. "Yeah, I'm sure. His face is pretty well burned into me mind. And I was with him in the car for a while, remember?"

"Tim, you need to show this to Sean."

"I can send it to him now," Tim said. "What's the e-mail?"

"Uh . . . I have no idea. By the time I figure that out, he could drive here. I'll call him."

Tim still looked puzzled, but Maura ignored him. She was lucky to find Sean at the station. "Tim's here, and he has something I think you should see, sooner rather than later. Can you stop by?"

"Yes, I can be there quickly." He hung up with no more comment.

Tim finally found his voice. "Doesn't he use e-mail?"

"Probably, but I know I don't." When it looked like Tim was about to lecture her on modern electronic technology, Maura stopped him. "Don't ask. Listen, maybe you should go through the other pictures on your phone and see if you recognize anyone else, or if that guy hangs out with anyone else for a while."

"Yeh think there might be more of 'em?" Tim now looked spooked.

"Probably not—there wasn't enough money for two people to follow up on." Maura was guessing, but her main goal at the moment was to reassure Tim. "Just look at the pictures, will you?"

He retreated to a corner table and stared intently at his phone as he scrolled through the photos. Maura went about the normal process of opening the pub. Mick came in; Jimmy and Rose weren't due for a couple of hours yet.

Sean arrived quickly, as promised. "What've you got?" he asked Maura.

"Talk to Tim." Maura nodded at him, in the corner. "He's got a picture of the guy who kidnapped him."

Sean didn't ask any more but went directly over to speak to Tim. They sat side by side while Tim went through the pictures, talking in low voices that Maura couldn't hear.

"What's that about?" Mick asked, nodding toward them.

"Tim took pictures of the show last Saturday, but then his phone went missing. He got it back, but he's been so distracted by everything else that he didn't really look at them until now. He thinks he's got a picture of the guy who grabbed him."

"Did you recognize the man?" Mick asked.

Maura shook her head. "You know how it was that night—busy and dark. I can recognize most of the local men, but not strangers. Tell me you'd be any more use."

"I doubt it. But I'll take a look." Mick walked over to the table, and Tim handed him the phone. Mick too scrolled through the pictures, but shook his head. He and Sean exchanged a few sentences, and Mick came back to the bar. "Never saw the man. Might be he didn't stay long—came in long enough to check things out then left. He must've figured Aidan wouldn't notice him in the dark, or maybe Aidan didn't know him. Anyway, there was only the one photo of him."

Sean had taken the phone and input some commands, and Maura guessed he was sending copies of the photos to his own phone or his computer at the station. He thanked Tim and came over to the bar. "The man looks a bit familiar to me—I've got to check somethin' back at the station. You'll let me know if you see him hangin' about again?"

"Of course I will. You really think he's still here in Leap?"

Sean shrugged. "Could be. Just be careful, will yeh?"

"Of course I will. Thanks for coming over so quickly, Sean."

"That's me job, Maura. Ta!"

Chapter 25

The pub had been open less than an hour when Sean called Maura on her mobile. "Yer man's a small-time drug dealer from Cork city," he said abruptly when she answered. "He's been in trouble before."

"Around here?" Maura asked. She had trouble imagining Leap as a hotbed of drug activity.

"Nah, he's never strayed from the city before. Which means he likely *was* after Aidan, or rather, after the money he was carrying. We'd like the man—his name is Donal Maguire—to assist the gardaí in our inquiries. As soon as we find him."

Maura recognized the formal phrase. "That means you want to question him, right? But you can't arrest him without some complicated process?" Sean had explained it to her in the past, but she hadn't absorbed all of what he'd said, except that all warrants had to come down from Dublin. Which seemed absurd to her until she reminded herself that Ireland was the size of Maine, so it wasn't like sending a request to the federal government back home—which could take years.

"Right so. Maura, if you see him, call me or anyone here at the station. Don't try to talk with him or hold him there. Just let the gardaí know he's there."

"Of course." She wasn't about to tackle a known drug dealer. "Uh, is he likely to be armed?"

"Less likely than a Boston dealer, I'm sure, but it's still possible. Like I said, be careful. You understand?"

"I do. What about Tim?" The boy was still sitting in the front window, alternating between staring at the tiny screen of his phone and scribbling notes in his notebook. He looked completely absorbed.

"It might be best if he were somewhere else for a bit. This Donal may have already chewed him up and spit him out, but Tim can't be relied on if things get nasty. Be careful," he said yet again before hanging up, leaving Maura in an uncertain mood. She was oddly flattered: Sean was worried about her.

Mick joined her behind the bar. "What's he got?"

Maura took a quick glance around—there were no customers in earshot. "Sean's identified the man who attacked Tim," she said in a voice low enough that only Mick would hear. "His name's Donal Maguire. He's from Cork and he does something with drugs. Sean thinks he probably followed Aidan here."

Mick didn't seem surprised. "Will he be back?"

"Sean or this Donal guy?"

"Donal. He'd still be after the money, wouldn't he?"

"Sean thinks maybe." A surge of lunchtime customers interrupted their conversation, and Maura was kept busy for the next hour or so. Jimmy and Rose came in together, but as soon as Rose saw Tim in the corner she went straight over to him and sat down. Maura didn't go after her—she didn't feel like playing the heavy today, not with a criminal lurking in the neighborhood. In fact, with Tim the only one who could identify him directly, maybe it would be a good idea to get both of them out of the way for the afternoon, or at least until she'd figured out what to do.

Billy Sheahan came in after his lunch and settled himself in his habitual chair. Maura delivered his first pint to him.

"Many thanks, Maura. Have you a moment to sit? You look troubled."

Maura checked the room before sitting down. "I am, I guess. You can probably figure out why."

"I can." Billy nodded. "It's a sad thing. But is that all that's on yer mind?"

"It's all kind of jumbled up. I mean, did Old Mick ever have any trouble here?"

"Trouble? Are yeh thinkin' of fights? Thefts?"

"Either or any."

"For the most part, it's a quiet corner of the country we have here. I'll have you know that West Cork has one of the lowest crime rates in Ireland."

That made Maura feel slightly better—at least her initial impressions and observations hadn't been totally wrong. "That's kind of what Bridget Nolan told me. But Old Mick was a guy, and I'm not."

227

"And the saints be praised for that! Many's the time I've said yer much nicer to look at." He beamed at her.

Maura smiled back. He'd used that line more than once, but it was sweet of him to say it. "Thank you—I think. But what I'm saying is, I can tell when guys are getting heated up, but I can't step in and stop them, not physically. At least, not if they've had too much to drink. I'm just not big enough or strong enough."

"You've Mick and Jimmy to look our fer yeh."

"Well, yeah, kind of. But this is my place, and I hate to have to call for help every time somebody picks a fight with the guy next to him."

Billy studied her critically. "I won't lie to yeh—it's the drink that starts most of the fights around here, mebbe everywhere throughout the country. It's not money or women. Although there's also times when a certain team's playing that people get a bit wound up."

"Somebody's going to have to explain all that sports stuff to me soon, so I'll know when to keep an eye out."

"You'll learn soon enough. It's the football yeh'll have to be watching out fer."

"Which one? I know there's more than one kind, and it's not what the New England Patriots play."

"Ah, see? Yer already on yer way if you know that much. There's the Gaelic football and the association football, or what yer side of the water calls soccer. When all this"—Billy waved his hand at the midsized crowd in the pub—"settles down, yeh can ask me again and I'll tell you more. But that's fer another day. Have I cheered yeh up, then?"

Maura had to smile again at his comment. "Enough, Billy. Thanks. Let me know when you'll be needing another pint."

She returned to her post behind the bar, where Jimmy was cleaning glasses. Rose was still in the corner with Tim, and they were deep in conversation. "What was that about?" Jimmy asked, nodding toward Billy.

"Billy was promising me an explanation of sports in Ireland, when things aren't so busy."

"Ah—you should've come to me. Are yeh a fan of the footie?"

"Not at all, but I figured I should know who's playing in case the patrons get rowdy."

"I'll keep you up-to-date on the schedules, then. Both winning and losing teams make for good business—the lads like to get together to cheer or to complain, and either way they need their pints."

"Got it." Something else to learn.

In midafternoon Maura caught Mick's eye and nodded toward the back room, and he followed her into it. "Is there a problem?" he asked.

"Not an immediate one. I was talking to Billy and I started to ask him about whether Old Mick had any problems with fights or crime here, and somehow he sidetracked me into a discussion about Irish sports."

Mick smiled. "Which probably are far more important to yer average customer than a quick robbery, and which may more often lead to bloodshed."

"Yeah, yeah, I get that. Guys care about sports teams and get pumped up, and then they take it out on each other, and then they buy a round for the house. Jimmy pointed that out. But I'm serious—do I need to be worried? I mean, there's a guy who may be a killer roaming around, and he still thinks we have something he wants so he may come back. And he's not from around here—and Billy insists that this is a really, really peaceful part of the country—but from Cork city, which I'm betting is not exactly a peaceful place. Am I right?"

Mick considered her question seriously. "Maura, are yeh really worried?"

"You mean, am I freaking out? You should know by now that I'm not like that. But I'm not exactly prepared to defend myself if some thug comes in, you know?"

"Give him what he wants and he'll go."

Maura snorted. "Oh, yeah, right—it's that easy?"

"I can't say what it's like in Boston, but around here, we don't attack people for the hell of it. And most of those who do are the fellas with no money and no job and no education and nothing better to do with themselves than make trouble. If one of those punks shows up and asks for money, just give it to him, will you?"

"That sounds nice, but this Donal Maguire wants his big wad of money back, and we don't have it. Then what? Am I supposed to tell him, 'Sorry, but the gardaí took it away. Would you like a note for your bosses explaining that?'"

Mick's mouth twitched. "I'd leave off that last bit, if I were you. Just tell him the gardaí found it and confiscated it in the course of their investigation of Aidan Crowley's death. You don't need to say anything more. Once he knows that, he might clear out."

"So you think I don't have anything to worry about?" Maura said dubiously.

"No. But if it makes yeh feel better, I'll stick around 'til closing. Look, Maura—thanks to Tim and his photo the gardaí know who they're looking fer now. At the very least they'll spread the word to their Cork pals and let them know that this Maguire man is not welcome here. That should cover it."

"If you say so," Maura muttered. A shout from Jimmy in the front reminded her that they had a pub to run. "Thanks, Mick—we'd better get back to work."

Back behind the bar, Maura noted that Rose was now collecting the empty glasses and Tim was nowhere to be seen. After Rose had deposited the glassware at the sink, she turned to Maura. "Sorry I've not been much help lately."

"Could it have something to do with Tim?" Maura asked mildly.

"Could do. Look, I hate to ask, but would you mind if I had supper with him tonight? He won't be around much longer, maybe 'til Sunday."

"I think we can probably handle it, if your dad stays here. Look, Rose . . ." Maura paused to choose her words carefully. "I know Tim's a nice guy and all, but you know he's going back to Dublin, and . . ."

"You don't have to say more, Maura. I won't be trailing after him like a lovesick calf. Only it's nice to spend a bit of time with someone near to me own age, yeh know?"

"I do. And I won't stand in your way. But keep your mobile on, will you? There are still some . . . loose ends here, and I don't want you to get caught up in it. Okay?"

"It is. Thanks fer lookin' out fer me, Maura. Oh, I've already seen to me da's supper, and I've told him where I'm goin', so you needn't worry on that account."

Maura was beginning to think that Rose was altogether

too good for Tim, at least until he grew up. But she'd said her piece and she could go back to worrying about her own problems, real or imagined, with Donal Maguire.

The rest of the day held no surprises.

Until closing.

Chapter 26

It had been a long day, and Maura was tired, not so much from the serving and smiling part but because under it all she was tense. Whatever lay behind Aidan's death, it wasn't over yet, but there seemed to be little she could do about it except jump every time someone came in the door, which was stupid but she couldn't seem to stop herself. Until now she had been comfortable in the shabby old building, and few people had given her any trouble. Then Tim had arrived and brought up the music and he had talked to Old Billy, going back to the days when Mick Sullivan had been in charge of the place and had somehow mysteriously drawn the bands to him in this forsaken corner of Ireland. And that had been all it took to make it happen again, years later: the word went out and the people came.

Yet with the new crowd, they'd somehow brought in

drugs and death. It wasn't supposed to work like that in Ireland, was it? Certainly not in Leap. Had the world changed that much?

Mick had stuck pretty close all afternoon, so much so that Jimmy had commented on it. So Maura had had to explain the situation to him. She was pleased that Jimmy's first reaction was concern for his daughter's safety, but he hadn't been happy with Maura's solution, which was merely to send Tim and Rose elsewhere until Sean told her she didn't have to worry. Now it was getting late and she hadn't heard from Sean yet.

The day had passed in fits and starts. The afternoon had been quiet, followed by a rush after five, then a lull for the dinner hour, then another rush after. No sign of any surly thugs looking for their missing cash. Maybe the man from Cork had decided to cut his losses and go home. After all, there must be bigger money to be made in Cork; was it really worth wasting time chasing around small villages? Or was it the principle of the thing? Maura had grown up with the whispered stories about Whitey Bulger and his associates, how they'd killed people who were "inconvenient" or had said something they didn't like.

Billy seemed to have caught her mood. When she swung by his table to pick up an empty glass, he looked up at her with less than his usual good humor. "Yer not yerself today, Maura," he said, unsmiling. "Is there a problem?"

She glanced quickly around, then dropped into the chair next to him. "I don't know, really. Sean figured out who went after Aidan the other night, but nobody knows where to find him. Or maybe he's already locked up and I'm worrying about nothing."

"You've heard no more from the gardaí, eh? So yer worried the man'll be back to finish up his business?"

"I guess I am. Am I being silly?"

"I'd rather see you worry and take a bit of care than not," Billy said. "But there's been no trouble today, I take it?"

"None. All business as usual, or maybe a bit better than usual, at the moment. I let Rose go with Tim to have dinner in Skibbereen, just in case. I thought they might be safer there."

"Ah, Maura." Billy shook his head. "What's the world come to? Cork may not be so far away by the road, but it used to be it was a different universe. I hate to see it spilling over onto our little village here."

"I'd be sorry too, especially if I had any part in bringing that here."

Billy shrugged. "Yer not in charge of the world, not even this corner of it. It would have come, one way or the other."

That was small comfort to Maura.

None of the musicians, or at least not the ones she was beginning to recognize, had put in an appearance. She had no idea what half of their names were, much less whether they lived near or far. She was more surprised that she hadn't seen anything of Niall. At least he'd had the courtesy to ask if he could use her place to honor Aidan on Saturday. If he'd changed his mind and decided not to go to the trouble, it would only be polite that he tell her that as well. Then again, could be Niall was operating on Irish time, which moved at a different pace than in Boston, and she should just stop worrying about it.

Niall seemed like a nice man. Almost old-fashioned. Not at all what she would have expected from someone who'd been "big," even if it was a while ago. How would Bono act if he stopped in for a quick pint? Would he have an entourage? A bodyguard or two? Or would he just show up, like a normal person?

Finally eleven thirty arrived, time for closing. Billy had gone home long before—he tired easily in the evening, and he'd had a busy few days. Maura shooed out the stragglers, although that involved a conversation with each of them. She hated to be a nag, but she was supposed to be following the local laws, and she didn't want to push the regulations too far, so she could give Sean an honest answer if he asked. She hadn't heard from him all day; was that good or bad?

"Jimmy, you should go see if Rose got home safely," Maura said.

"I've been calling her each half hour, and she's there. That young man went back to Keohanes' a while back, or so she tells me."

"I'm sure she's telling you the truth. But go on home anyway."

"I'll do that. See yeh tomorrow, Maura."

"I'll check the back for yeh, Maura," Mick volunteered. He disappeared into the back room, and now that it was quiet, she could hear his steps on the stairs leading to the balcony, then around it as he made the circuit, checking that the locks were turned. Still the same useless locks, but they had to try, didn't they? He came down and turned off the lights and pulled the doors shut as he left the room. "Oh, and one of the tap lines needs cleanin'. I might as well see to it now."

It was close to midnight. "Can't it wait until morning?"

"Now's fine," Mick said curtly, and went down the stairs

to the dark basement. Maura pushed the cellar door closed—more than once she'd almost taken a tumble down the stairs, since there wasn't much room behind the bar and it was dark. And Jimmy had had that accident on the old stairs, not long after she'd arrived, and broken his arm . . .

She turned the key to lock the front door and made a final sweep of the room, mopping the rings off the tables with a damp cloth, and was returning to the bar with the empty glasses when there was a rapping at the door. "Sorry, we're closed," she called out without looking.

The rapping became a pounding, and Maura stiffened, then turned to see through the glass of the door who it was. She couldn't say she was surprised that it was Donal Maguire: the very man Sean was looking for, the drug dealer from Cork. Or his twin brother. She froze for a moment, wondering how well the darkness inside concealed her expression. The man didn't pound again, just stared at her, waiting.

Now what? Mick was downstairs: did the guy at the door know that? If she waited too much longer, the guy would probably just break the glass and let himself in. Her phone was in her bag, and she couldn't reach it in time to do any good. But he didn't know she knew what she knew, right? She went over to the door and yelled through it, "It's past closing."

"Let me in," the man said, without changing expression.

"We're closed," Maura said again. That was the way a normal person would act, wasn't it?

"I'm not leaving 'til we talk."

Maura considered her options. One: wait him out, hoping he'd go away. That didn't seem to be working. Two: shriek like a banshee, which she hoped would bring Mick running—she knew that there was no one else awake in Leap who would hear her this late, particularly through the thick stone walls of the pub. Mick could handle this guy, couldn't he? She'd never seen him confront anyone physically, because it had never been necessary. The guy at the door wasn't much bigger than Sean, but he looked like he'd fight dirty. Of course, she'd never seen Sean do more than wrestle handcuffs on to someone, so she wasn't sure how he'd fare in a fight either. Three: walk calmly over to her bag, find her phone, and hit 999 to bring the gardaí running. Which would give the man plenty of time to smash his way in and stomp on her phone. Four: paste on a silly smile, open the door, and pretend she knew nothing about anything, like his missing cash—all the while hoping Mick was listening and could put two and two together and get help.

Maybe three seconds had passed, and Maura was still standing like a lump, staring at the man who didn't know she knew who he was. Maybe she really could convince him that she was clueless. She took a breath and strode over to the door, unlocking it and pulling it open.

"Are you in trouble? Hurt? Car problems?" she asked brightly.

He shouldered her aside and walked into the pub. Maura quietly closed the door and turned to face him. "Excuse me? What did you want?" she said, sounding like a feeble-minded idiot to herself.

"Don't play the fool, Maura Donovan. You know what I'm after."

So much for option four. There was no use in stalling. "I don't have it," she said.

"Who does, then?"

"The guards. We found it a couple of days ago."

The man let loose a string of curses, half of which Maura had never heard and didn't want to guess at. He was not a happy camper. She almost felt sorry for the guy, who was clearly out of his element here in the sticks. In her mind Maura turned over several things she could say, but none of them promised a good ending.

She hadn't made a decision when she heard Mick coming up the stairs. He paused at the top to take in the scene; Maura didn't dare turn to look at him.

"We're closed, mister," he said, giving nothing away.

"So the lady said," the man replied. "I guess I'd best be on my way."

Maura felt a wash of relief: was he really giving up that easily? But another part of her was getting mad. What gave him the right to walk in here and kill Aidan, whether or not he meant to? Over money? Was that all Aidan's life was worth? She felt Mick come up behind her and lay a hand on her elbow. Could he tell what she was thinking?

And then they were all distracted by something else. Maura looked past the man through the window to see Old Billy weaving along the sidewalk. He reached the door and found it open, and glee washed over his face as he stepped in. "Ah, yer still open, me darlin'. Could I trouble you fer a pint? I know it's late, but an old man gets thirsty."

Billy knows the closing hours better than I do, Maura thought. What did he think he was doing here? "Sorry, Billy, it's after hours."

Billy staggered his way into the room, bumping into Donal, who shoved him away. Billy kept his balance, then looked at the man with hurt in his eyes. "Ah, surely there's no reason to push around an old man? All I'm after is a pint." He wobbled closer to Donal again.

Donal looked disgusted and seemed to decide that his best option was to leave. He turned to head for the door, still open, but somehow Billy's cane became entangled between his legs and he fell heavily to the floor. The stream of curses began again, and he struggled to get back to his feet. But Billy's cane kept getting in the way, and Maura was beginning to suspect that Billy wasn't anywhere near as drunk as he made out. If he was drunk at all. Her thought was confirmed when Billy glanced at her briefly—and winked.

"Mick Nolan, yeh might give me a hand here, if you don't mind," he said. Mick moved quickly to grab Donal before he could get up again, and then Old Billy sat on his back. "I've already called the gardaí," Billy said.

Mick grinned at him. "So have I."

Donal on the floor issued a few more interesting curses, but he couldn't escape the two men.

"I'm guessin' this is our man from Cork city?" Billy asked Maura.

"So it seems. He should have left while he still could. I can't believe the two of you!" She could hear the distinctive sound of the garda siren coming from the west, and it was no more than two minutes later that not one but two cars pulled up in front of Sullivan's.

Sean came in first. "What's going on?"

"We've captured Donal Maguire for you," Maura said, feeling giddy now that the crisis had passed. "You can have him now."

Sean looked down at the man under Billy. "Mr. Maguire, I'll have to ask you to accompany us to the station in Skibbereen. We have a few questions for you."

"Then get this old fool off me," Donal Maguire spat out from the floor.

Sean suppressed a smile. "Billy, I think we can handle it from here."

Mick held out a hand and helped Billy to his feet, and the garda from the second car, a man Maura didn't recognize, grabbed Donal by the elbow. Donal Maguire seemed to have lost the will to fight and allowed himself to be maneuvered into the waiting car.

Sean said, "Thanks fer the call, Billy. And yours as well, Mick. We were ready to find a crime wave, what with all of you ringing us up. So was it only the one man?"

"Wasn't that enough?" Maura demanded.

"Sure, if it turns out that he's the attacker, which all things point to. Well done, the lot of you. He didn't happen to say anything about Aidan Crowley, now, did he?"

"No, he did not, and we didn't ask him either," Maura retorted. "All we did was catch him—there wasn't much time for conversation. Now you can take over."

"I'll do that." Sean turned to leave, but Maura followed him out the door.

"Why were you at the station so late?" she asked.

He looked down at her. "I thought things might come to a head—if the man was goin' to make a move on the place, it would be tonight. I didn't want you to be, well, unprotected tonight. I hadn't counted on Old Billy's assistance."

"I have no idea what Billy thought he was doing, but he managed to keep Donal Maguire here until you showed up."

"He's a smart man, even if he plays the fool a bit fer the tourists."

"And I'm sure Billy will collect his share of pints with this story! Listen, Sean—thanks for looking out for us. I've been worried all day that something like this was going to happen, and you got here fast."

"I'm glad it all worked out for the best." For a moment he looked like he wanted to say something else, but then he decided against it. "I'd better go start processin' our man from Cork, so I'll talk to you tomorrow, Maura. Take care."

"Thanks, Sean," Maura called out to his retreating back. She wasn't quite sure what she was thanking him for, since Billy and Mick had taken care of the hard stuff. All she'd managed to do was not panic. She had some reason to be proud of that, didn't she? She'd stood her ground, at least. Defended her place.

Her place. And the battle, such as it was, had been won with the help of her friends. Something to think about.

Chapter 27

When Sean had left, Maura took Billy's arm. "Do you want that pint now?" she asked with a smile.

He patted her hand. "Thanks fer the offer, but I'll wait 'til tomorrow. I wouldn't mind it if you'd walk me to my door, though."

"Of course. Are you all right?" Maura hadn't even had time to wonder if he'd been injured in the brawl, such as it was. Surely tangling with a thug like Donal Maguire would have taken a toll on a man far younger than eighty.

"I'm fine, just not as young as I was."

Maura called out to Mick, who was busy righting the tables and chairs that had been knocked down in the scuffle. "I'm taking Billy home. I'll be back." Mick nodded and went on picking up the furniture that had been overturned.

Maura kept her pace slow to match Billy's. The night

was completely still, and there were no cars in sight. It was hard to believe they'd just caught a criminal drug dealer and possible killer, yet nothing had changed outside the pub. "Billy, you didn't just happen to show up tonight, did you? And you weren't drunk."

He slowed his pace even further, to look at her. "You've served me every drop I've had today, so you'd know I wasn't. The truth of it is, I was keeping an eye on the front. I figgered the Cork man would have reached the end of his patience, so tonight would be his night to make a move. He woulda done better to go home last night. I thought the cane might come in handy. And nobody pays much attention to an old man like me, so I had surprise on my side."

Maura had an image of Old Billy, cane at hand, sitting by his front window, waiting up and watching well past his usual bedtime, and she was touched. When they reached his door, Maura said, "Billy, you were wonderful. You caught him completely off guard, and you were even smart enough to call the gardaí first. I can't thank you enough."

He brushed away her compliment. "Ah, a pint or two'll see me right—I'll come by tomorrow and claim my reward. And you woulda been fine with Mick on the lookout too. Plus young Sean sittin' by the phone waiting fer the man to do somethin' daft." He paused before opening the door and looked at her again, and this time his expression was more serious. "Maura Donovan, here we look out for our own. Yer one of our own now. Good night to yeh, then." With that he turned and went into his home, leaving Maura on the doorstep fighting tears.

In all the time she'd waited on tables or served drinks in Boston, she'd never personally had to break up a fight, and she'd never had to stare down a killer (at least no one she'd known to be a killer, although she'd had a few suspicions). Most of the bars where she'd worked had kept a bouncer on hand for things like that—and there could have been any number of killers who had come and gone without making any trouble. But here in Leap, at Sullivan's, she had thought she was on her own. Instead, she had just learned that she had Mick and Sean and even Billy backing her up. She was surprised—and moved. It was hard for her to let other people help; she was so used to managing on her own. But this place was different, as she was constantly being reminded. Was she really one of them now? Not the odd outsider from America, who had dropped in from the sky and taken over the pub from under the noses of Jimmy and Mick?

She walked slowly back to Sullivan's, where she found that Mick had finished erasing all signs of the scuffle. The old clock over the bar read half past midnight, but she suddenly felt too exhausted to move. She dropped onto a bar stool and shut her eyes.

"Yeh look like yeh could use a cuppa." Mick's voice broke through the fog.

She opened her eyes again and managed a small smile. "The Irish solution to everything: a cup of tea."

Mick busied himself with making the tea. "It's hot, it's sweet, and it's got caffeine in it. What more could you want? Better for yeh than a shot of whiskey, fer sure."

"I wasn't going to ask for that—I'm not much of a drinker."

"I've noticed." He slid the mug of tea across the bar toward her, and Maura wrapped her hands around it. "And you runnin' a pub."

"If I'd known that was what I'd be doing, I might have

developed a taste for it. Luckily most people only want their pint." She sipped. Mick was right: hot and sweet seemed to be working. "What just happened here?"

Mick poured himself a glass of whiskey from a bottle on the top shelf and came around the bar to sit on a stool next to her, resting his elbows on the bar, cradling his glass. "I'm thinkin' the proper phrase would be, 'You apprehended a criminal.'"

"Hey, I didn't do much of anything. I just stared at the guy while everybody else did the work."

"You faced him down, did you not? Knowing who he was and what he might have done?"

"I guess. What else could I do? Hide in the loo?"

Mick's mouth twitched, and he took a swallow from his glass. "And leave me to take him on alone?"

Maura waved a dismissive hand at him. "Ah, you could've taken him, easy."

Mick nodded. "I might have done. Point is, you didn't run or hide."

Maura swiveled on her stool to face him. "This is my place. I'm responsible for it, and for the people who work here. Including you. And don't tell me you can take care of yourself, because I know you can, and this isn't about that. I *own* this place; I run it. So I have to be ready to deal with thieves and killers and God knows what else. Do you get that?"

"I do, Maura," he said quietly.

Maura fell silent, drinking her tea, staring at the ranks of bottles on the shelves behind the bar. Most of them were dusty. The people who came to Sullivan's were not fancy drinkers. Most of them could stretch out a single pint for an hour or two, but she felt no need to hurry them along or to force more drinks on them. She wanted Sullivan's to be a place people were happy to come to, and she didn't want them to feel rushed or pressured once they were here. Was that the best thing for her bottom line? Probably not, but she wasn't going to fiddle with the system.

The sugar and caffeine finally kicked in, and getting herself out to her car and driving home didn't seem to be quite the mountain it had a few minutes earlier. She straightened up on the stool, but before she could gather herself to stand up, Mick laid a hand on her arm.

"Maura," he began, then stopped. But didn't remove his hand.

She turned to look at him. "What?"

"Are yeh seein' Sean Murphy?"

That she hadn't expected, not here, not now. "Seeing, as in dating? Going out with? Whatever it's called around here? Is that what you're asking?" Where had this come from?

"Yes." He didn't elaborate, but only watched her, his eyes dark.

Oh. Well. That was complicated, mostly because she didn't know *why* he was asking and she wasn't sure she wanted to explore what that might mean. Or what she wanted to tell him, for that matter. And why had he picked this of all times to get into it?

Maura took a deep breath to steady her nerves. "Sean and I have been out on exactly one date, when he took me to dinner in Skibbereen, though we barely got to eat before he got a call from the station. Which everybody in the village knows. He's asked me to go with him to one other thing, if we ever get all this . . . stuff here sorted out. Why do you want to know?"

Mick shook his head, more to himself than to her, as he turned to stare into what was left of his drink. "I didn't want to put myself in the middle of anything."

Maura was beginning to be glad that she hadn't had anything alcoholic to drink, because even sober she was unprepared for this conversation. Was Mick trying to ask her out? "There is no 'anything,' at least, not yet. But I haven't noticed you putting yourself into anything either. What are you asking?"

Her question hung there in the air between them. As the silence went on, Maura again realized how little she knew about Mick Nolan. He had to be in his midthirties—but no attachments, other than his grannie Bridget, that she knew about. He was always here at the pub when he said he'd be, and he didn't seem to mind covering for Jimmy, who was far less dependable. But she'd never heard him talk about family or friends or much of anything else—which, she realized, was a lot like her. But she was the outsider, the intruder, and she had no ties with the living around here. Why was Mick so closemouthed about *his* life?

He still hadn't answered her question, so she plunged ahead. "Mick, why are you still here? Not tonight, but in general? I know you must have hoped that Old Mick would leave you Sullivan's, and you should be mad at me for snatching it away from you the way I did, even if I didn't mean to. But there must be something else you could be doing that has more of a future for you than this place." She'd stopped herself just in time from saying "this dump."

"So now yer givin' me career counseling?" he asked with a slight smile. "If you want to know, I did wonder how Old Mick had left things, not that we'd ever talked about it. And then you showed up, looking like a half-drowned kitten, and it took a bit to sort out what was what with the ownership."

"And once you knew, you still could have cut and run," Maura said.

He nodded. "I could have done. But it was clear that yeh were in over yer head, and I wanted to see how you took to runnin' the place."

"Do I pass?"

"There've been a few bumps in the road, but yer gettin' the hang of it."

"And you're still here," Maura said bluntly.

"I am."

This is a very lopsided conversation, Maura thought. He'd opened the can of worms but he wasn't going fishing with them. God, what a pathetic metaphor—she must be more tired than she knew. Well, from everything she'd ever heard, Irish men were kind of slow, at least when it came to women. There was probably a long history to that, but that didn't help her at the moment, when she was sitting in a pub past midnight confronted by a thirtysomething man who seemed to be trying to tell her he might be interested in her as something beyond his boss. Did she really want to get into it, here and now? If she shot him down now, would there be another chance? They could always blame whatever came out of it on the stress of the moment—all that life-and-death stuff they'd been dealing with for days. But should she? Did she want to? She didn't know.

She was surprised when Mick suddenly began speaking again. "Sean Murphy is a good man—smart, hardworking, ambitious. He knows the people around here. He likes his work. He's got a strong family behind him."

"True. But?" Maura demanded.

"But . . . he seems a bit young," Mick answered.

And Maura knew exactly what he meant. She'd had the same thought many times. Sean did seem kind of . . . innocent, for all that he was a policeman. Though being a policeman here meant something very different from what it did in Boston. "And you're saying I'm not?"

"Not in the same way. You've seen more of the world, or mebbe I mean the darker side of it. You haven't had an easy life, especially lately, but yer tough."

What few romantic fantasies Maura had entertained in her life, none had included being called "tough." "Well, I've had to be," she said cautiously. Where was he going with this?

Mick seemed to be choosing his next words carefully. "It seems there's no one you've left behind in Boston—no relatives, I know, but no friends either?"

Or lovers? Maura added mentally. "Not really. Looks like I'm a misfit, right? No attachments." Except for Gran, and she was gone. "Mick, I'm tired. It's been a long day, and I have no idea what's going to happen tomorrow. Was there something else you wanted to say?"

He gave her an odd look, and Maura knew she wasn't playing by any rules that he would recognize. Heck, she'd never figured out the him-and-her rules back home either, and the best she could do was to be direct, and try to be honest.

And now she seemed to have scared Mick off, because he said only, "You're right—it's late. I should let you get home. Will you be all right, driving the lanes?"

Right now she wasn't sure whether she was relieved or

disappointed, but she knew this was not the time to decide anything. "I've been managing fine—I know the way."

Maura slid off her stool and stumbled, and Mick was quick to grab her arm to steady her. They stood for some indeterminate period, inches apart, frozen. Maura felt something like panic: did she lean in and let happen what maybe they both wanted, or did she do the sensible thing and run for the hills? In the end it was Mick who stepped back, gently. "I'll lock up, and I'll be in early tomorrow. *Slán abhaile.*"

Safe home indeed. Maura tried to make her exit look like anything but flight.

Chapter 28

Maura wasn't sure how she got home, but it seemed she knew the way without thinking now. Or maybe the car knew the way, and it was probably older than she was and had done the drive plenty of times. Whatever the case, she arrived home and fell into bed without thinking of anything other than sleep. Not Sean, not Mick. That was for another day.

The next morning, Thursday, she overslept, in part because it was raining—not a gentle, misty rain, but rain that was determined to darken the day and soak everything. Maura fought against letting the weather dampen her mood, but in truth she was confused and a bit overwhelmed after the events of the day before. She dragged herself out of bed, pulled on sweats and socks, and wandered downstairs to boil water for tea. Then she sat at her table and stared at nothing, trying to figure out what had happened.

The bare outline was simple enough, at least at the beginning. Donal Maguire, recently identified as a low-level soldier in the drug trade in Cork city, had shown up at the door of Sullivan's at closing. He'd demanded to be let in, and she had no idea what might have happened next if Old Billy hadn't hobbled in and confused and distracted Maguire, and then Billy and Mick had held him down until the gardaí rode up on their white horses—well, police cars—to her rescue and carried Maguire away to the station to do whatever they needed to do to hold him.

She had been warmed to learn that she had Old Billy's official stamp of approval, that he now considered her "one of them"—"them" being the people of Leap, or West Cork, or maybe all of Ireland. She hadn't known she needed it, but she was glad she had it, and she owed him big-time— at least free pints for as long as he wanted them, and a permanent spot by the fire in the pub.

And then she and Mick . . . that was where she got confused. It wasn't that she didn't remember what had happened, but that she didn't understand it.

She sliced some bread for breakfast, to keep her hands busy, but she couldn't stop thinking. Mick had asked, in a roundabout way, if she was interested in Sean, and she had somehow managed not to answer the question. Was she? She liked Sean. He was a good guy—honest, decent, kind, thoughtful, a whole string of positive things. He clearly liked her, since he kept asking her out. He could probably have his pick of neighborhood girls, and he'd be a desirable boyfriend, since he was actually employed, unlike most of the few young men who were still around. So why'd he pick her? She didn't know, and she hadn't asked.

Come on, Maura—can't you at least be honest and get to the point in your own head? Did she "like" like Sean? She wasn't sure. She hadn't been looking for any kind of relationship because there was so much else going on in her life that she had to get sorted out first, and it wouldn't be fair to anyone else to give them only a small part of her.

Uh, Maura—that "honest" part? her inner voice reminded her. All right. First of all, she'd never given her real self to anyone who mattered. Second, she . . . wasn't quite sure that Sean was the right one. She liked him, she trusted him, sure. Still, she didn't want to give him false hope or send him the wrong message. He deserved better. But were there any sparks? None that she'd noticed. Not that that meant there might not be, eventually. But not yet.

And that was where things had rested until yesterday, when Mick had jumped into the middle of it. For a start, he'd put his finger on one thing that had troubled Maura about Sean: Sean seemed young. It wasn't just his age: he seemed kind of unfinished, untested. He was going in the right direction, but was he there yet? When would he be a real grown-up? *What, like you, Maura? You're not exactly a prize in that department.*

And what the hell was Mick trying to signal by indicating that *he* was interested in her? She sure hadn't noticed any sign of that in the six months they'd known each other. Maura sat, her tea cooling, and reviewed her interactions with Mick over the past six months—and came up with nothing. He'd been polite and punctual; he'd always done what he'd been asked; and he had kept the pub running while she was learning the ropes. He hadn't asked for much of anything from her. As she'd said to him, she had started out thinking that he was kind of pissed about not getting at least a part interest in the pub from Old Mick. At least Jimmy had been up front about his resentment, since he'd wanted a share too, although he seemed to be coming around. Mick she'd never been able to read.

He hadn't volunteered much of anything either. She knew very little about him. He was a nice-looking, eligible bachelor; why *hadn't* some woman snapped him up by now? He couldn't be gay, not if he was coming on to her. If "coming on" was the right term—she still wasn't sure about that, because he'd been so vague. Did he have some deep dark secret? A dead wife? A not-dead wife? A divorce or three? No, this was Ireland, and divorce wasn't all that easy. Illegitimate children scattered all over County Cork? A fatal disease? A criminal record? Sean would know that last one, but how could she ask Sean? Or was Mick just a very private— or did she mean secretive?—person who didn't like to share personal details? And who was she to criticize that? Because she was the same way. Except that everybody in Leap knew her life story before she opened her mouth.

God, she was a hot mess.

Or had been when she arrived. Since then, she'd been working on it, and she'd learned to open up a little more; to let people in and to trust that they wouldn't take advantage of her. It was hard. And she'd had an awful lot on her plate, hadn't she? A new country, inheriting then running a pub in an unfamiliar place, trying to make friends. She'd been overwhelmed, and that was only now beginning to fade.

Maura, you're making excuses. All right—she felt more settled in Ireland; the pub was running smoothly and she'd even made some small improvements, and the music this past weekend had been amazing and at the same time had handed her a solution for how to keep the pub in the black; and she had friends. And not one but *two* guys asking her out. She was going to have to take a hard look at herself and figure out what she really wanted. One of them? Neither?

She wished she could talk to Bridget, but wasn't sure she should. She had a nice relationship with the old woman, who'd kind of stepped into the role Maura's grandmother had held. Did she want to jeopardize that? And hadn't it seemed that Bridget kept nudging Maura toward Sean Murphy rather than her own grandson? Was she imagining that? Was Bridget concealing something about Mick? Or was Maura simply being paranoid and reading too much into simple things? How unsettled was she about everything that had gone on during the past week? Just when Maura had thought she was getting a handle on the situation, everything had shifted. Like bringing the music back: it had seemed like a good idea, but it had brought a whole batch of problems along with it. Well, it looked like those problems had been solved—with help from Sean *and* Mick. So maybe the music could go on without anything else going wrong.

Enough, Maura! She slapped both hands on the table and stood up abruptly. She'd get dressed and then she'd go talk to Bridget and tell her about facing down a wanted criminal, and maybe test the waters about the Sean versus Mick problem, and then she'd go to the village and open her pub and see what surprises that might hold for the day.

Ten minutes later she was knocking on Bridget's door.

Bridget opened it promptly. "Come in, come in, before yer soaked through."

"I'll get your floor all wet," Maura said. "It's really coming down out there."

"And the floor's never been wet before?" Bridget asked. "The tea's in the kitchen—take yer coat off and tell me all the news."

"What've you heard already?" Maura asked cautiously, as she shed her coat and helped herself to a mug of Bridget's strong tea.

"That grandson of mine called me this morning and said you'd had a bit of trouble last night but that it was all settled. Does he have any part of that right?"

"More or less." Maura outlined the events of the prior evening, but ended lamely with, "Then Mick and I talked for a bit and I came home."

Bridget gave her a searching look, but said, "Ah, Billy Sheahan—he was a fine lad in his day. I'm sure he's pleased as punch to be able to help you out. Have you heard from Sean Murphy yet today?"

"Shoot, I haven't even looked at my mobile. I suppose I'll have to give my official side of the story sometime today, unless there's enough to hold on to Donal Maguire without it. I mean, they've got breaking and entering, assault, kidnapping, and maybe even whatever they call accidental murder in Ireland to charge him with. But there are bound to be loose ends to tie up." Maura sipped her tea. "Did you hear we're planning on having another do this weekend, a wake to honor Aidan Crowley? Niall Cronin's putting it together. If the gardaí have their killer now, all the more reason to go ahead with it, I guess. And I'm still

257

trying to decide whether it's worth taking on planning music events like we just had."

"Ah, Maura, it'll be easy once you get the hang of things. And wasn't it grand?"

"I think so, or that's what other people have been telling me—I was so busy managing the front of the house that I couldn't spend any time in the back just listening. I only heard bits and pieces of it."

"Did you not draw a good crowd?"

"Yes, we did. I know I made a very nice deposit in the bank this week. But there were problems too, you know."

"Like Aidan Crowley? That wouldn't be happenin' each and every time. But I won't tell yeh what to do, and if it's too much fer yeh now, there'll be time enough later. Like you saw, people remember."

Maura read between the lines and decided that Bridget was in favor of the idea, even though she'd taken no part in the event. "Maybe. Look, Bridget, I know a lot of people around here talk to you. Can you let me know what they thought about that night? No rush—it's not like I have to decide anything right now. Anyway, I'll see how the wake on Saturday goes."

"Sure and Mick will help you out with it all."

Well, there was her opening. Maura took a deep breath. "About Mick . . ." And then she stalled, not sure what she wanted to say. "Bridget, I don't really know what I'm asking, or if you're the person I should be talking to, but . . ." Another fumble for words. "I got the idea last night that maybe Mick wanted . . . wanted to ask me out." *Lame, Maura, lame.*

"I've been wonderin' when that would rear its head,"

Bridget said, more to herself than to Maura. Then Bridget's eyes sharpened. "And would that be a problem fer yeh?"

"Can I be honest with you?" Maura asked. When Bridget nodded, she plunged on. "I really don't know. I haven't thought about it, but maybe I have to—think, that is, and either say yes or put a stop to it now." A stop to what? Nothing had started. "Bridget, Mick is pretty much a mystery to me. I've been working alongside him for six months now, and what I know about him would fill a postcard. Is there something he's not telling me? Something I need to know?"

Bridget looked down at her hands in her lap, with a half smile on her face. "I learned long ago not to put myself in the middle of these things—there's seldom any good comes of it. And if there's any tellin' to be done, it should come from him, not me." Bridget looked up at Maura then. "He won't press you, if you say no. But know this: he's a good man. Decent, honest, fair-minded. Mind you, he's also a closemouthed devil and you seldom know what he's thinkin'. Is that what you want to hear?"

Maura shook her head. "I don't know what I want. I need Mick to help run Sullivan's—if we started seeing each other and it didn't work out, that would make things harder all around."

"Here yeh go endin' what hasn't even begun," Bridget said, smiling. "I won't tell yeh what to do, and if you do nothin' at all, I won't hold it against you. I'm old enough to know not to meddle in the lives of others. Yer a friend now, Maura, and that won't change, whatever happens with Mick."

"Thank you, Bridget. That helps." She still didn't know anything more about Mick, but she figured that Bridget had more or less let her know that there was nothing awful lurking under his surface—although there might be some-thing she *should* know, but she wasn't going to get it from Bridget. And that Bridget would let her work it out for her-self and stand by her either way. That was good. "I should be going now—I'm sure there's going to be follow-up to the capture of Donal Maguire yesterday, and planning for Aidan's wake, and I'd better be there."

"Not to worry. I'm sure half the townlands will be stop-ping by to tell me all about it today."

"I'll come by later, to give you the real story," Maura said. She took her mug to the sink and rinsed it, and on her way to the door she leaned over and kissed Bridget on the cheek. "Thank you."

"Ah, go on wit' yeh. Get yerself into the village—there's work to be done." Despite her words, Bridget seemed pleased.

"I will. 'Bye, Bridget."

Chapter 29

The rain didn't let up as Maura drove cautiously toward Leap. She knew she wasn't likely to meet any other cars, but the heavy downpour had nowhere to go but down the lanes, which in some cases were hardly paved, meaning she had to fight unexpected streams and mud. Besides, she wasn't in a hurry, and the ride gave her time to sort out her thoughts. As she kept her eye on the road, she reviewed her to-do list for the day. Had it really been only a week since Tim had arrived, all starry-eyed about the rich music history at Sullivan's, which she had known nothing about? Somehow he had started something that had produced that amazing gathering of musicians by last Saturday. And then Aidan Crowley had died.

She parked her car but didn't get out right away. *Nervous, Maura?* Mick had said he'd be in early. Jimmy and Rose would be in around noon. She could check in on Old Billy, but she didn't want to disturb him after the late night he'd had. She could go looking for Tim at the Keohane house, but he would probably come looking for Rose anyway. After the week he'd had, she wouldn't blame him if he'd scurried back to Dublin. Now she had no idea what was going to happen. Tim had had his own agenda for coming here, and he'd been disappointed, at least by Aidan. Would he try again, or would he give up his hunt for his father? What was really keeping him in Leap? Was it Sean asking him to stay until the crime side of things was settled? Was it Rose's sympathetic eyes? Or was he actually interested in the music, and he still entertained hopes of seeing another gathering of the bands at the Saturday wake?

But if that was going to happen, she wasn't ready for it—she still hadn't sorted through what she had learned the last time around. Of course, if Niall wanted to do it, as a tribute to Aidan, she was sure Mick would help him out with the details. She could veto the whole thing—but why would she? Actually, as she'd said to Bridget, she hadn't seen or heard much of the previous weekend's music, and she thought she should take a hard look—or did she mean listen?—before she made any decisions about bringing it back on a more regular basis. And this second event might solidify the success of the first one.

Well, Maura believed in facing things head-on. Sitting here was stupid. She climbed out of the car and headed for the front door of Sullivan's. It was unlocked, and she could see Mick moving around inside. Taking a deep breath, she walked in.

"Hello," she said. And stopped: she couldn't think of anything else to say.

"Good mornin'," Mick replied, curiously formal. He glanced at her and then went back to sweeping the floor.

No help there. "Any damage we didn't notice last night?"

"Nothin' that matters—these tables and chairs are as old as the hills, and a few more dents won't matter."

"I stopped by to see your grandmother this morning."

"Did you now?" Mick replied, his eyes on the broom.

"She said you told her only that there was a bit of a fuss here last night but nothing important. Is that right?"

"I didn't want her to worry."

Maura almost laughed. "Mick, you know every friend she's got is going to be calling her or stopping by today. You can't exactly hide it from her."

He leaned on the broom and looked at her then. "Do I take it you told her the whole story?"

"I did, right down to the drug dealer. I don't think Bridget is stupid, any more than Old Billy is. By the way, have you seen anything of him yet today?"

"No, but it's early yet. He'll be fine."

"Mick, he's the same age as your gran," Maura protested. "Her you protect, but Old Billy can take care of himself? Jeez, he assaulted a drug dealer last night!"

"He did," Mick agreed. He pushed the broom around the floor some more before saying, "Maura, what's this about?" Again without looking at her. "Yer a bit sharp this morning."

She didn't know how to answer that, because it was about at least four different things, all jumbled together—starting with the fact that she was now nervous to be around

Mick. She was saved by the arrival of Jimmy and Rose, much earlier than expected.

"What's this I hear about a brawl last night?" Jimmy demanded immediately.

How did the word spread so quickly? "Good morning, Jimmy," Maura said. "Only a small one, and Old Billy took care of it for us." That stopped Jimmy in his tracks, but Maura didn't expand on what she'd said. Instead she turned to Rose. "So how was your dinner with Tim?"

"Lovely, thanks so much. He said to tell yeh he'll be stopping in later today. I'm guessing that he and Niall are hatching a plot between them."

So Niall still had his eye on a farewell do for his late friend. It would be nice if somebody kept her up-to-date on their plans, since it was her pub. "So Niall will be along too?"

"Looks like. Mick, do you need help with the sorting out of the place?" Rose asked.

This was *her* place, Maura thought indignantly, and she was the one who was supposed to be giving the orders, not Mick. "Could you check in the back, Rose, make sure it's cleaned up?" Maura asked, instead of acting like a spoiled brat.

"I will," Rose said and disappeared in the back room.

Mick was still sweeping, with a great show of energy, and Jimmy was watching them both. He seemed to sense there was something off. "So the boys in the bands will be back?"

"Maybe," Maura said. "I haven't heard anything final from Niall, since we first talked about it."

"Speak of the very devil!" Jimmy exclaimed, and Maura turned to see Niall standing in the doorway, looking sheepish.

"Am I welcome?" he asked.

"Of course," Maura said. "Come in and dry off by the—oh, Jimmy, could you make up the fire? Niall, can I get you something?"

"Coffee would be grand," he said, settling on a bar stool as Jimmy bustled around with kindling, logs, and lumps of turf. Mick took the opportunity to disappear toward the back of the building, and a few moments later Maura could hear the clanging of barrels.

Maura fixed Niall a cup of coffee, passed it to him, and then waited for him to speak. He'd come to her; let him figure out what he wanted to say. She wasn't going to make it easy for him, even if he was a superstar, or a former one.

Finally he said, "Maura, I owe you an apology, for bringing all this down on you."

"All what?" she asked cautiously. *The musicians? The drugs? The death?*

"When I heard that Sullivan's might be startin' up again, I wanted to be a part of it, because I remembered the way it was. I didn't stop to think what that meant, but the word spread and you saw what happened."

"Yes, and I'm still trying to process it. But you don't have to apologize for that—Old Billy was the one who started things rolling."

"He knew who to talk to, and the rest took care of itself, true. But I haven't been exactly honest about Aidan."

Ah. "What do you mean?"

Niall stared into the depths of his coffee, as if there were an answer there. Maura noticed Jimmy was moving very slowly and quietly to build his fire, hoping not to be noticed and shooed away. She could almost feel his ears stretching in their direction.

"It was true that I ran into Aidan in a pub in Cork," Niall began, "but it wasn't by chance. I went looking fer him."

"You'd kept in touch?" Maura prompted.

"Barely. We started out together—you'll know that. He had some talent, and he played with a lot of people, although he never took the lead. He was never a happy man, and you'd have to say he took the easy way out."

"Drugs?"

"Not so much the using of them—his heart wouldn't stand that—but being on the edges of the drug trade made him feel important. He's related somehow to one of the families who run the business in the city, which got him in the door. He was a bit of an odd-jobber—he'd run errands, make pickups and deliveries for the boys, that kind of thing. It gave him enough cash to get by, and at least he felt he was part of something."

"You knew this all along?" Maura asked. "Why didn't you tell the gardaí?"

"I didn't know at first if that had anything to do with his death, and even if it did, I didn't want that to be the one thing that anyone remembered about him, that he was killed over the drugs. He was a brilliant fiddle player, and his last night was a happy one, with the music."

Jimmy gave up all pretense of keeping busy and came over to lean on the bar. "So what part of yer story isn't true, then?"

"I found Aidan at that pub and told him what was going on at Sullivan's, and I persuaded him to come along— offered him a ride and a place to stay, though he took me up on neither. It wasn't easy to convince him, but in the end I won him over, and he came."

"And he never happened to mention that he was carrying money for the drug gang?"

"On my mother's grave, he did not! I thought he was embarrassed by the idea of facing his old friends and that was why he said no at first. But he had his fiddle case with him, at the pub. I thought—I hoped—that meant he still kept his hand in. So I twisted his arm and made him promise to come along. And that's what got him killed and brought the trouble down on yer head. For that I am truly sorry."

He sounded as though he meant it, Maura thought. "It's not your fault. You couldn't have known. But you need to tell the gardaí this."

"I will."

Rose emerged from the back and did a double take on seeing Niall at the bar. Then she squared her shoulders and marched over to where they were gathered. "Pardon the interruption, but there's something I must say to this man."

Jimmy was about to stop her, but to his credit Niall took her seriously. "And what would that be?"

Rose looked around the group briefly before addressing Niall. "We all know why Tim came here, so I'm spillin' no secrets. He wanted to find his da, and he thought Aidan might be that. So he asked him, and Aidan told him no. Was he lyin', do yeh think?"

Niall shook his head. "It's hard to answer that. You'd have to know how things were back then, and yer too young to recall them. It was a wild scene, no mistake, with some of us on the way up, and some of us scrabbling to hang on at all. We slept where we could, when we could. And we didn't always sleep alone. Did Aidan cross paths with Tim's mother? Might be. Would he remember? Most likely not. And there's nothin' to be done about that now. Even if some kind soul wanted to test everyone's DNA and offer some proof, Aidan's gone now, and he never would have been the father Tim wanted."

"I think he'd still like to know for sure," Rose said stubbornly. "Is there anyone else who might know somethin'?"

"Rose, you've done more than enough," Jimmy interrupted. "It's not yer problem."

She turned quickly to face him. "Da, I'm tryin' to help a friend. And before you ask, that's all he is, and no more. I know he'll be leavin' soon. But right now he's hurtin', and he feels like he started somethin' here and it got out of hand and he's very sorry. So, Niall Cronin, is there anything yeh can tell me that might help Tim find what he's after?"

Niall smiled ruefully. "If this was a show on the telly, I'd stand up and declare that I am that very man, and we'd have a grand reunion. But I can't do that. If ever I met his mother, I have no memory of it either. I admire what yer tryin' to do, young lady, but Tim would be better off if he stopped worryin' about the past and got on with his life."

Rose nodded, once. "Thank you fer listenin' to me, then. Would you tell the same to Tim?"

"I will, when I see him today. He's got a good friend in yeh." Niall turned back to Maura. "Now, Maura Donovan, can we talk about wakin' Aidan Crowley?"

"What did you have in mind?" Maura said cautiously.

"Giving the man a good send-off, with his friends in attendance. Put out the word, like the last time," Niall said with a grin. "I know, yeh still don't see how it works, but you've seen that it does. Trust me—and I'll see to it that things don't get out of hand."

Maura had her doubts about his ability to do that, especially if he was lost in playing his own music, but could lightning strike twice? No one else could possibly die this weekend, could they? "Then let's do it. Mick can see to the music and the back room, and I'll cover the front again, with Jimmy. Let me know if there's anything special you want."

"Ah, that's grand!" Niall told her. "Old Mick would be proud of yeh." He lowered his voice. "One other thing— seein' as Aidan has no family, and even if we found any they're probably worse off than he was, I'll see to buryin' him. If anybody asks."

Just as she'd hoped, and she'd let Sean know. Maura decided that Niall Cronin really was a good man.

Mick had returned from the back in time to hear the latter part of Niall's conversation with Maura. "Niall, if this is going to happen I need to talk to you about some of the amps . . ." he interrupted, and they went off toward the back, deep in a conversation about amplifiers that could have been Greek for all Maura could tell. She sighed.

"Do you not want to be doin' this again, Maura?" Rose asked softly.

"I really don't know," Maura said slowly. "I think it's very nice that Niall wants to honor his friend—but after last time, I have to worry, don't I?" When she heard that come out of her mouth, Maura laughed out loud. "Don't answer that!"

Chapter 30

Maura opened the pub before Mick and Niall finished in the back; there were already customers waiting in the rain outside the door. She spent the first hour or so reporting on the excitement of the night before, as some people left and more replaced them. She tried to stick to the facts, knowing that the story would grow through many retellings, and who knew how much it would be changed along the way? She feared that by the fifth version they'd have her facing down an entire gang from Cork armed with machine guns. At least that version might bring more people into Sullivan's, if only out of curiosity.

It was close to one when she realized with a pang of guilt that she hadn't seen Billy yet. She turned to Rose. "Can you cover for a bit? I'm going to check on Billy."

"No problem—you go on, then," Rose said, already smiling at the next customer.

Maura grabbed her raincoat, slung it on, and dashed up the sidewalk to Billy's rooms at the other end of the building, mentally kicking herself for not checking in on him earlier. She knocked on his door and for a long moment heard no sound from inside. She found she was holding her breath, picturing the worst, until finally she could hear movement inside, a slow shuffling of feet, and Billy pulled open the door.

"Good mornin', Maura! What brings yeh all this way on this wet day?"

"I was worried about you, after last night. Can I come in?"

Billy stepped back and opened the door wider. "Please. Don't mind the mess—me servant hasn't been by today."

Maura realized that she'd never been inside Billy's rooms. She owned the building now, but she'd inherited Billy along with it and hadn't wanted to invade his privacy. He'd had some rent-free handshake agreement with Old Mick, and she hadn't had any reason to change that. She wasn't about to start demanding rent from him now. In fact, she had no idea how he got by financially—maybe there was a pension or something. But she didn't think she could or should ask. She stepped in and pulled off her coat and, finding there was a peg waiting for it by the door, hung it up.

"Can I fix yeh a pot of tea?" Billy offered.

She didn't need any tea, but she didn't want to offend Billy by turning him down; this was the first time he'd ever had a chance to offer her his hospitality. "Sure, fine. Need any help?"

"Nah, I know me way around. Please, have a seat."

Maura sat down in a sprung armchair and watched as he made his slow way to the other end of the room, where she saw a small sink and a stove that was as old as the one at her cottage. There was a steaming kettle sitting on the back of it, so all Billy had to do was fill the metal teapot with water and add some teabags.

"Sorry, there's not milk, but there's sugar," he said, and he rummaged about and found a pair of mismatched mugs.

"That's fine." Maura waited while he assembled the tea things, making more slow trips back and forth across the room. When he was done, he dropped heavily onto a sagging couch that might once have been blue but was now a greasy gray.

Billy looked very pleased with himself. "I can't recall the last time I entertained a lady here. Oh, I forgot the biscuits. If I have any."

"Please don't get up, Billy! I don't need any biscuits. I only came by to make sure you were all right after last night. And to thank you for what you did."

"Ah, go on wit' yeh! You and Mick would have handled it fine if I hadn't stuck my nose in."

"Maybe. But it was very brave of you to try to help. You could have been hurt."

"Thanks fer worryin', but I'm tougher than I look. Have you had any word from the gardaí?"

"About what they're going to do with Donal Maguire? No, not yet. I don't know how this arrest business works, or if they have enough evidence to charge him with Aidan's death. It may be that he was only trying to scare Aidan and Aidan's heart gave out, so I don't know if that means it's just assault or what. Or if we'll have to give evidence of anything," she ended dubiously.

"The gardaí'll sort it out. How's yer tea?"

"It's fine." *If you like drinking furniture polish.* It was incredibly strong stuff. Maybe that was what had kept Billy going to past eighty. "Niall's back, and he wants to hold a wake for Aidan Saturday. Is that a good idea?"

"And why wouldn't it be?" Billy replied. "The man played here at the prime of his life, and he played his last session here. I've no doubt the others will want to come as well."

"The musicians, you mean?"

"The same. They'll want to honor their own and say their farewells to him. Even if they hadn't seen him in years. Do yeh not want to do it?"

"I'm happy to do it. I'm just still trying to understand it, how people know when and where to come."

"Why don't you call it magic and leave it there?"

"Might as well." Maura drained her cup and managed not to make a face. "Will you be down later? You sure you're all right? Nothing broken?"

"A few bruises, no more. Now, me cane may never be the same. But I'll want to hear the craic, and I'll wager there'll be plenty of it today."

Maura stood up. "It's already busy, so I'd better get back. I'll see you later. And thanks again, Billy. I mean it." She slid into her coat, pulled up the hood, and went out the door. The rain hadn't slowed.

When she dashed through the door to Sullivan's, she found Sean sitting at the bar talking with Mick. His face lit up when he saw her.

"Maura, I've been tellin' Mick here what's to be done with yer intruder Maguire."

"Did you arrest him?" Maura asked, shaking off her coat and hanging it up.

"You might remember my telling you that there's nothin' so simple as that. We can't arrest the man without a warrant, and we must petition Dublin to obtain such a warrant. It'll take a bit to sort out. But no worries—he won't get off," Sean said. "And we've sent the money that we found to the Cork lab for testing, to see if there's drug residue. If there is, likely the Cork gardaí will be looking into it, along with taking a hard look at Maguire."

"I guess so. That means there's nothing we need to do?" Maura asked. "I mean, given all the charges you collected, do you need anything more from me?"

"I think not. The man won't be troublin' you anymore, and I wanted to let you know meself, is all. Oh, Mick here is after tellin' me that you'll be wakin' Aidan Crowley here come Saturday."

"That's what Niall wants to do. Do we need to give the gardaí official notice or anything?"

"I'll pass the word around, but you should be fine with it. I'll come by if I have the time off."

"As a garda or as a music lover?" Maura smiled at him.

"Just fer meself, if I can. I've been a fan of Niall's since I was in school."

"So we'll see you then."

For a moment Maura wondered if Sean wanted to say something more, and she felt a spurt of panic. She wasn't ready to say anything of a personal nature to Sean, at least not before she'd had time to talk with Mick, and certainly not in front of Mick and a crowd of local men. She was relieved when Sean decided not to add anything, and he merely raised a hand to her as he dashed out through the rain to his car. She waved back as he pulled away.

Then she turned to Mick. "Billy's fine, and he'll be along later. Did you and Niall get things worked out? Where is he, by the way?"

"He's gone off with Tim. They'll be back."

"Is that a good thing?"

"I think so," Mick said. "I have to say, I admire the man—not the public one in all those posters on young girls' walls, but the one we've seen here. I think he'd like to help Tim, even if he's not his father."

"That's nice of him. It's good to meet a real musician who's also a decent human being. By the way, Billy thinks the wake is a good idea too. So now we can expect a crowd of people to mysteriously show up on Saturday?"

"More or less. Listen, I need to show you something in back."

Maura took a quick look around, but Jimmy and Rose seemed to have serving the crowd well in hand. She followed Mick to the back room. "What is it?"

"It's not about the room here, although I think there are some rotten boards on the stage that I ought to see to before someone falls through. It's more that I, uh, thought we left some business unfinished last night."

Maura could not believe that Mick had voluntarily brought this up. Had Bridget put him up to it? Maura still wasn't sure what she wanted to say.

"I'm not sure we even started any business, Mick." *No, that isn't really true.* Maura hesitated, gathering her courage, before speaking again. "Look, you should have figured out by now that I'm not a girly girl. I don't know how to play those kinds of games. I've always found it a lot easier just to be honest, even though I know that puts some people off. Probably a *lot* of people, since I don't have many friends. So if I've got it right, you're asking if I'm involved with anybody who might be more than a friend, and the answer is no. Not even Sean. I mean, I like Sean, and he seems to like me. But we've had one-half of one date, and that's as far as it's gone. So you're saying that you, uh . . . ?" She *really* wasn't comfortable with conversations like this—which was why she tried to avoid them. She couldn't even come up with a good term for . . . whatever.

But Mick seemed to understand. "Mebbe," he replied, then he flashed a smile.

Maura couldn't hold back her sarcasm. "Well, thanks a lot—that clears things up just fine. If this was some other century, you'd be asking my father for permission to court me, but there's only me to ask. Am I right?"

"Kinda," he said, still smiling.

Maura stared at him for a long moment, then burst out laughing. "Damn, I wish Ireland came with an instruction manual. Half the time I have no idea what people are saying, and I'm not talking about the accent. Okay, sure, I'll take your application under consideration. Will that do?"

"Fer now. We'd best get back," Mick said.

"Everything shipshape in here for this wake thing?"

"It is. We need to talk about orderin' more supplies."

"We can do that out front." When Maura walked into the front room, both Rose and Jimmy followed her with their eyes. Maura slid behind the bar, and Rose leaned toward her. "Everythin' all right?" she asked in a low voice.

"Fine. Honestly. Wait—do I look like things aren't all right?"

Rose shook her head. "No more than usual."

Great. Maybe she should spend more time in front of a mirror: did she always look ready to bite someone's head off?

A couple of hours later, Niall and Tim came in, looking very pleased with themselves and talking a mile a minute. Tim looked much more cheerful than he had the last time she'd seen him. He came over and dropped onto an empty bar stool. "Hey, Rose, wait 'til yeh hear what we've been plannin'!"

Niall was lucky to find a second stool, a few over. He greeted Maura. "All plans subject to yer approval, of course."

Maura smiled. "Don't worry—everybody's looking forward to this Saturday, now that the rest of it's been cleared up. You talked to the gardaí?"

"I did. We're all square. And I think I cheered up young Tim. He's a bright lad, and he has a real feelin' for the music. I'd be proud to be his father, but we've worked it out that I was in England at the time in question." He leaned farther over the bar and lowered his voice. "But I'll talk to me brother—he's out of the music business now, but we were tight back then, and sad to say, there were girls who thought that getting close to him was near as good as me, if you know what I mean. But I don't want to get Tim's hopes up."

"I understand, and it's very kind of you. Will you keep in touch with him?"

"I will. And with you, if you want to bring the old place back."

"You know, I think I might, and I'd appreciate your help. Unless this old building collapses with your crowd on Saturday."

"No worries. It's lasted this long, and it's got strong bones. You'll see."

Chapter 31

Friday proved to be an ordinary day without any of the disruptions that had plagued Sullivan's over the past week. Business remained strong: there were still curious local people wanting to know what had happened and what was going to happen. They'd come in for a pint, and maybe stay for a second one. More than that, Maura couldn't put her finger on it, but there was a new undercurrent of excitement in the place. Because of the wake? And the music it would bring?

As soon as the pub opened on Saturday the music makers started arriving. Maura directed them to the back room and kept the door to that space closed while they tuned up. The patrons had started arriving as soon as Sullivan's opened, staking out a table or a stool and watching the arrivals eagerly, nudging one another and identifying them one by one. And they kept ordering pints. It was going to be a good day.

Niall arrived just after noon, with Tim in tow. Tim looked like an eager puppy following his master, but Niall didn't seem to mind. Rose smiled and waved at both of them from behind the bar, and then the two men disappeared into the back room.

"Tim seems excited," Maura commented to Rose, between pulling pints.

"And well he should be! He's followin' his dream," Rose retorted.

"You mean Niall?"

"Nah, the music, of course. Niall's a part of all that, but there's a lot more to it."

"You're okay with Tim leaving?" Maura asked softly.

"Sure, and why wouldn't I be? He's a city boy, and I always knew he was goin' back to Dublin at the end of it all. You've no call to worry about me."

But Maura did anyway. "Rose, sometimes I think you have an old head on your shoulders." *Like me,* Maura realized. She'd never had the time or the patience for teenage angst and romantic drooling over unattainable boys. Mostly she'd kept her head down and kept on working— just like Rose was doing. With a small sigh Maura turned to the next patron. "What can I get you?"

Jimmy was schmoozing the crowd, spending more time talking than actually distributing drinks, but that was normal for him. Mick was in the back room, helping with the physical setup for the bands. He'd found time to repair the stage so no one would put a foot through it, and he'd checked out the old wiring more thoroughly—it wouldn't do to have the power go out in the middle of the session, and Maura had no idea who to call to fix it, and no faith that anyone would show up late on a Saturday night to make it right. Unless, of course, they were a big fan of Niall Cronin's.

Niall was kind enough to come out now and then and mingle with the local people—which now included a surprising number of women. Well, maybe not so surprising: Niall was still an attractive man, and he'd aged gracefully since his heyday. Maura found it was kind of fun to watch the women in the room jockeying for position, which happened every time he emerged and asked for another pint or six for his friends in the back. On one of those trips Maura leaned forward to say, "You do know you're giving the ladies here a thrill."

He smiled. "Of course I do, and I won't let them down." He scanned the room while waiting for the pints to settle. "Looks like yer doin' a good business today."

"Thanks to you and your pals, I am," Maura said, "and I'm grateful. And we've a long night ahead of us—again, because of you. Do you know, I think people around here will be talking about this day for a long time."

"Old Mick helped me get my start, and I owe him fer that. I'm sure he's watchin' all the fun down here."

"I'll believe it," Maura replied and passed him his pints.

Old Billy came in at midday, and the crowd parted respectfully as he made his slow way to his accustomed seat—and then swarmed back around him; or at least, those did who wanted to hear the tale of his bravery from him directly. Billy held court like a king, and the admiring circle around him didn't dwindle, as new people kept arriving. When there was a break in the crowd Maura smiled across the room at him, and he smiled back.

She almost panicked when she realized how full the house was getting; she tried to envision either Mick or Jimmy turning people away from the door and almost laughed out loud. The crowd was polite but they were also determined, and no doubt they'd brush off either of the men if they stood in the way. But as the afternoon wore on, Maura realized that the crowd seemed to have an organic life of its own: the space never got too packed. There were never more than a few people standing outside waiting, and they weren't impatient about it. Thank goodness the weather had cleared since the day before. Some people left, and others replaced them, but somehow it all achieved a balance. Maura hoped that balance would last the night.

Darkness came early, despite the fine weather—or maybe it was all the bodies blocking the light from the windows that made it seem dark.

"I've never seen such a crush," Rose said, awed. "You'll let me stay, won't you? Fer the music?"

"Of course. This may be historic, for all I know," Maura said, wondering how she'd find any time to listen herself. She'd promised herself that she'd give it a chance, at least.

Mick made one of his periodic forays into the front room. "Everything set?" Maura asked.

"As ever it'll be. Nervous?"

"I don't know. Should I be?"

"I don't know what you've seen in Boston, but here there's a kind of respect for the performers. There'll be no brawls, and if anyone gets out of hand, the others will show him the door. They're here for the music."

"When will things start?"

"They start when they start. Nine, maybe? Are you ready for it?"

"I hope so," Maura said fervently, pulling yet another batch of pints. She'd lost count of the total a few hours earlier and thanked the stars that Mick had laid in an extra supply of barrels in the basement.

Just past nine she sensed a change in the mood of the crowd in front, a sort of electric surge, and realized that someone—Mick?—had opened the doors to the back room and people were flowing that direction. From the back came the sounds of a few last tune-ups on the various instruments.

Rose edged closer to her. "Here we go. Are you excited?"

"I think I am," Maura told her, and she realized it was true. Whatever songs or styles were played that night, the energy of the crowd was undeniable. Even after all these years, the people here cared about that motley bunch of musicians. And then someone struck a chord and the back room erupted with cheers.

The next time Maura looked at the clock, it was nearly midnight, and the music was still going strong. An hour or more earlier Sean Murphy had come in out of uniform, and they'd exchanged a few words.

"You're off duty, Sean?" Maura had asked loudly as he edged his way up to the bar.

He grinned. "What gave me away? Was it the denims?"

"That, and you don't look so serious. Pint?"

"Please." He looked around him. "Quite the lively crowd yeh have here."

"Don't you dare think of taking anyone into custody! This is nothing short of a miracle."

"I wouldn't dream of it," he replied. "I told you, I'm a great fan of Niall's. Has he been on?"

"More than once, and he's still there. Go on in," Maura said, sliding a full pint toward him.

"I'll do that," Sean replied, tossing a few euros on the counter before wading into the crowd once more.

At midnight Jimmy came around the bar. "Why don't you go on back and have a listen?"

"Are we good for staying open?"

"It's taken care of," Jimmy said vaguely, and Maura didn't feel like questioning him. After all, there was a garda on the premises, and he would know if there was anything amiss, wouldn't he?

"Then I'll take you up on that offer. Holler if you need help," Maura told him, but he'd already turned away and was serving someone else. Actually, she decided as she stepped out from behind the bar, the majority of the people had moved themselves into the back room, and in the front the mood was a bit quieter—Jimmy could certainly handle it. She wove her way toward the back, smiling at those who greeted her along the way.

When she stepped into the back room it was like jumping into a storm. The group on the stage was going full steam, and the sound of guitar, drums, fiddle, concertina, and whatever bounced off the walls and washed back again. She'd never been in the room when the music was live, and it was an almost physical thing, and overwhelming—and that was with the wall-to-wall bodies absorbing at least part of it. She looked up to see that the balconies were packed as well, and she was glad Mick had checked their stability.

Although if anyone fell over the rail, they'd land on people, not the hard floor.

Actually, looking around she realized that it was not a rowdy or belligerent crowd: people looked happy. She waved at Rose on the far side of the room, standing next to Tim, whose eyes were gleaming as he bounced to the beat. Sean stood a few feet away from them, but there was no way Maura could cross the room at the moment. The performers segued from one song to another, swapping out one or another player seamlessly. Every now and then they'd pause for a drink before picking up where they'd left off. Maura recognized a bit of a tune now and then, but most of the music was unfamiliar. Still, there was a constant thread running through many of the songs—a hint of the old sounds that even she recognized as coming from traditional music, a style that she had been told went back centuries. No one would identify this lot as anything but Irish.

Niall led many of the songs, although he stepped back to let some of his colleagues have their moment as soloists. He caught sight of her and gave her a smile, without breaking stride, and she smiled back.

She nudged her way to a corner and leaned against the wall, listening. She could feel some of the bass notes reverberating through the wall of the old building, almost as though there was a beating heart in it. The performers were glistening with sweat, and Maura realized how hot the room was; she looked up to see that the upper door wasn't open. Might as well open it now, for ventilation. She wasn't worried about crashers this late, and what did it matter? Everybody was having a good time.

It took her five minutes to wriggle her way to the staircase and up the stairs, where quite a few people had taken seats. Once on the balcony, she had to fight her way to the back door, but nobody took offense when she stepped on a toe or elbowed someone accidentally; they were all too busy watching the stage below. Only when she reached the door did she realize that Mick had stationed himself up near it at the back of the balcony. He too looked completely absorbed by the music—and as happy as she'd ever seen him.

"Trying to keep the riffraff out?" she yelled into his ear.

"What?" he yelled back.

"Are you guarding the door?"

"No, I was trying to keep out of the way. You want it open?"

"Yes—it's about ninety degrees down there. Fahrenheit, I mean. We could use the air."

"No problem." Mick reached past her and unlocked the door, and she slid outside, glad for a momentary rush of cooler air—and the muting of the music. Mick followed her out. "What do yeh think?"

"It's amazing. Niall is really something—you can see why he made it big. But everyone is working together—it's not all about him. I think I finally get it."

"The music, you mean?"

"Yeah. It's wonderful."

They'd been leaning against the outside wall, cooling down, so Maura wasn't prepared when Mick swung around to face her—and then kissed her. Not a tentative peck, but a full-on, full-out kiss. She froze for a fraction of a moment, and then she found she was kissing him back. *Maura, what the hell do you think you're doing?* She didn't care, because it felt like part of the music and the excitement. Maybe she'd regret it in the morning, but right now it felt right.

Before things went too far, though, she pulled back to look up at him. "You're not drunk, are you?"

"Sober as a judge. Why? Are you hoping I'll forget this?"

"I'm not sure. I'll let you know tomorrow. We should go back in."

"Right so. The boys should be wrapping up soon enough, I think. Hold on"—he reached out and tucked a stray strand of hair behind her ear—"that's better. You go on in; I'll follow in a minute."

Maura turned and went back inside, hoping her cheeks weren't flaming red, or if they were, that people would think it was the heat and the music. No one seemed to be paying her the slightest bit of attention—except Sean Murphy, who was watching her from across the room below. Had he seen Mick follow her out? Did it matter? She wasn't sure.

As Mick had predicted, the song ended and Niall stepped forward. "It's been grand to play fer you all tonight, I think we all agree." Cheers from the crowd. "But this is also our way of saying good-bye to Aidan Crowley, who most of us up here on this stage knew. He and I started out together a long time ago, and I'm sorry we didn't keep on the same path. But this room here was where he played his last session, and I want you all to raise yer glasses in his memory."

The audience quieted, and a forest of glasses went high. Then Niall stepped back, and the group began one more song, this one slower and without amps. Maura didn't know the lyrics, but the boys sang it with care, and she could pick out some of the words. Mick came up behind her and leaned to whisper in her ear, "It's 'The Parting Glass.' Good choice."

Maura could only nod, because by the time the song ended, tears were running down her face.

Of all the money that e'er I had
I spent it in good company
And all the harm I've ever done
Alas it was to none but me
And all I've done for want of wit
To mem'ry now I can't recall
So fill to me the parting glass
Good night and joy be to you all

When the song ended there was a moment of silence, and there wasn't a dry eye in the place, that Maura could see. Then Niall stepped forward again. "Before we all go our separate ways, we also need to thank Maura Donovan, who's taken over for our old friend Mick Sullivan. Come on up here, Maura. I think she's done Mick Sullivan proud."

Maura fought down a wave of shyness and began to struggle her way to the stage, wiping the tears from her face along the way, trying to think of something, anything, to say. But she knew she had to do it, because that was her job now—she was the owner of the pub. When she reached the edge of the stage, Niall extended a hand and helped her up, then smiled his encouragement. "Go on, then."

Maura turned to face the crowd, filled with both familiar and unfamiliar faces. "I don't know how you all found your way here tonight, but I'm glad you did—and I hope you'll be back. I never had the chance to meet Mick Sullivan, but I've tried to do right by him." That met with cheers and clapping. "And this wouldn't have happened without the help of a lot of other people, starting with Billy Sheahan and Tim Reilly, and of course Niall here. If you're all willing, we'll make it happen again." *Minus the death,* Maura reminded herself. But despite it being his wake, it seemed Aidan was not on people's minds, and they all cheered—for her. "Thank you all for making it a wonderful night, and safe home to you all."

The crowd quieted slowly, and people began drifting toward the front of the building. Maura saw Mick making his way in that direction, probably to manage the traffic. She turned to Niall. "Thank you, for a lot of things. I've never seen anything like this, much less been part of it."

"It's what we do," Niall said simply. "We make music, and that makes people happy. That's all it is."

"Will you be back?"

"I'd like that. But you've got to see what yeh can do with it on yer own."

"Deal. Are you guys set for the night?"

"Not to worry—we're grand."

"Then I'd better make sure everything's okay up front."

In the front room the crowd had thinned, with only a few diehards finishing up their last pints at the bar. Billy had disappeared, which didn't surprise Maura—she only hoped she had his stamina when she was his age, in a half century or so. But Sean was waiting near the door, leaning against the jamb, and he straightened up when he saw her, and she crossed the room to talk with him. "What did you think?" she asked when she was close enough to be heard.

"It was brilliant. Really. Niall was right—Old Mick

would be proud of yeh. Listen, uh," he said, looking down at his feet, "I've got those tickets fer the show we talked about. That is, if yeh still want to go?"

He looked back at her then, and his expression tore at Maura's heart, it was so eager and so hopeful. Had he seen her and Mick? Or seen her face when she'd come back in? No, he couldn't have. "Sure, I'd love to. Next week, is it?"

Now Sean looked ridiculously pleased. "That's grand. I'll let you know the details. Thanks again for an amazin' evenin'," he said as he turned and left.

Maura, still smiling, turned and found Mick staring at her from behind the bar. Her smile faded. "What?"

After a moment he said, "Nothin'. Want me to close up?"

"Why don't you let me? I'd kind of like to be alone in the place, just for a minute."

"Right so. I'll be on my way, then," he said. He set the broom carefully in the corner, then went out the door without looking back at her.

Maura sighed: this Sean versus Mick thing was going to get tricky fast, but she wasn't going to do anything about it right now. She was in no hurry. It was her choice to make. Or maybe she'd choose neither of them. It would all work out in the end, and she had plenty of time.

She smiled, though there was no one to see. She'd turned a corner, somehow. She'd hoped the place would be profitable, and now she'd proved it could be. Better: she'd found something that was unique, that would draw people in. It was an unexpected gift, and she'd be an idiot to ignore it. She pivoted slowly, taking in the room. Everything was in order. All the people had gone. Did some hint of the music linger, embedded in the walls? Maybe.

So what if she'd also found some trouble here; that was the exception, not the rule, at Sullivan's. There were people she could turn to for help, and, what was more, they *wanted* to help. They had accepted her. Some knot inside her, balled up tight since she had arrived, could untangle now. She was staying.

FROM *NEW YORK TIMES* BESTSELLING AUTHOR

SHEILA CONNOLLY

Scandal in Skibbereen

A County Cork Mystery

As the new owner of Sullivan's Pub in County Cork,
Ireland, Maura Donovan gets an earful of all the village gossip. But uncovering the truth about some local
rumors may close her down for good. . .

"An exceptional read! Sheila Connolly has done it again
with this outstanding book . . . [A] must read for
those who have ever wanted to visit Ireland."

—*Shelley's Book Case* on *Buried in a Bog*

sheilaconnolly.com
facebook.com/TheCrimeSceneBooks
penguin.com

M1424T0114